THE SEELIE QUEEN

This book is dedicated to my husband, for every moment you have loved me, for every word of inspiration you have offered, for every time you have encouraged me.

I love you always,

~ Your Loving Wife

Acknowledgements

I want to start by thanking one of the most influential people in my life, Mike Bixby. Who always told me I could do whatever I put my mind to. This advice stuck in my fifth-grade brain and carries me through even now, in adulthood.

Editing by Blazing Butterfly Edits and The Night Owl Editing. Both excellent editors who pushed me hard and were my cheerleaders throughout the end stages of the book.

Thank you to my dad, my rock, my boulder. The very man who has sacrificed everything to watch his children grow and succeed, I love you more than words could ever tell.

To my insane children, thank you for giving me character inspiration and keeping every day interesting.

To my erratic, hilarious, and fantastic mothers for supporting me and my writing so whole-heartedly.

To Nikki Cornett and Lauren Raybould, thank you for being motivational, inspirational and so supportive it hurt sometimes, I could not have finished my book without you.

PROLOGUE

"Run, Delly! Run," the haunting voice screamed.

My whole body convulsed momentarily before springing to life and running in an unknown direction.

My feet ached as I ran across the grass. I looked down to see they were bare, toes reddening from the cold. My stomach turned in circles as I attempted to gain enough courage to see what I was running from.

Peeking behind me, I saw three large figures in black gaining on me. Was I fast enough to outrun this? I looked ahead, and a small person with crimson hair grabbed my hand and pulled me along. Her speed and strength were impressive for her short stature; her identity was unknown, yet somehow familiar enough that I trusted her completely.

"Run, Delly, run!" My deceased mother's voice rang in my ears and pushed me forward. I picked up the pace, digging my numbing feet harder into the ground to gain traction. I increased the distance between me and the threat.

I looked over to see the small red-haired girl climbing a tree, and I quickly began to climb the one next to me. My feet and hands skidded across the moist bark as I attempted to scale the tree. They slipped down, again and again, leaving my skin tender and raw.

I reached my left leg up as far as it would go, finally landing on a tall, broad branch that could hold my weight. But I was too late. I felt a cold, constricting hand wrap around my right ankle and pull.

I

I could sense it: her presence. It was incredible how fast the connection happened, considering I had only agreed to the duties in the letter moments ago. Yet there I was, thinking that today was going to be another average, dull day, but I could *feel* her. I sensed her hesitation at the front doors, the anxiety that coursed through her aura. But scariest of all, I was conscious of my insatiable need to be with her, to be *near* her. I had this undeniable feeling that only I could keep her safe. Only I could be her protector.

Sometimes I wondered why me? Why again? I approached the front doors for the first time. My hand trembled as I reached for the long silver handle on the gigantic red door that led into the place of my nightmares: high school. I looked up and saw a light green girl with electric purple hair placing her books in her locker. She set her things on the shelf and gave me a tiny smile through the glass window.

I let go of the handle, and stumbled back in shock. I squeezed my eyes shut and shook my head quickly.

Not again, not now.

I opened my eyes a sliver, to see a perfectly average blonde girl glaring at me with her eyebrow furrowed in confusion. *Great, I'm not even in the doors yet, and I bet there will be rumors that I'm weird.* I reached for the handle again, and the wide door swung open, inviting me into its warm, hormone-driven hallways.

I walked into my new school alone, yet I kept my head held high. Hopefully whatever new experiences today held would be quick and relatively painless. *Although I highly doubt it.*

Wearing my new purple ballet dress and black flats, I stared straight ahead as my peripherals caught numerous sets of eyes ogling me, their stares weighed heavily on my already uneasy stomach. Another first day, at another new school, in yet another new town.

So far, I'd enrolled in three new schools, just in my freshman and sophomore year alone. I didn't necessarily mind moving, it was the locations we went to that I didn't prefer. We were always far from cities, and they were all abnormally hot. Our newest location was a little town in Tombstone, Arizona. Hot, brown, and small; the only words that could possibly be used to describe my new world.

As I walked down the hall, I counted all the school's population of 400. For some reason, all eyes were still on me. Only one question crossed my mind as I averted eye contact, focusing on posters decorating the wall as I walked: how could I fly under the radar until my dad decided we needed to pack up and move again? It was the same question I'd asked myself on the first day of every new school. I turned the corner and spotted a small handmade sign that clearly stated: "New students this way," knowing all too well this sign was made just for me; I was the only new student in this town in the last two years.

I turned another corner and found a little door marked 'Office.' I hesitated, steadying myself for a second and ended up focusing much too hard on the doorknob. I closed my eyes and prepared myself.

As I opened them again, I saw a hand reaching in front of me. It twisted the doorknob and opened the door. I swiveled around to look up at the stranger's face and could feel my jaw drop. I quickly shut my mouth and met his eyes. I *can't believe I just gaped at him. Did he notice?*

He smirked in return and raised his eyebrows at me questioningly, as if he'd wondered why I couldn't possibly turn the knob myself. I clenched my teeth and rolled my eyes, refusing to give him the time of day. Ignoring his all-too-genuine hand gesture towards the desk, I made my way in.

The room was humid and only had enough space for a tiny desk and a couple of padlocked filing cabinets.

"One moment please." The receptionist had a frantic kindness to her, big round eyes, and a face full of freckles that almost hid the wrinkles around her nose and the laugh lines near her mouth. I glanced around in anticipation to see if the boy was behind me, in the close proximity of this small office, but the room was empty besides the receptionist and me. *Ugh get a grip.* I turned back around trying to control the annoyance on my face and provided the receptionist with my undivided attention.

"Okay, what can I do for you?" She glanced up at me quickly before returning to the paperwork in front of her. After a slight pause, she looked back up.

"Oh! You must be Adella, Adella Shenning? Let me grab your schedule." She seemed to answer her own questions. I liked that. The less conversation I had to make, the better.

A manila envelope full of paperwork landed with a thud on the table between us.

"Here you are, Adella. The first papers are your schedule and locker number, behind that is paperwork you and your father will have to go through together, sign and bring back." She gave me a reassuring smile, before carrying on. "My name is Mrs. Detter. If you have any questions, let me know. For now, you better get to your locker. The bell will ring in about seven minutes."

Grabbing the paperwork, I nodded and left. Extra dialogue wasn't necessary. She was a one-person-show kind of lady, and I certainly admired that.

Finding my locker was the easy part. There's only 350, all lined up down one long hallway, half-sized, and I was near the end of them.

Heading to Homeroom was a daunting task, but one I felt compelled to complete before an overly helpful individual tried to start up an unnecessary conversation. I walked through the halls glancing this way and that way, keeping my eyes on the door's numbers ahead. The classrooms weren't in chronological order as I assumed they would be; instead, they seemed to be ranked by some kind of leveling structure.

"Ouch!" I collided with someone and fell hard. My books flew across the hallway and into the oncoming student traffic, the thud was deafening and echoed across the corridor. I glared upward as I lay on the floor, only to see a guy staring incredulously at me with his all-too-familiar face. *It's him!* This time, he was only half-smirking, with an expression that looked as if he had a question, but it also seemed as if he knew the answer too. I found myself staring back at him, mesmerized. His eyes captured my complete attention; they were an odd shade of green, almost dark enough to be forest-colored, but they had bright yellow grassy specs throughout them. I watched him run his pale hand through his jet-black hair, I shook my head a bit trying to break myself from this daze. He smiled down at me apologetically, and to my extreme irritation, I noticed that he was completely unmoved. *What was this guy, a brick?* Yet I could see physically he was lean. *Maybe he's a bit dense, possibly by both definitions of the word with the way he is staring at me. Wait: he's still staring at me!* Part of me was ecstatic about his unswerving gaze, the other part was annoyed.

With impeccable timing, the bell rang. Hastily, I broke eye contact and began to gather my scattered books from across the floor. The frustration inside me built, as I realized I was going to be late on my first day. *Ugh.*

"Do you run into people often?" The words felt like an accusation and a joke at the same time.

"I'm looking for my class. Room 204 Homeroom." I didn't know why my face was getting so hot. He was a perfectly ordinary boy. *If totally gorgeous and perfectly ordinary are the same thing.*

"What a small world," he said. The inflections in his voice told me what I said wasn't exactly a surprise to him. "I'm heading that way. You can follow me." With that, he headed off. Much to my embarrassment, he started walking the opposite way to where I was originally going.

Snatching up the last book on the floor, I jogged after him. He walked slowly, for my benefit no doubt. He slid easily through the door marked 204, and I followed closely behind.

I didn't quite pull off a smooth entrance because my backpack strap caught on the door. It jerked me backwards, and my shoulder crashed into it causing it to slam loudly. *Ow.* I struggled to free it

13

for a moment with my arms full. When I finally got the strap out from the handle, I glanced up through the curtain of hair shielding my face. My cheeks flushed crimson. Of course everyone noticed this mortifying display, and they were staring.

"Ahhhh Miss Shenning. My name is Mr. Hendrickson, I see you found your way and met my son, Luxor." Something was amiss. It was the teacher's voice, but I wasn't sure how. "Luxor is a teacher's aide in my class this year until he finds out what he wants to major in next fall. He will also be showing you to your classes this week. He already has a copy of your schedule to make things easier." Pity. I detected pity in the teacher's voice. *Great, just what I needed.*

I made my way to my seat, holding what little dignity I had left. I plopped my books loudly onto the top of the desk. I might as well own the attention I had already earned. I gave Luxor nothing more than a slight nod; no wonder he'd been smirking at me, he knew I was heading the wrong way.

"Thank you, Mr. Hendrickson," I replied simply. Looking quite satisfied with himself, and thankfully taking the attention off me, Mr. Hendrickson started the class where he'd left the previous lesson, I assumed. Today's lecture was on how to care for your books, not that I needed a lesson. I loved reading; I'd spend all day bundled up on my floor, with a pillow stack in the corner of my room if time allowed it.

I settled into my seat, as the teacher talked on. I decided to spare a glance in Luxor's direction. To my surprise, more than half

14

of the girls in the room were sitting near where he was perched precariously on the countertop next to the window. Some were on the edge of their seats, while others were all noticeably leaning in towards him. I glanced over again but this time allowed my eyes to linger, only to make direct eye contact once again with him; I felt the breath catch in my chest. *Why is he staring at me?*

He had that ridiculous half-smirk plastered on his face again like we shared secrets only we knew. My stomach fluttered slightly, I bit my tongue so the blood wouldn't rush back up to my cheeks. The blonde in front of him did a full 180-degree-turn in her seat, solely to glare at me. *Great, your first day and you already made an enemy, Dells, way to go.* I quickly lowered my gaze and daydreamed for the rest of the lecture.

When the bell rang, I sprung up from my seat with a bit too much enthusiasm and bolted for the door. I almost made it when I felt someone's hand grab my arm firmly, but also gently. Electricity shot through my entire arm; I paused momentarily, before yanking my arm free.

"Whoa, speedy, didn't you hear? I'm your personal chaperone for the week." My stomach did circles again as I turned around slowly. He was standing close, much closer than I had originally anticipated. His smug face took my breath away. *How did he do that?*

"I don't like to be touched," I barely managed to say with what felt like no breath left in me. It came out as nothing more than a whisper.

If we were the same height, we would have been nose to nose. But alas, I was a proud five-foot four inches.

He has to be at least six foot, I thought, letting my eyes wander from his head all the way down to his feet.

I took a couple of breaths to steady my heartbeat. I looked back up and saw the pain in his face as if he'd taken it personally that I didn't like being touched. He chewed his bottom lip and his eyes drooped slightly.

"But of course, I appreciate it. Math is my next class." I spoke softer than before, trying to show there were no hard feelings. *What are you doing? He's a big boy, he will be fine.* Being around him was slightly unnerving.

"I know. I have your schedule, remember?" he said, flashing a smile and pulling a folded piece of paper from his pocket. Before I could respond, he darted past me. I stood frozen for a second, trying to process his emotional lightswitch. He stopped in the doorway, holding it open for a moment with an amused look. I sighed and followed him through.

The math class was right next door — not that I needed someone to lead me there, a simple hand gesture would have sufficed. The class was smaller than the last; one of the perks of being in AP calculus. A whopping six people sat around me. Well, six kids and Luxor.

I leaned over to him. "You don't have to stay, you know. I can meet you back at your dad's room after class."

He took a moment to ponder that. *Maybe he really likes you.*

16

"Nah, it's easier this way. Since we'll be spending most of our day together, I might as well stay in your classes. The teachers all know me anyhow, so it's no big deal." *Easier, of course it was simply easier.*

I didn't quite know what he meant by us spending a lot of time together. If he just showed me to my classes and left, we'd only spend around 30 minutes a day together, at most. *Did I want that? Did I want him to go away?* My stomach knotted at the idea of him leaving and continuing on with his life. The feeling that I wouldn't be okay if he walked away and did not return left me unsettled. *Why wouldn't I want him to go away?* I gave him a friendly smile, he gave me one in return which made the knots in my stomach feel like butterflies.

I would be fine. *I will be fine.* The pull I'm feeling toward Luxor was probably because of how friendly he'd been, the kindness he'd shown to me on my first day. *It will fade, I think.* I quickly averted my gaze and turned to the whiteboard, where the teacher was explaining today's work.

As if the day wasn't confusing enough, Luxor's presence was distracting. He managed to perch himself on any counter or windowsill he could find, separating himself from the students on purpose I was sure. He sat just far enough behind me to be outside my peripheral vision. I had to noticeably turn my head to look at him, but he was close enough that I could smell the cologne he wore and hear small movements he made, which in turn, made me

17

want to see what he was doing. Maddening, it was maddening. I gripped the corners of my desk. *Show a little self-restraint. Geesh.*

My next two classes went by quickly, and I decided on gardening for my elective. The greenhouse was massive, as soon as I stepped outside the aroma of honeysuckle and lavender filled the air. They complemented each other well. When I walked up to the greenhouse, the roses growing along the inside wall stole the attention with their sweet, floral smell. Their glistening petals shined in the sun infiltrating the walls. Thorns protruded from the stems, giving the flowers strength. They remained delicate-looking though, thanks to careful contrasting with the velvet petals. Inside the greenhouse were many rows of flowers, fruits, and vegetables. As I stood there next to the roses, I already knew this was where I was going to spend most of my time.

Luxor stood behind me as I pruned the rose bushes and dug up some soil to add fresh fertilizer, trying to produce extra buds to the plants that were already blooming. I focused hard on my work, trying to distract myself from his unforgiving stare. It was beginning to make me feel a bit self-conscious. He watched me so intensely, as if everything I did held interested him.

My last class before lunch was creative writing. Time flew by and I now had my first assignment to do at home. I'd never been much of a writer, but I was positive I could write a two-page essay in no time. When the bell rang, I couldn't have stood up any faster. I was ready for lunch. I could feel my stomach growling impatiently.

Luxor was already standing next to my table. He reached over to grab my books. I sighed. His scent was intoxicating. I rocked back and forth on my feet for a second before grounding myself. The effect he had on me was infuriating. My body seemed to react to his actions in a way I could not control. I dug my nails into my sweaty palms in an attempt to slow my heartbeat to keep the blush from returning to my cheeks. He flashed me a smile as he turned to walk out of the classroom. I admired the essence of confidence he portrayed when he walked. Always with his head up and shoulders back as if nothing in the world could bring him down.

We were the first to enter the lunchroom, which was always bad, especially when you're new to school. Odds are most of the tables were already claimed by students who had been here since day one. I looked around for any signs of where we should sit and dread filled me. The tables were almost all away from walls and relatively close together. However, I still wanted to sit on the outskirts of the room, so I could watch people and get a feel for the different groups in the school—particularly I wanted to know which were the popular crowds. I would be avoiding them at all costs. With moving so often, I like to keep my friend circle small, fewer people to say goodbye to.

Sitting at the wrong table, especially one that was taken, messes up the whole dynamic of the lunchroom. Luxor walked to the side of the lunchroom next to the door, and as if reading my mind, and set my books down on one of the tables on the outskirts. We were at the perfect angle to see people entering and leaving the room, and could peer at those busy with their lives around us. After we reserved our seats, he continued to the lunch line and began to grab an abnormally large tray of food.

"I hope you don't mind sharing a tray, it's easier than grabbing two." *It's practically a lunch date.* My cheeks suddenly felt as if they were on fire.

"No, that's fine." I glanced at the ground and followed him through the line. *Play it cool Dells, play it cool.* I turned my face away so he couldn't see the blush. I'd never had a crush on a guy before, this is maddening.

At the end of the line I pulled my wallet out, and to my embarrassment he set his hand gently on mine. I looked up to him, and he shook his head slightly. *DEFINITELY A DATE.*

"My treat." He winked at me, causing my heart to flutter in an unnatural pattern.

"Will you just stop already," I whisper screamed at myself.

"What?" Luxor asked, raising an eyebrow at me.

"Nothing," I wasn't going to give him the satisfaction of knowing I was yelling at myself over him.

We walked back to our seats. Luxor sat across from me and set the tray of food in between us. We ate in silence but I couldn't help but to allow my eyes to wonder every few minutes to avoid any direct eye contact. Looking around the room I realized sharing a lunch tray was a common occurrence here. *Maybe not a date.* However, the number of eyes on us was a little uncomfortable, so, I focused on my food instead and the task at hand: eating.

Luxor cleared his throat loudly, I peered up at him through my lashes and the wall of hair separating us.

"So, what are you? If you don't mind me asking."

Wow, that was unexpected. It was the type of question I hadn't put much thought into and so I needed time to answer. I knew I got my looks from my mother; my dark complexion comes from my mom's side, along with my shoulder-length, thick brown hair, and deep brown eyes. I took a couple of bites from my food, chewing slowly to buy myself some time as I contemplated what to say. It doesn't help that his eyes never wavered from my face, almost pressuring me to answer.

I looked at the back of my hand, concentrating on the thought of my mother, the last time I saw her as I answered his question.

"My dad is Scottish and Irish and I don't know what my mom was. I look more like my mother did though."

Luxor seemed to hold a perfect poker face as he continued his interrogation. "And what is your mom's name?"

My face fell as I spoke of her. "My mom's name was Jennette, but she was in an accident and passed away four years ago."

Saying her name caused a lump to form in my throat. My mom and I were always close, then one day, dad told me she passed away in a gruesome car accident, and I'd never see her again. That was the first time we moved homes, leaving all of her things and memories behind. Besides the jewelry set she gave me, I grabbed the necklace dangling from my neck and held it for a moment, and looked up at the lights to stop the unshed tears that brimmed my lashes from running down my cheeks.

"Was she summer or winter?" *Uh, what?*

I looked at his face again to see if he was joking. He stared straight back at me, like he was concentrating hard on something, or trying to see through me instead of what was right in front of him. Having his undivided attention tightened the knots in my stomach. It was a sensation that I'd never felt before.

My eyebrows knit together as I looked directly at him. These questions were confusing. "I'm not sure I follow."

"Oh, some people prefer Seelie or Unseelie. But it's alright for now, we have to get you to your next class."

We finished lunch without any more questions, thankfully. I
started to get up, but Luxor lifted his hand, giving me the wait here
sign. He got up and walked to the garbage to toss the leftovers. I
waited until he came back towards the table to stand up and follow.
My last class was by far the most confusing. History and Mystics
1-1; it took up the time usually allocated for three classes.

As we walked into the room, I noticed a vast difference from
the rest of the lessons I'd had today. This class had to have at least
100 students sitting in rows at long tables. The room was
abnormally silent, which was odd for a history class in my
experience. Luxor walked to the counters on the side and I found
an open seat in between two girls who looked friendly enough. The
teacher wasn't in the room yet and I arrived early enough that I

didn't attract much attention. The girl on my left turned to face me as I sat down. Her eyes widened.

"Hi, I'm Annabelle. My friends call me Anna though." Her voice had a familiar, yet somehow unrecognizable ring to it. She tucked a strand of her curly, fiery red mane behind her small ears and reached out her hand to shake mine.

"Adella. It's nice to meet you." I mustered up the friendliest smile I could. I grabbed her hand and shook, measuring her slightly against myself. She was noticeably shorter, even sitting, I towered over her.

"What are you, Adella? Your skin is beautiful!" The question itself seemed innocent enough, although the context still baffled me. Just like Luxor's line of questions earlier. I looked at her for a moment, her freckle covered eyebrows scrunched together, noticeably uncomfortable under my stare.

"It's complicated, but thank you." I caught a little glimpse of something sparkly on her wrist and noticed the vast majority of jewelry she's wearing. Bracelets traveled up her left forearm and earrings, partially hidden under her unkempt hair, lined both ears entirely. Her freckled face almost hid a shiny dimple piercing in her right cheek.

She raised one of her eyebrows at me, giving me an incredulous look and turned slowly in her seat to focus on the front of the room. She must have thought it odd that I was staring at her for so long saying nothing.

Just as I turned, I saw our instructor walking into the room. She was beautiful, to say the least. Tall with dark black hair that swayed behind her as she made her way to the center of the floor. "Good afternoon class." Although her voice was quiet, it somehow filled the large room without the need for a microphone. The board behind her stated her name as Professor Hendrickson, she sent a quick wink in Luxor's direction, and I knew she must be his mother. Only then did I notice the large scar that decorated her face. A thin line formed from the right temple, went across her nose and down to the left side of her chin. "Last week, we covered the basics of sight and the histories of the Seelie and Unseelie court. Any students who missed a lecture from last week can pick up the reading pages and assignments from the front of the room." Once I saw the scar, it became unsettling to look at, almost as if it was an accessory she put on that morning that didn't actually belong to her, I found myself almost fixated on it.

I was so distracted by my own thought I almost missed what was just said, a couple of the new words stole my attention. This wasn't right. I took a moment to rethink the teacher's statement. *Seelie? Unseelie? Sight? None of these sounds like history.*

"To begin today's class, let's practice using our sight. How many of you practiced over the weekend?"

I was certain that every hand in the room raised. All except mine.

"Alright class, since we have a new student, we will cover what we did last week so everyone is up to date on what we are learning

25

about. As most of you know, sight comes naturally at 18, but it can also be practiced and used before then. Can anyone tell me what sight does?" Anna's eager hand flew up and Mrs. Hendrickson nodded her way.

Anna cleared her throat. "Sight is the ability to see the true form of someone else and of the world around them." She smiled smugly.

"Very well Anna." The professor closed her eyes. "Now class, practice with me. Everyone close your eyes. I want you to focus on your breathing. In one-two-three, out one-two-three-four."

The whole class followed her example; I could hear their long, drawn in breaths. The entire room was still silent. Everyone listened carefully to the professor's bell-like voice ringing in our heads.

But meditation? What could History class possibly have to do with meditation? I leaned over to Anna.

"Anna," I whispered but got no response. She was either ignoring me or so deep in concentration she couldn't hear me.

"Hey," I whispered at her and poked her shoulder.

She shook her head no at me and kept her eyes closed. I sat back in my seat waiting for it to be over, for everyone to open their eyes again and start talking about the Civil War. I opened my notebook in front of me and began to doodle on the blank pages.The professor cleared her throat.

I looked up at her, and she gave me an encouraging nod. I nodded back and closed my eyes reluctantly, listening carefully to her breathing instructions. I didn't know how long this went on, but eventually, she stopped speaking, and we began breathing in the pattern on our own.

"Now class. I want you to focus on the person to your left, everything about them. Picture them in your mind. Think of their hair, their eyes, even the outfit they decided to wear today."

That was easy enough. Anna was an extraordinary person; she's wearing a beautiful green blouse that complimented her bright blue eyes, a pair of shorts and suspenders, accompanied by large amounts of jewelry.

"Now, think of their aura." Her voice echoed throughout the classroom, weaving between the sounds of breathing, and almost felt as if she was standing right next to me.

I didn't really know how to picture an aura, but if I had to give Anna one it would be like a sunset — warm and friendly. She was approachable and beautiful at the same time. A deep red center with flickering orange and yellow bounced off her. I imagined it dancing and moving around. Anna didn't seem to be the kind of person who just liked to stand around, she's full of energy, and happiness.

"Okay class, keep practicing your breathing as you slowly open your eyes, remember to remain calm or your sight will leave."

I took a deep breath and opened my eyes slowly. I was not sure what to expect exactly, but it was certainly not what I saw. There's a wave of colors in the room, so many that my eyes couldn't focus

27

clearly. Instead, I concentrated on Anna. She was somehow paler than before, her freckles appeared black against her new pasty complexion. She has pinched ears and her eyes suddenly seemed much too large for her strange, small face.

I gasped, throwing myself back as if I could escape her. Searing pain radiated throughout my back when I hit the table abruptly behind me. "What are you?"

My vision blurred. I closed my eyes and tried to clear them out a couple of times, only to open them to see the Anna I originally sat next to. She snickered.

"You're supposed to remain calm, remember? I'm part Elf and part Fata, but mostly elf. My dad's half-Elf and my mom's a quarter Fata." Her lips curled up in a shy smile. Or maybe it was mischievous — I didn't look long enough to differentiate. I turned to stare at my empty desk, trying to calm myself down, but to no avail.

"Part Elf? Elfs aren't real Anna."

"Aren't they though? I'm sitting right next to you Adella," her voice was filled with pity, which only irritated me further.

Fragments of fractured nightmares flashed across my closed eyes. Thick red blood everywhere, the smell of copper made me gag. A high pitched wail belonging to me rang in my ears, but I knew I didn't make a sound. Explosions and destruction showed next, black thick smoke filled my lungs forcing a cough. Anna in a field, fighting people twice her size, us getting captured and stuffed into a room. I put my hands to my head and held my

28

temples, hoping it would somehow slow them down, at least enough to make sense of them.

"I know you," I barely whispered, my now pounding headache made the words feel like yelling.

I looked up at her familiar face again, the face of the partner in crime that had run with me through my bad dreams a hundred times, running from the terrifying black figure, running for what feels like our lives. I heard a familiar scream in the background, "RUN DELLY, RUN." I couldn't help but think it belonged to my mother, which only told me this dream is all the more unreal. I looked at her again. I must be mistaken; how could a girl I'd never met appear in my dreams?

Anna stared back at me in disbelief with her head cocked slightly to the side, clearly confused by my odd display. I tried to relax a bit and took a closer look at her face, trying to understand, to make sense of it all. Elf and Fata? Was that even possible? It would have been impossible to believe if I didn't see it for myself, although I swear I'd seen it a hundred times before, even just this morning before school. I closed my eyes trying to relax, as I scooted back into my spot. I wanted to see it all again. I wanted to take in the changed forms of everyone around me. It was as if being able to see it all again would make me understand everything that was happening. But the confusion was making my head spin, which made concentration nearly impossible.

That was when I realized the room was silent. I took a peek, but everyone still looked relatively normal — if normal was a standard. Everything seemed back to how it was, except for one thing: every set of eyes in the room were on me. *Oh no*. I shrank into my seat a little as my eyes met with the teacher, hoping for an explanation as to why I was the center of attention.

"What is she?" I heard the whispers begin. I scanned the room and made eye contact with multiple sets of eyes staring at me. Some were curious and wide, others were envious and upset. They seemed to chide me for, once again and much to my embarrassment, demanding the attention of over a quarter of the student body at this school.

Thankfully, Mrs. Hendrickson hushed the class and began to speak again. "Well class, let's describe her characteristics, which will allow us to categorize her into a species."

"She's shining gold!" One of the girls shouted.

I looked at my hands. Nope, I was still the same dark caramel I'd always been. I looked to Luxor, as if one approving look from him could give me a little guidance; instead, he was fixated on the instructor, his mother.

"Not shining," chimed another student. "Luminescent. She has a slight luster with a gold tint, and deep brown eyes with very bright golden streaks."

"That's right, Trevor! And what does gold represent in the Seelie court?" She scanned the room, so she could pick on someone to answer. "Uhm, Rachael?"

I turned to face this Rachael and to my dismay, recognized her immediately as the same blonde girl from homeroom. *Anyone but her.*

"Summer, gold represents summer. But only the Seelie Queen and Seelie Queen-in-training are supposed to represent gold. My father told me I was supposed to be one, that's why my skin is almost as shiny as theirs," she bragged, holding her arm out for the classroom to see, which I would hate to break it to her, but wasn't shiny in the slightest. "Also, Gremlins are gold. She could be a Gremlin, Mrs. Hendrickson." Rachael sat right up front, and held a shrewd smile as she spoke. She was enviously beautiful, with long golden hair and flawless skin. Her nasally voice, however, made her unattractive somehow.

I was wrong before. I thought there would be rumors going around school that I was weird because of the way I sometimes saw people. But no, that was perfectly normal, apparently. Instead, there will be rumors that I'm a freaking *gremlin*. I honestly would have settled for weird at this point.

"That's a good point Rachael. Can anyone tell me why Adella is *not* a Gremlin?" Rachael's expression soured immediately; she carefully studied every detail of my face. It took every fiber of my being to relax my shoulders and keep a calm demeanor; I wouldn't let Rachel know she was getting to me.

Just as I thought things couldn't get any worse, Luxor finally decided to make eye contact with me. He looked proud and smug that I was already waiting for his gaze. In my peripherals, I saw

31

Rachel turn away in annoyance, apparently she wasn't too cool with sharing attention.

"Because today, exactly one hour ago, I received a letter from the Seelie court, assigning me to be Adella's protector-in-training. Only those who hold the utmost importance in the Seelie court are assigned a protector. Gremlins are considered a part of the Unseelie court." Luxor broke eye contact and glanced at his mom, who was beaming with pride. *MY protector. Do I want a protector? Do I need a protector?* I liked to think my dad had kept me safe all these years. How would he feel about me being assigned some random guy?

"Exactly, Luxor. Adella will be one of the three chosen Seelie Queens-in-training. The next Queen will be chosen in three years on the winter solstice, when all Queen trainees are 20 years of age. Please open up your textbooks to page 79, and we will begin our lecture on the Seelie Queen training rituals."

I raised my hand timidly and without even looking at me Mrs. Hendrickson called on me.

"And why do I need a protector?" I asked.

Mrs. Hendrickson's eyes settled on my face, she appeared as if she was trying to understand me. She looked perplexed by something.

"Luxor will keep you alive Adella," goosebumps raised on my arms. "The trials you will soon face are not easy, or for the faint of heart," she added.

Vomit raised in my throat, although I had at least one thousand more questions, my body was threatening to throw up at any moment. Sealing my lips, I swallowed hard, clearing the sour, acidic taste, and I put my head down on my desk. The professor hesitated momentarily, then went on with her lecture.

I wanted to pay attention to the people speaking of my future as though I wasn't in the room. I wanted to open my book and follow along. If it was about anyone but me, I probably would have. Instead, I found myself completely lost, attempting to come to terms with a future that's already been decided for me. They wanted *me* to train to be the Queen of a world I'm just learning exists — a world I'm not sure I even believed existed. If I hadn't seen it for myself, I would have probably gotten up and left this room.

When the bell rang, I charged towards the door, my goal to be the first one out, so I could suffocate in silence on my lonesome. Loud familiar footsteps sounded from just behind me. Luxor was already on my trail, foiling my plans.

"You really didn't know, did you?" He sounded breathless as he chased me out of the room, but there was no disguising his incredulous tone that had a hint of, to my annoyance, concern in this voice.

"Which part? The part where I glow like a neon light, or where I don't get to decide my future?" I snapped back, as if I didn't have better things to do than answer endless questions all day.

"I wouldn't say glow, it's more like a slight shine. They just aren't used to using the sight yet, so it startled them a little." He was trying to explain but it didn't make things any better. I just needed to be by myself in a silent place.

"Awesome. So, I'm a freak and startling. Just what I needed on my first day of school."

I wasn't sure if it was my condescending tone, or if I was being too blunt, but Luxor decided to follow along silently as I went to my locker and left the building. I couldn't help but be extremely aware of Luxor's presence while we walked together, his shallow gruff breaths, and his sweet yet musky scent that enclosed around me every time he got too close. I tried to stay far ahead as we walked home but I did slow at times to see if he wanted to walk closer than I was allowing. I was not sure what I wanted, exactly. I waited for him to turn every time we reached a new block, but he didn't. I realized we were getting close to the stairs that lead up to my apartment. Was he trying to be nice and walk me home? Or was he just curious about where I lived? I couldn't stop my irritation from getting to me, I hated having unanswered questions.

"Are you going to follow me into my home, too?" Glaring was probably too harsh, but controlling my expression wasn't an option right now.

He looked at me innocently. "I don't know what you're talking about. I'm just going to walk around the new apartment the Seelie court assigned me."

It took me a second to understand, then he turned around and walked into the apartment directly parallel to mine. Frustration coursed through me, or was it confusion? Maybe a little of both. I stomped into my apartment, slamming the door behind me.

3

My dad wasn't going to be home until at least 6 pm. The independence was freeing. He worked close enough that he could come home if I needed him, but there was enough time to myself to gather my thoughts. Today had been overwhelming enough without the slew of questions I knew my dad would ask about my first day of school. He did it on the first day of every new school.

I started loading my laundry into the washer, scrounged myself up a bowl of cereal (not exactly my favorite meal, but something easy), and headed straight for my room. I went to my pillow corner, the fluffy pillows and fuzzy blanket enveloped me; it felt like a warm, homely hug. Looking around, I noticed my dad had finished hanging all the string lights in my room. The familiar warm glow made the new apartment feel less like a Bed Bath and Beyond brochure, and more like home. The familiarity helped me relax a little as I pulled out my history and mystic 1-1 textbooks.

I hesitated before opening it, the implications of opening this book felt heavy. Opening this book meant that I was admitting that everything going on around me was real. I still hadn't decided if all of this was anything more than a terrible nightmare.

Finally summoning the courage, I scanned through the pages, trying to take in as much as I could, as fast as I could. Pictures scattered the book of a beautiful forest, covered in wildflowers, and I squinted closely at the page. My eyes took a while to adjust. Was that a fairy? Sitting on top of a tulip, it's little wings spread out in an array of colors that matched the many flowers surrounding it. The outskirts of my vision began to blur as my mind reeled. Annoyingly enough, I had a hard time concentrating on all the information before me.

This can't all be real. Why have I not heard about it before? Wouldn't my dad tell me if I was Fay? Or supposed to be a Queen?

Too many questions and not enough answers floated around my head. I couldn't concentrate on reading it properly.

A knock on the door roused me from the questions clouding my brain. Jumping up, I sprinted down the hall to peek through the peephole at my visitor. *OMG HE'S HERE.*

I sighed, dramatically, and on purpose, refusing to let him know I was excited to see him.

"What do you want, Luxor?" I called loudly through the door.

"A cup of sugar?" He gave me a big toothy smile right into the peephole viewer. "Well, not really. My apartment is still empty, so a cup of sugar wouldn't help. I just want some company, I'm going to order some take out if you want some. I could help you study, too?"

Well, Chinese food sounded better than my bowl of half-soggy cereal. I felt like my dad wouldn't mind — I mean, Luxor was supposed to be my "protector" and all. *Does my dad even know about all of this, about where he has sent me? Or was all of this one big mistake? Maybe he will homeschool me if he finds out.*

Luxor cleared his throat, disrupting my train of thought.

I unlocked the door and walked away, knowing he wasn't going to wait for an invitation. Luxor was the physical embodiment of over-confidence, taking it to the point of cockiness.

I grabbed the book from my room, I heard him letting himself in, closing the door and making his way to the living room.

"Do you want anything to drink?" I called to him.

"No, I'm alright," his voice was calm, maybe even bored.

I grabbed myself a cup of water before heading to the living room and plopping myself next to him on the couch.

"Where do you want to begin?" He eyed my book curiously.

"Well, there are two courts. Seelie and Unseelie? Seelie is light Fay and Unseelie is dark Fay or Fata. So, good and bad?"

"Yes and no," he said. "Let's start with what Fay and Fata are and what they represent. Fay and Fata are anywhere from one third to full-blooded fairies. Fay are light because they draw their energy

38

from the sun. Fata are dark because they draw their energy from the moon. However, one group wasn't completely 'bad' or 'good;' they're just different energy sources. The Unseelie court draws off the dark; it also includes Dark Creatures like Gremlins, Goblins, and Imps. Although a lot of them are bad, you will occasionally run into a good creature. Elves and Sprites are typically part of the Seelie court, but don't let that fool you; they're quite mischievous. You can't put one group into good and one into bad, because there's a mix of them in each, and some who prefer to ride down the middle."

"Hmm," I wondered aloud. "Do you get to decide whether you're Fata or Fay?"

"Yes, you can pick as early as your 18th birthday or as late as your 21st. If you don't pick, one side will pick you based on the prior choices in your lineage. You can also be chosen by the Seelie Queen or Unseelie King to be part of their court at any time. That's what happened to you, and the other two possible Queens. You were chosen based on abilities and family bloodlines."

"Abilities? What abilities?" *Can I fly?*

"Fay and Fata are both born with natural abilities, such as green thumbs like when you naturally knew what the roses needed and how to tend to them, and natural optimism. However, some Fay and Fata have additional abilities. Like for instance, I have the ability to draw people closer to me. I can't control what they do when they get close, but I can make them want to get closer. I've seen Fay who can do the opposite, they can repel people whenever

39

they wish. Some can influence mood, emotions, habits, and sleep patterns of others. There is one premonition Fay born every year that can foretell future events, and I've met a dream-walking Fay once."

"Wait a second," I interrupted, stopping his explanation as I attempted to understand all the powers he was listing for me. "So, you can draw people close to you?" Well, that's interesting — not that I could get any closer than I already was.

Maybe that's it! I wasn't crushing on Luxor. I wasn't obsessed with him. I was more drawn to him because that was his gift.

"Most of the time it's unintentional. I can't always control the gift. It takes a lot of practice and time. But yes, in essence, I can if I'd like to. Although I've never felt it myself, my friends tell me it's like an emotional gravitational pull. They want to be around me, and they don't know why."

"That explains the girls around you in the homeroom." I rolled my eyes, smiling.

"No, that's just my devastatingly good looks." He gave me a sly grin.

"Ya, okay," the sarcasm rolled off a bit smoother now that I was getting more comfortable with Luxor.

We sat in silence for a bit, scrolling through pages in the history book. Occasionally, he pointed to a page and made a note on the importance of it. One page explained the courts' hierarchy, Starting with the Unseelie King and Seelie Queen, going to their second in command and personal protectors, then down the latter to those who trained their leagues of protectors and the Army that protected the courts. And luckily, Luxor could help me understand parts of the vocabulary I was unfamiliar with, for example, the word hierarchy. The courts sounded like magical places filled with beautiful people and locations, not small areas like a castle sitting on a court, but a small village in which the castle is the heart of the area.

The textbook said the Queen or King of the courts helped their people worship their elements, also known as the sun and the moon. More people practicing would give the court, as a whole, more power and magic to utilize. The rulers were less like sole lawmakers and more like colleagues, working with and for the better of the people.

The idea of having magic, or powers, and worshiping an element to strengthen those abilities sounded ludicrous to me. I am still having trouble believing this foreign world was real. I needed hard evidence.

As I was taking in all this information, I couldn't help but notice that Luxor sat close enough to read over my shoulder, but far enough away so that we weren't touching. I assumed he noticed that I was distracted by him because he paused his reading and we exchanged glances. An awkward silence filled the air and I quickly looked away.

"Well, I want to feel it. Pull me in." I scooted away a few inches and eagerly waited to feel the magic, staring at him in anticipation.

I could tell my request shocked him. He sat there, staring wide-eyed at me for a long moment, before finding his words and speaking carefully.

"Are you sure? It's nothing special. It's certainly not as cool as dream-walking. The only thing I can control is making you physically come closer, and you seem to do fine on your own." There was a hesitation in his voice. *Maybe he doesn't want me closer.* That stung a bit.

"Haha. Yes, I'm sure. Show me the magic!" I forcibly pushed the words out with a thick layer of enthusiasm and looked away to try to cover the rejection I felt. Underneath, my excitement grew. I wanted to know what magic felt like. Reading about it wasn't enough; I wanted to experience it first-hand.

Just then, he turned to face me. I felt his gaze on me, so I closed my eyes and tried to focus. I didn't feel anything special, maybe a slight tingle, but it wasn't a magical feeling I would say. I wondered if his powers didn't work on me because I was part-Fay. Maybe I was just a freak and that was why his powers didn't work on me, or maybe repelling his powers was a power of my own.

"Is this close enough?" His voice was nothing more than a breathy whisper, and my eyes flickered open. *Gulp.* He was close, very close. Or maybe technically I was close to him since he was still in the same spot as before. However, as far as I knew, I didn't move a bit. I took a deep breath and smelled his cologne for a moment. Sweet like the subtle taste of the first breath you take when walking into a candy store, yet spicy somehow too, and I liked it. My breathing quickened as I leaned back an inch and looked up at him. It was only now that I realized just how close we were.

"I won't touch you again unless you want me to," he whispered. There was something in his eyes I couldn't read. I studied them, trying to decipher it and came up blank.

Answer him! To my utter surprise, and without my mind going through the possible outcomes, I nodded gently.

That was when his lips first met mine. A pleasant burning sensation flowed through my entire body, gasping into his lips. It must have been the magic I was feeling. From my head to my toes, there was a strong tingle — no, a magnet, pulling me closer to Luxor.

I wrapped my hands around his neck and snaked my fingers through the hair on the back of his head. I flexed a little at the weak attempt to pull myself closer to him than I already was. He didn't object. I felt icy cold, hesitant but somehow comforting hands resting on my lower back, as he helped me climb up onto his lap. The kiss deepened. I feel a desperate need to be closer to him, as his tongue traced my lower lip. The places where his bare skin was against my own burned in an odd and pleasant way. I allowed my hands to wander, and they started following the line of his collar around his neck, and down his shirt.

His hands were slow and gentle as they followed the outline of my spine. I jumped a little at his touch, and he slowed down as if to relax me and show me he wasn't going to do anything I objected to. I felt safe, comfortable.

Being in charge of this kiss, maybe even being the one that initiated this kiss, was empowering. My first kiss and I wanted more.

4

I woke with a jolt. Startled and out of breath, I gasped for air, not able to get enough air into me quickly enough. I realized I was in the corner of my room on my pillow stack, with my textbook laying open upside down next to me. *No!* My bowl of cereal was a complete pile of mush. I put my fingers to my lips as if I thought they would feel different somehow.

There were a few knocks at the door before it opened partially, and my dad peered in. I snapped my hand down into my lap and it hit my book. I grimaced but tried to control my face as pain shot through my hand and radiated up my entire arm. I closed my eyes to hold myself together and control my breathing, the flurry of questions flooding my head already brought tears to my eyes.

"Sorry if I woke you up Addy, did you have a good day at school?" he asked warily. The bags under his eyes were

45

particularly prominent; it must have been a long day at work. He looked the same as he had for years, no extra wrinkles or gray hairs, yet at the same time, I could tell he was older. I was not sure if it was the way he presented himself or the way he spoke.

"It was...informative." I paused, not only to gather myself and my sanity but to decide if that could have possibly been a dream? So vivid, so real. I quickly brushed the thought away; now wasn't the time, there were more important things requiring my attention.

"I know, Mrs. Hendrickson called. She said you seemed a little shocked about the events in class today. Not that I can blame you." He looked at the carpet, clearly ashamed, and maybe slightly confused himself.

I needed to focus on my questions and decide how to continue this conversation to get the answers I needed, but I wanted to do it without making him uncomfortable and scaring him away. "Dad, have you ever heard of Fay, or the Seelie courts?"

My dad slowly nodded, the look in his eyes told me this was a much overdue discussion. He took in a breath that seemed to last forever, then he finally spoke.

"Yes, and I should have told you about us sooner. Every time we moved it was to find you a protector so that we could safely introduce you to the Fay world." He looked down again, but only for a second, before returning his gaze to me. "But, the last two cities we lived in, the protectors assigned to you were killed, so we had to leave immediately."

My eyes widened, and my heart rate increased. I wasn't worried for myself, but because Luxor was in danger.

My dad's eyes appeared watery — tears were beginning to form. I saw the wheels turning in his head as he gathered his thoughts. I could have only imagined how hard this had been for him. My dad and I didn't talk about death much, he took it hard. Whether it was terrorist attacks, old age, or even an accident, dad had never handled death well. Needless to say, we didn't watch the news much.

"I can only imagine how confusing this is for you. Your mom was full Fata and I'm only half-Fay. She was expected by grandma and grandpa to keep the bloodline pure. We were only 16 when we met. Your mom was the most amazing woman I've ever met. She could make you feel safe, secure, and insane — all at the same time, she had a gift at manipulating emotions I've never seen before." He was laughing through his words as he thought about mom. "I was assigned to be a hunter at 18. Do you know what a hunter is, Addy?"

I shook my head, but only slightly, as to not interrupt his story. I was not ready for it to be over yet; I was not ready to stop hearing about mom. Sometimes she seemed like a figment of my imagination, rather than someone who once existed.

"A hunter is a boy who is chosen by Seelie and Unseelie courts before the age of 18. There is a pool of names of every boy under 18, and 15 names are drawn every year. Those 15 are trained as hunters. They are trained in both Fay and Fata ways and used as an

47

asset against any potential threats to the Seelie or Unseelie courts. It's like a small private army to protect the Seelie world." He quickly glanced at me as if he was checking I'm still paying attention.

"At that point, I wasn't going to go. It's an amazing honor to be chosen, but I didn't know what it would mean for your mom and I. Training took at least 24 months, and who knows where we would end up being assigned when I was done? But your mom insisted I go; she wrote to me twice a week. Those two years were easily the longest years of my life. The day I came home, I looked at your mom and I knew nothing had changed. I was assigned to move to New Braunfels, Texas, where Dark Creature uprisings were happening against the Unseelie court. So, we asked your grandma and papa for permission to be together, and to our surprise, they said yes."

The look in my father's eyes was almost dreamlike, as if he was reliving the memory. He moved further into the room and took a seat on the floor close to me, his slightly tense demeanor told me he was contemplating something. Awkwardly dad reached an arm out, patted my shoulder a couple of times, then returned his arms to his lap, looking perplexed. Unsure of how he could comfort me, he settled for just sitting nearby.. Like me, my dad didn't like being touched.

"On the day of our wedding, your grandma handed us an unopened letter from the Seelie court. Why they sent it to your grandma I'll never know; she's a premonition Fata, so I'm sure she saw it coming. The Royal Sight Fay predicted we would have a daughter in a year, and that you, our daughter, would be special in the Fay world. For reasons unknown, you would spark change in Fay everywhere. The moment your grandma and grandpa heard you were going to be blessed with summer, they packed up and moved to the Seelie Kingdom. Since your mother's accident, they haven't left the Seelie Kingdom, not even to cross back over to the Unseelie Kingdom." He spared me a glance again. I heard the gentleness in his voice, as if he was gauging whether or not grandma and grandpa's fear to leave the Seelie Kingdom hurt me or not because they never came to visit. It didn't.

"However, predictions aren't always accurate, especially now your grandmother is living in the Seelie courts; her premonitions are few and far between and when they do happen, they are fuzzy and sometimes inaccurate. Without being on Unseelie grounds she isn't able to channel as much energy. Grandma would send letters to keep us updated on what was happening in the courts. Sadly, things have changed since then. With your mom's passing and the recent events making us move homes, I couldn't find the right time to sit and talk to you about everything. Grandma and grandpa have become more and more distant; with us moving so often, it made it difficult to find the schools we needed to put you in, so you could learn about the Kingdoms."

Dad leaned forward and put his hands on his knees, I scooted over to sit by him and rested on his shoulder, he wrapped an arm around me and gave me a smile. It was good to know more, even though I could tell through his unsteady voice talking about all of this was painful for him too. I couldn't help but wonder if now that I knew about this world, if I would be allowed to see my grandma and grandpa again. That however, would be a question for another day.

"When you were born, it was like seeing the sun for the first time. You were gifted with the representation of summer. Your mom was so filled with joy she wept, held you closer, and cried some more. I thought she'd never stop crying. You were nothing but perfect, you always have been. We decided then and there that we weren't going to tell you until you were assigned a protector on your 16th birthday."

I took a moment to picture it. The past my dad described sounded like the typical boy-meets-girl fairy tale — with a special golden child twist, of course.

My dad moved slightly so he could see my face, and I plastered on a smile. Overwhelmed, I felt totally and helplessly overwhelmed, not that I would let my dad know that. He had enough on his plate.

"It's okay Dad, I'm learning quickly. It's just a lot to catch up on," I said, trying to reassure him I wasn't going to lose my mind. Or maybe I had already lost it. "Dad, I don't know if I want to be a Queen. I don't know if I want to go through trials. I don't think I can be the ruler everyone seems to think I can be." The words spilled out of me in a panicked rant.

"You're going to make an amazing Queen, honey; the premonition Fay have seen it. Fay from hundreds of years ago, up until this day see several possible future rulers, from those rulers only three are gifted. Dells, you were one of those three; they saw something in you. You'll catch up quickly. Soon you will be traveling to the Seelie court to meet the Seelie Queen and the two other potential Queens. This will give you the chance to meet the people, see what you're fighting for, and see what you stand to lose if you give it away." He turned his head away, but it was too late. I saw what flashed across his face: pure fear.

It felt as if my heart skipped a beat. My dad was not one to be afraid, he was one of the strongest people I knew

"Just remember that life in the Seelie Kingdom is dangerous honey," he whispered cautiously. "Not everyone wants a new Seelie Queen. Keep your protector close."

My face flushed immediately. *My protector.* I glanced at my feet, hoping he'd mistake my sudden display for awkwardness and confusion, instead of embarrassment. Not to mention, I had to be assigned my own living, breathing human just to keep me alive. *With two protectors dead already, maybe Luxor was a lost cause. Perhaps if he died too, they would give up and just let whoever wanted me to have me. After all, there were two others selected for the trials who probably knew a lot more than I did.*

Being close didn't seem to be an issue. In fact being too close might've been more problematic for us. I didn't know if there were boundaries for this sort of thing.

"Protectors are chosen for several reasons: compatibility, abilities, and recommendations. So, Luxor will make a good partner. You just have to be open to working together."

Of course, my dad knew who it was already. We wouldn't have moved here if they didn't already have a protector lined up. Maybe this meant we wouldn't be moving again so soon.

Standing up, my dad kissed me on the forehead and walked out of the room, giving me the silence I needed to try to comprehend the changing world around me.

From the floor, I crawled into my bed, somehow still exhausted, even though I'd just had a nap. I was not physically tired but mentally drained. I'd never had a dream about a boy before, and I was not entirely sure what to make of it. *Maybe it wasn't a dream at all.* I shook my head in confusion and covered myself in blankets. Was I looking forward to spending more time with Luxor, or was this a sign that maybe I was letting him get too close to me?

A plethora of emotions flitted around my head as I closed my eyes: confusion, sadness, loss, despair, and just a glimpse of hope. The emotions swirled behind my eyelids in a mixture of colors. The longer I lay there; however, the colors slowly faded away into nothing, until finally, blackness surrounded me.

5

The crisp, autumn air flowed in as the leaves changed from bright green to a comfortable red-brown. They fell in circular patterns everywhere, dancing soundlessly through the air as the trees shed their old foliage to make room for their new sprouts in spring. I took a deep breath as Luxor and I walked in silence to school. The cold, sharp air filled my lungs, making me feel more awake.

School seemed to move smoother, now that I knew where I was going. Luxor still walked with me everyday, close to my side rather than leading now though, sometimes even tracing behind me. I hadn't dared to bring up my, well, what I thought was a dream. Sometimes when he got too close, I could still feel a tingling heat radiate through my body.

If anything really happened, Luxor didn't let on. He blended into all my classes effortlessly. Well, except History 1-1. During my last class of the day, Luxor had to take extra self-defense and advanced mystics courses. To become a protector, he had to pass a field exam at the Unseelie court and, from what I'd heard from the whispers, it was going to be intense.

Our lunch table naturally filled on its own now. By my side was Anna, whose outfits were becoming bolder every day. Her choice today was a metallic pair of golden skin-tight pants, and a simple black blouse with ombre bracelets up both arms in hues of golds, oranges, and reds. It gave the impression that she was physically and fashionably on fire.

Her current fling, Dustin, sat dutifully next to her, and his best friend, Devon, sat by him. Dustin and Devon were a funny pair; they were about as "boy"' as "boys" could get. You name it — comics, boots, bugs, and dirt. Dustin was the complete opposite of who I would have imagined Anna fancying, yet for some reason, they were good together and it worked.

Then on Luxor's side was Rachael (of course), and her posse (whose names I hadn't bothered to learn yet). Luxor still sat across from me; we still ate together from one big tray, which I could see bugged Rachael, although she remained strong and confident — I would have almost admired her if she wasn't annoyingly persistent in her attempts to ask Luxor out.

I had a theory about our lunch tray. I didn't notice until recently, but Luxor took a small piece out of every item of food on the tray. I used to think it was a sweet gesture — him getting my lunch for me, that is. Now I wondered if he was just checking for poison. The thought of needing someone to check my meals for any signs of poison made my stomach churn. I turned the apple back and forth in my hand wondering if my next bite could be my last. I need to remember to ask Luxor about it later.

"Adella? Hellooooo, earth to Adella?" Anna waved her hands around my face in big sweeping gestures.

"Oops. Sorry, Anna, I guess I was a little deep in thought," I said.

She eyed me suspiciously; I gave her my full attention. She wrestled with something in her head for a moment, almost as if she wanted to argue something. "That's fine," she conceded, apparently the argument to herself did end well enough to say out loud. "I just wanted to know if you got your letter silly? I'm dying to know." She bit her bottom lip and her eyes widened as she leaned closer to me onto the edge of her chair.

Even Rachael stopped staring at Luxor for a moment and looked at me, the whole table immediately became uncharacteristically quiet.

"Letter? No, I didn't get a letter. Why would I get a letter?" I shook my head slightly. Once again, I felt like I was the last to know things.

"Maybe she's not really a chosen one, and it's just a mistake," Rachael sneered. Or maybe it was just her voice. *An ugly voice for an ugly person.*

"Oh, pipe down Rachael!" I swear Anna was my savior. She continued, despite Rachel's remark. "The selected three are starting to receive letters about the weekends they're supposed to go to the Seelie court to meet the Queen. And I heard you get to bring your protector *and* a friend..." She wiggled her eyebrows at me. No guesses were needed to know what she was not-so-subtly hinting at.

"Okay Anna," I laughed way too hard. "If I get a letter."

"You mean, *when*," she corrected me.

"Okay, *when* I get a letter, and *if* I can bring a friend. You are the one."

"Yaaaaaaayyyy!" Anna squealed, attaching herself to my side. She reminded me of a koala.

Luxor met my eyes; I could see him quietly chuckling to himself as he watched Anna's display of affection. It appeared Anna and I had officially hit the best friend zone. I was certainly fond of having her around, and I was starting to get used to all the hugging.

As far as I remembered, I hadn't visited the Seelie courts before; however, dad said we visited grandma and grandpa at their home, which was just on the outskirts of the courts. But I probably didn't remember, I was too young. I was really looking forward to returning and getting the chance to explore the new world, my new world. Although I was internally freaking out about everyone's expectations of me and who I was and who I would become. But I did hear that as soon as I entered the Seelie court, I didn't need sight; I could see everyone in their true forms.

I'd practiced my sight a couple of times over the last few days, only on myself in the mirror, and my dad. I almost couldn't see a difference with my dad; his skin appeared a little paler, with a blue tint. Hardly noticeable changes unless I focused really hard. His eyes were brighter, and I could see light scars across his arms and legs. He told me the reason I couldn't see a big change was because, as a hunter, he was taught to hide his true form, even from the sight of Fay and Fata. I wanted to learn to do that someday, but he said it took a very long time to learn.

Closing my eyes, I prepared to do it again. I counted my breaths, picturing Luxor across from me, his black hair was just long enough to run his fingers through. I saw his green eyes and his broad shoulders. Next, I attempted to pinpoint his aura, which was the real trick to opening sight. Knowing someone's true colors would help to reveal their true form. I concentrated as hard as I could.

I decided his aura was warm, brown, earthy, and comforting. *Umber.* The deep shades of a hot latte on a cold day, or like a handful of cool, moist dirt right after the rain. I pictured the color surrounding Luxor. Taking one final deep breath, I opened my eyes one at a time, a little excited and afraid at the same time at what I'd see.

Anna's large elf eyes appeared in front of me unexpectedly.

"You're getting good at your sight, Dells! But it's time to head to class, Luxor is putting your lunch tray away." She giggled, knowing full well it wasn't her I wanted to see. I didn't reply, so she grabbed my hand and led me down the hall. "Come on we have to get to class."

As she continued half-dragging me, I smiled and sighed. Seeing Luxor would just have to wait.

After class, I made plans for Anna to come over to my house; she wanted to be there when I got my letter. Not to mention, when I told her my dad was a hunter, she almost begged to meet him. My dad promised a couple of good stories over dinner if I brought any friends home. It would have been nice having someone to walk with since Luxor was going to be at his training.

The class flew by, and before I knew it, Anna was pulling me out the door, and we were walking down my street — well, really, she was leading me down the street.

"I'm so excited to see the Seelie courts. Maybe there will be a ball! I wonder what I'd wear, I don't own any ball attire. I wonder if it would be near the gardens. I hear the gardens there are beautiful year-round. Full of color and liveliness, *oh,* and sprites! I can't wait to see the sprites! I hear they flutter around the blooming flowers and cause quite a bit of mischief with all their little tricks," Anna rambled to me.

"What's a sprite?" I asked, it felt a bit silly needing her to dumb it down for me.

"I forget that you started school a bit late!" She sounded sympathetic, which made me feel better about asking the question. "Sprites are little creatures, no bigger than a few inches, who like to cause problems — practical jokes, basically. Well, if you're on their good side." She moved her fingers showing me the rough size of the sprite, then began moving her hands as if they were jumping up and down.

"Like tapping your shoulder when no one's really there?"

"Not quite." This time, Anna rolled her eyes at me. "Sprites can put ideas or thoughts in people's heads when they get close to them. They can't force you to do anything, but they can certainly give you funny ideas. My mom says one day, she and my dad were picking flowers in the Seelie gardens, and 20 minutes later, my dad was making a crown with the flowers and dancing around the court in them."

I couldn't help but laugh; that certainly did sound mischievous. We had officially stopped in front of my apartment door and Anna tapped her foot eagerly.

I reached over to unlock my apartment door, with Anna still leading the way. She wasted no time with any formalities as she brazenly explored every inch of my apartment before I had the chance to take my shoes off.

"Your apartment is so big and colorful!" She said as she swept down the hall and peaked nosily into my room.

"Thanks!" My dad called from the kitchen.

Wheeling around, Anna headed toward the kitchen.

"Hi Mr. Shenning," she called as she approached. "I'm Anna. I thought you'd be at work, sorry." Her cheeks flushed slightly.

"It's fine Anna, call me Dan. I came home early to cook us all dinner tonight. Addy doesn't bring home friends often so it's more of an occasion. I invited someone over myself, too. As for the apartment, I hired someone to decorate it right before we moved in. I'm not much of an interior decorator."

"It's perfect!" Anna was gushing at this point. "Did you get any mail today *Daaaannnnnnn?*" I could only imagine what my dad could really see; because to me, Anna's eyes looked wide and her eyebrows were raised high as she put way too much emphasis on my dad's first name.

"I'm not sure." My dad gave Anna a curious look. "You're welcome to check if you'd like, box 24."

My dad threw Anna the keys. Without hesitation, she smiled and ran out the door. She must have seen the mailboxes on her way in because she waited for no instructions.

"Anna's kind of an odd one, I like her." My dad grinned at me.

"Me too, Dad. Who did you invite to dinner tonight?"

"Well, I'm not certain he'll come. But I left an invitation taped to Luxor's door. It's about time I get to meet him. You know he puts a lot of effort into keeping you safe, right? The least you could do is introduce us." His comment seemed halfway between a lecture and a joke. With my dad, it was always hard to tell.

I was unsure if he felt hurt that I hadn't brought Luxor home to meet him yet, or if he was scolding me for being rude and taking advantage of my new protector. His words weighed heavily on my shoulders either way. Thankfully, Anna came rushing in the door.

"A letter, a lettterrrr, Adella got a leettttterrr." Her voice was high and melodic as she skipped into my house, tossing the keys back to my dad, who caught them with ease. I could see a hint of amusement and joy in his eyes as he watched Anna skip around. It was certainly refreshing being around her.

"Well, what are you waiting for?" My dad looked almost as excited as we were. Maybe he's just humoring us. "Open it!"

Anna did one more victory lap around the kitchen before she skidded to a halt in front of me and handed me the letter; I ripped it open in one quick movement. I took the letter out, the color of it reminded me of a sunflower with gold embellishments. It read:

Ms. Adella Shenning

The Seelie Court requests the presence of you and a guest of choice for three days' time from March 3rd to March 5th.

On March 3rd you are requested to join us for dinner at 6PM in the Grand Room.

On March 4th at 7PM you are requested to join us for a ball in the Gardens.

Attire will be provided by the seamstress for you and your guests. Measurements will be taken upon your arrival.

We look forward to meeting you, Adella.

Queen Wyvette Leaure

Anna was practically hyperventilating. "That's me... I'm '*and one guest*,'" she squealed excitedly.

I read it a couple more times. It didn't specify if I should bring parents or protectors. I glanced at the little calendar that sat on the fridge next to us, that was this weekend!

"You girls will have so much fun." My dad gave Anna a friendly smile, then turned to grab something out of the oven as the timer went off.

"You're not coming, Dad?"

"No Addy, I've had enough time in the Seelie court for one lifetime. You'll have Anna and Luxor; they'll be all you need, trust me."

Well, that explained that. Whether the invitation for a protector to come along was in my letter or not, he would be there. I wondered if Luxor received a letter too. As the thought crossed my mind, there was a small tap on the door. My dad leaped out of the seat at the island and half-walked, half-ran to the door. Almost as giddy as Anna was when she arrived, it must have rubbed off on him.

"Luxor!" I heard my dad exclaim like they were old friends. Maybe just a bit too enthusiastically for a greeting.

"Hey Dan," I heard Luxor say before a weird, "oomph" sound escaped his lips.

Did my dad hug him? I tried to imagine my dad hugging a stranger. There was no way he would have done that. Would he? Just as I tried to imagine the strange display, Luxor and my dad walked in side by side. One of my dad's arms hung oddly around Luxor's shoulders. It would have been a normal sight, only Luxor was a few inches taller than my dad, so it looked very uncomfortable.

"Hey, Luxor! Long time no see," Anna said sarcastically. She showed no mercy and laid it on thick. I could tell that it was going to be a fun dinner.

I decided to set the table; it wasn't a hard task, but it kept me busy while dad, Anna, and Luxor talked in the kitchen. I did my best to tune them out and keep my nerves calm. I heard my name occasionally, but not too much. The conversation seemed to be heading down a good road, with no raised voices or serious tones.

Luxor came out first, holding my dad's famous green beans and bacon, followed by Anna holding the mashed sweet potatoes. It was like a food runway show; my stomach grumbled, making me aware of how famished I was. Just then, my dad walked in with the main attraction: a maple-glazed whole ham garnished in pineapple rings and maraschino cherries.

Everyone sat down, mouths drooling, as my dad made a show of carving the magnificent ham. As soon as he finished, he thanked everyone for coming, and we dug in. I was mid-face-stuff when my dad looked right at me and Luxor and asked us an odd question.

"So," he stated solemnly. "How long have you officially been together?"

I half inhaled my food and had to cough a little to get it out of my throat. My eyes began to water as I struggled to take in oxygen quickly enough.

"Not that I approve, you're not supposed to have romantic relations with your protectors. You can't let anyone find out; Luxor could get his title taken away." He looked at Luxor. I followed his gaze. Luxor played it much cooler than I did.

"We're not together sir," Luxor said, as confident as ever, giving my dad his half-smile that made my heart skip a beat.

"That's too bad." As Dad said the words, I could see the relief in his face. "But that means he's still available, eh Anna?" Anna turned redder than a tomato; the deep red contrasting with her pale face was very flattering; nearly the same color as her hair. I was just thankful the attention was off of me, even if it was at Anna's expense.

"Dad, this doesn't seem like a very appropriate dinner conversation." I did my best to give him a stern look. I could see in his face that I failed. *Who's the adult here again?*

"No, please continue," Luxor smiled. "I'm a catch." He gave me a quick wink.

Luxor and my dad then burst into laughter, this time at mine and Anna's expense. I didn't know if a family dinner would happen again any time soon. I did my best to divert the conversation.

"Didn't you promise me a good, action-filled story, Dad?"

"Are you sure you want to hear one while you eat?"

Luxor and Anna both nodded enthusiastically. I hesitated before I nodded as well. If my dad was double-checking, I just knew it was going to be gruesome. "Okay then Addy, I'm going to tell you the story of how I met your uncle David."

This story was going to be good. My uncle David is one of the scariest, yet most amazing people I knew. He's not my uncle biologically, of course, just a close friend of the family.

"I met David on my first day of hunter training. We were frightened, away from home, and nervous for the days ahead. We happened to be assigned bunks together. After David put his things on the top bunk, he turned to ask me if it was okay, and I was scared to disagree. Anyone in their right mind would be scared to disagree with him, you see." My dad's expression looked as if he was seeing uncle David for the first time, wide-eyed and a tad frightened.

"David was a savage! He was covered in strange bite mark scars from head to toe — in some places you could see parts of his flesh had been taken out. Not to mention he's *huge*; well-built, and is at least 6'5. I was speechless. I don't even remember shaking his hand or responding for that matter. I remember I cowered slightly as he looked at me, afraid to stay, but even more afraid to run away. Honestly, I can't even recall if I ever actually answered his question. As the days went on, David and I became friends. The day I'll never forget, is the day I asked him about his scars."

My dad took in a deep breath, preparing himself. I could see how hard it was for him to talk about; he was white knuckled, clenching the side of his chair and his face was hard.

"Some of the best people in the world are given burdens that only they can handle," he said through clenched teeth. "His family was attacked by a group of Dark Creatures attempting to overthrow the Unseelie King. His dad was part of the guard, and on the night of the attack, the guard's quarters were raided. The families were all burned and beaten — some were even eaten, depending on who found them first." My dad cringed from the memory. This wasn't a story he enjoyed telling, but my dad believed no story of character deserved to go untold. He closed his eyes for a minute as if he saw the events replaying in his head.

"David was just a boy; he was hiding in the closet when the Gremlins attacked. As kids, we're taught that Gremlins no longer

66

prefer flesh, that they can survive on a diet of fresh meat as well. But this wasn't always the case. Evil Gremlins still exist, those who refuse to adapt to the new ways. That night, David's mom and dad were examples of just that, and they were killed. David could hear their screams from where he was hidden, but they didn't say a word about where he was or even muttered his name. When David thought the Gremlins had left, he peeked his head out of the closet door. It made just enough noise that two of the Gremlins returned. David, only ten years old at the time, was attacked mercilessly. He doesn't remember exactly how it happened, or where he found the strength, but when he could no longer take the pain and when the numbness of his parents' death faded — only then he began to struggle. He screamed, flailed, and kicked as much as he could, feeling the burning sensation of teeth tearing at every inch of his body. He dared to open his eyes, and it was just in time to see guards charging into the room. That's when he finally blacked out."

My dad blankly stared at the center of his plate, reliving the horrors of the past. He looked back up at us all. Luxor was engrossed in the story, Anna on the other hand, looked pastier than normal.

"David told me that story and smiled at the end. He considers himself a survivor, a fighter. I consider him so much more than that. David is one of the most respectable, considerate, and loving people you will ever meet. I wouldn't be here today if he wasn't by my side for the battles that came after."

I never knew how or where Dad and David met. I never inquired about his scars, although now I wish I had. We sat in silence for a short time, before Dad started to recount a couple of more lighthearted, funny tales about the trouble he and David got into. Suddenly, I remembered I had a question for Luxor.

"Luxor, did you receive a letter?"

"Nope, not that I know of. I just checked the mail on my way up, why?"

"Well, I was formally invited to the Seelie court and I wasn't sure if you were coming too or not."

"Protectors are expected to follow at all times, so I'd be going regardless. Though, I'm given a little slack because I'm in training; as long as I know where you are, who you're with, when you'll be there, and for how long, then we can be apart a few blocks. However, no formal invitation needed for me to attend trips and events. We also get trained and tested on our skills and abilities by the Queen's protector while we're attending," he said easily, as if everyone had known this.

"That makes sense, I guess." I ate another forkful of food, unsure of how I felt about having an adult babysitter. Somehow, knowing it was Luxor gave me a warm, comforting feeling. When dinner finished, Luxor stood and began clearing the table.

"No, I've got it," I offered.

"Me too, you guys go relax," Anna chimed in.

Luxor followed my dad into the living room where they turned on a football game and began to talk quietly. I couldn't hear the

68

details, but it sounded like questions regarding the trip to the Seelie court.

"You rinse and I'll load."

Being Anna's friend was easy. She didn't require constant conversation, and she offered plenty of topics when I needed someone to talk to. We worked quietly for a while; the silence was peaceful. Letting my mind unwind after a long day was always a difficult task.

I heard the T.V. turn off and Luxor said goodbye to my dad; he'd been in training almost all day today, I was surprised he was not passed out already.

Luxor walked slowly by the kitchen, waved to Anna then took my hand as he passed and squeezed it.

"See you tomorrow, Adella."

"Bye," I barely whispered.

A painful heat seared the palm of my hand and radiated from where he touched, up my entire arm. I cringed, and he let go quickly. He hesitated and gave me a small wink before he left. *Well, that was odd.* I wanted to follow, to be near him. I froze, staring after him as he walked out the door. When I snapped out of it, I looked over to Anna, who was staring at me, grinning.

"You're not together...*yet,*" Anna proclaimed loudly.

"Oh, quiet you." I laughed and threw the dish towel at her.

"Seriously Adella, he likes you."

"It's so hard to tell. Sometimes he's friendly and sometimes he's so serious. Either way, I don't have time for a boyfriend right now. But you know what I do have time for?"

"Help picking out clothes for the Seelie court?"

"Of course!" I smile as we head to my room to raid my closet.

Finding clothes didn't take too long, as I decided to pack light.

Before I knew it, it was morning time, and we had to leave. I didn't sleep a wink all night and now somehow, we were in the car.

"How do you get to the Seelie court again?" I asked my dad.

We'd been driving into nothing for about 30 minutes now and brown dirt surrounded us from all sides.

"We'll be there soon Delly, we just have to find the spot. Keep your eyes peeled for a greenhouse."

A greenhouse? Why in the world would I look for a greenhouse?

Anna and Luxor kept an eye out of each of their windows in the back, and I focused my eyes straight ahead.

"I see it! Right over their guys!" We could barely understand Anna. She pressed her face completely against the glass, and used her index finger to tap and point.

My dad turned the car and sped up. His accelerator climbed as we made our way straight towards the greenhouse. The closer we got, the more I started sweating; my dad didn't show any signs of slowing or stopping.

I looked back at Anna and Luxor, whose faces mirrored the same fear and shock that mine had.

We were at 75 miles per hour already; my dad's expression was that of pure recklessness as he'd hurtled the car towards the side of the greenhouse.

"Hold on guys!" My dad semi-shouted as we drove into the side of the greenhouse. I held my breath and squeezed my eyes shut, waiting for the impact, only we didn't crash into anything.

I slowly opened my eyes, knowing we should have made contact with it already. Blurs of greens and various shades of yellow whizzed past us, and the scent of fresh lavender filled my nose as we went right through the wall and landed in a field. Hundreds of wildflowers surrounded us now, in colors and hues I'd never seen together all at once. The sight was overwhelming.

"I didn't think we'd make it! The car didn't wanna pick up speed fast enough, we needed to reach at least 88 miles an hour," my dad said, as he half-laughed. Beads of sweat trickled down his face.

Luxor joined in; he and Dad laughed harmoniously. Anna and I made eye contact again, with her still clutching her chest, trying to get her breathing under control. I saw in her face that I was not the only one who thought the boys were going crazy.

My dad jumped out of the car and started to unpack our luggage. We jumped out quickly to lend a hand and that's when I really noticed the change. I was so used to seeing Anna's true form that I didn't realize it was all I could see when I looked at her the first time. I looked over to my dad grabbing the luggage. He was dark blue, and his scars were baby blue. His hair was dark with white streaks; it complemented his skin nicely. But somehow this unfamiliar person wasn't a stranger, he was somehow even more familiar than the dad I knew and loved.

I looked down at my hands and stared at the strange fluorescence my skin emitted. I tried to imagine my skin being the same as my dad's — if I wasn't gifted the representation of summer. I couldn't help but wonder what my mom's complexion was.

"Where are we headed next Dan?" Luxor asked.

I looked up and flinched. Luxor looked... exactly the same. He was almost out of place when I compared him to our odd little group. His eyes were as beautiful as ever against his pale skin and black hair. He looked back at me like he always did. I guess that made sense. At 18, he could use his sight all the time.

Anna, on the other hand, stood there, just staring at my dad. He glanced back but continued to work. He took a deep breath in and let out a low chuckle.

"You know it's rude to stare, Anna," he teased her.

"Oh, sorry Dan! I was just wondering about your arms. They're...they're hurt! Or well, they were hurt," Anna fumbled with her words as she continued to count the scars that trailed my dad's arms.

"I wasn't always ready for my fights, Anna. I had to get some sense knocked into me before I learned to always be ready. One eye open and all that."

We grabbed our luggage and walked across the field. As we walked through the flowers, I ran my hands along their soft petals. With every different color, a different, intoxicating scent arose.

I could see a small line that stretched as far as I could see either way in the distance. As we approached, it became more evident it was a large wall. It was large, the wall had to be at least 30 feet high, covered in ivy and moss, and it looked like something right out of a fairy tale. Dad stayed on the path and led us to a small gate. A shiver ran up my spine, and I couldn't help but wonder if we were being watched. I looked over my shoulder. No, I was still in the back of the group.

My dad led and we followed down the path through the gate so narrow it put us in single file. Towards the end, the path widened again. Luxor forcefully moved Anna and me right behind dad and made his way to the back of the group. I protested in annoyance, not wanting to be rushed. Anna grabbed my hand and pulled me forward gently. I ignored her for a moment, readying myself to argue with Luxor, when she tugged on it again. I turned to talk to her, and that was when I first saw it.

A white and gold castle glistened brightly in the light. Pink and white intertwined roses climbed up the tall columns and walls. Moss and wildflowers covered the path leading to the castle.

On either side of the colorful path, was a carefully designed garden display. The colors blended into each other seamlessly, creating a perfect color wheel of reds melting into pinks, pinks into purple and purples into deepening shades of blue. Sprites danced

73

around the petals of the flowers, humming a melodic tune. It was mesmerizing. I let go of Anna's hand to get a closer look.

I didn't notice that I was veering off towards them until a hand grabbed my arm.

"Whoa, Dells. Don't go that way. Those sprites are nasty little things," Dad squinted at them and Luxor nodded in agreement.

"I heard they were just mischievous, like little pranksters."

"Only if they like you," my dad chuckled. "Not everything they do is always so pretty." The way he said it sounded threatening.

I walked back onto the path, jogging a little to catch up to Anna. She wasted no time making her way to the castle. When I finally caught up to Anna I linked our arms together.

"I heard they last all night long!" Once again, Anna was gushing about the ball.

"We need to make it through dinner tonight before we can think about the ball Anna." Luxor shrugged his shoulders and laughed.

"That's right," I chimed in. "We need to go straight to the seamstress, Anna. We're a little late."

As we walked up the steps, a man waiting next to the entrance whispered something into his radio and opened the front door for us. The interior was minimalistic. I ran my fingers along the intricate carvings in the wood along the champagne walls. The floors were a beautiful white marble and a large glass chandelier hung suspended in the middle of the room.

A small woman stood under the chandelier. She was shorter than Anna, with pointed ears and sharp features. Her outfit was a bold, red knee-length dress accompanied by minimal accessories. Her lips pressed into a tight line, her foot tapped incessantly, and her eye contact, which lasted just a bit too long, made me feel as if she was already judging me. Next to her stood a man of average height with green skin and white hair, waiting with one hand on a large cart.

"Adella, Anna, and Luxor." It sounded like a statement, but I might have been a question.

We nodded our heads. The woman gestured towards the large cart.

"Please put your things on the carts; they will be brought to your room. You three are late for your appointment with the seamstress. Follow me."

We quickly placed our items on the cart.

I turned to hug my dad, who held onto me tightly and whispered in my ear, "Stay safe and have fun, honey. I love you."

"Love you too, Dad," I squeezed him one more time before he left.

The lady's foot tapping grew louder, and quickened in pace, so I broke away from my dad, gave him one last smile, and joined the others. We followed her up the large staircase, through what felt like endless hallways, decorated in pictures of what I assumed were past Queens and their families. *For someone so short, she sure walks at a brisk pace.*

We walked through a large, dark door at the end of the hall. I bit my cheek to hide the shock that threatened to display on my

75

face as we entered the room. As we walked down the center aisle, none of the women working on their antique sewing machines bothered to look up at us. They were holding what seemed to be an endless amount of different fabrics in deep blues and reds; some held a beautiful gold swirling pattern, that, judging from the amount of material they had on hand, must have been a fairly common color scheme to wear in the Seelie Kingdom.

However, the fabric didn't even come close to all of the different skin hues of the women working on them—pink, gold, maroon, and blue. I counted at least twelve different ones in various shades, just on one side of the room.

I wonder what decides their beautiful hues?

Down the middle of the row was a tall man, wearing around ten different fabrics. A pad with pins in the side was attached to his hip. He held a pen and a notebook in his hand. Charcoal-black rings coated around his eyes and colorful shadow on his eyelids. A dark liner lined his lips. The color showed a clear contrast with the actual lipstick he was wearing. Weirdly, it complemented his face.

"RayRay!" The short elf woman squealed, hugging the designer, who was like a statue coming to life. "These are your subjects."

She turned to us, her demeanor changing again, transforming into the woman we met in the lobby. "I must be leaving. I have to welcome the next selected. If you need anything, ring for me, my name is MaryAnn."

She handed us a small card with her name and number, then swiftly left the room. Somehow the invitation to "ring for her," wasn't all that inviting.

I focused my attention on RayRay, who was examining us like a pack of lab rats. I was not normally super self-conscious, but I found myself holding my breath and sucking in my stomach a bit as he looked me up and down. He called for his helpers to take measurements while he talked to us individually to get an idea of our preferences.

Anna's turn took forever, luckily. When it came to clothes, my mind was blank. However, the extra amount of time she was taking didn't help me think of any ideas. My turn had finally arrived to sit and talk to RayRay.

"I know exactly what you need," he said, seriously.

"That's great because I have no idea what I want." I tipped my head back and sighed, so he could see my relief.

"I'm thinking dark blue, with jewels around the hems — like a starry night to complement your gold skin. Nobody else will be wearing blue, they'll stick to the Seelie Kingdom colors: yellows, pinks, and golds." He was elated to be sharing his expertise with me.

"That sounds perfect."

He beamed at me, then gestured for me to stand. He helped me up and gave me a quick spin, seeing how I move, no doubt. Hopefully, my clumsiness showed him I need some mercy in the practicality of the dress.

77

He measured under my bust, and diagonally from my shoulder to waist again. I was not sure what for, since his assistants had already measured me from head to toe. RayRay threw me a pair of heels that were sitting on a shelf on the wall. I put them on and he watched me struggle to find balance. Then I haphazardly trudged down the small hall in the room a couple times before falling into RayRay. He caught me, when I looked up at him he returned my gaze with a look of confusion.

"No makeup?" he inquired.

I shook my head no in response. He gave me a small reassuring smile as I slipped the heels off and handed them back.

"I will find someone to help you with your makeup, and we will have to do something about your lack of skills in heels," he said in a tone of dismissal as he opened the door and gave Luxor a small wave to come forward.

Then I sat waiting quietly on the side until Luxor's turn finished.

As if she knew that we'd finished, MaryAnn walked back into the room just as Luxor was stepping away from RayRay.

"Follow me and I will take you to your rooms where you can prepare for dinner."

She walked back out without so much as a backward glance to see if we were following. We walked down several long halls until we reached a set of doors.

"Anna, Adella, these will be your rooms."

I gave Luxor a nervous glance. I wondered how far away they would put his room. Just as he opened his mouth to say something, MaryAnn pointed to a room across the hall.

"Luxor that will be your room."

Relief washed over me. It was comforting having Luxor stay close. Luxor's shoulders visibly relaxed too.

"Don't forget dinner at 6 pm. The dress code is semi-formal."

That was also good news seeing as my entire wardrobe consisted solely of semi-formal attire. We thanked MaryAnn and entered our rooms. For dinner, I settled for a pair of long gray slacks and a black blouse that had a big bow across my back. I pinned my hair up and threw on some lip gloss and mascara. I was just about to head out the door when I noticed flowers on my bed.

"Were those there a minute ago?" I whispered to myself, puzzled. Certainly, I couldn't have missed such a huge arrangement as I walked back and forth in my room, while I was getting ready. *But, my door hasn't been opened since I shut it, and no one has knocked, so they must have been.*

Red, white, and pink roses — at least three dozen laid on my bed in a simple but elegant arrangement. A small handwritten poem accompanied the flowers.

Join me for a dance
Alike yet distant we stand
Your presence I crave

My heart skipped a beat; these were beautiful. *Maybe they're from Luxor.* A small part of me held onto that hope. I smiled, inhaling the deep scent of the roses before walking out my door. Anna was already there, and Luxor walked out at the same time as me. They both looked great, Luxor in a button-up and slacks and Anna had toned down her jewelry — kind of. She donned a knee-length pencil skirt and dark green blouse that complemented her fiery red curls.

MaryAnn left instructions to the grand room, where the dinner was going to take place. It wasn't hard to find. We walked down a few hallways, asked some kind strangers who pointed the way for us, and then, we found ourselves entering a grand pair of double doors that had elegant, intricate carvings in the wood.

The table was large enough to seat 16 people. All the seats had placeholders, so we had to find our name. It didn't take long; we found our spots next to the names of the Seelie Queen and her attendant James. When Luxor sat down his arm brushed mine, sending heat throughout my entire body. With Luxor on my left and Anna on my right, I felt like we could take on the world together — or at least dinner.

The other two candidates arrived shortly after. I knew straight away who they were because their skin shined like my own. One looked small in stature, with big beautiful round eyes. The other was the exact opposite, lanky with features that seemed to be perfectly balanced. They were both stunning. I stopped focusing on them to mentally reevaluate my ensemble and hairstyle. They were simple compared to the other two and I couldn't help but compare. They were followed in by their friends, but only one had a protector, and she looked fierce.

"Madeline," she said her name as if no other introduction was necessary. I could tell she was a protector from a mile away. She sat down stiffly as if she was ready to jump up and take a bullet at any moment. I peeked at Luxor from the corner of my eye. He was watching me, as always. He was relaxed, as if to say "Come at me, I dare you."

Madeline's curvy body was toned and extremely frightening. Her blonde ponytail was pulled back tightly, and she wore plain black slacks and a blouse. It looked like she was ready for a battle at any time. I wondered how many weapons she carried on her right now. She made eye contact with Luxor, and they nodded to each other, almost as if they knew each other. *Of course, it's always the blondes.*

The Queen's arrival was announced, and so was her right-hand attendant. They entered the room, and so we stood and waited until she gestured for us to be seated.

"Welcome to my home, young ladies and gentlemen. I am Queen Leaure, and this is my protector, James." *Leaure, sounds French*, I thought. "Thank you for taking the time away from your schedules and school to come for the weekend. I understand times aren't the safest right now, but I assure you no harm will come to you while you're in the castle. I am deeply sorry for the loss of your protector Lilah, and we will work vigorously to find you a new, suitable one." Queen Leaure's voice was soft, almost mouse-like, but she spoke with such authority and grace. It was difficult not to want to listen to her.

I assumed it was Lilah, the taller girl, who let out a small sob and lowered her head. I couldn't help but wonder what my life would be like if I lost Luxor, and just how real that possibility was.

A small tap on the wall redirected our attention to the service doors as the food began flooding in by the tray full.

"The Unseelie King and his protector won't be joining us tonight, he had urgent matters to attend to and won't be back until tomorrow. As for introductions, Anna, Adella, Luxor," she moved her hand gracefully in each of our directions. "Madeline, Jaqueline, Lilah. You will have plenty of time for a more formal

introduction later this week when your first challenge is assigned."
The Queen sat down; everyone waited patiently for her to take a
bite, then began eating.

Responding with anything other than a nod would be too
difficult. I couldn't seem to stop eating, the food was amazing. I
glanced over at Anna who looked like she was in pain while she
took small appropriate portioned bites. She was much more
graceful than me in many ways.

I glanced up to see if the other competitors also noticed my
horrid eating habits. I sat back a little, I guess I didn't realize there
was a specific way to eat in the courts. I did my best to copy Anna
from out of the corner of my eye. Jaqueline attempted to stifle a
small giggle with a cough and returned to focusing on her food.

When dinner finished, the dessert trays were brought out, and
the atmosphere changed. it was time for conversation, now that full
mouths were not an excuse we had no reason to remain silent any
longer. It seemed as if no one wanted to start though. Anna gave
me a funny look, as if I was supposed to somehow initiate the
evening's dialogue.

"Well, the ball will be quite difficult for all of you if no one is
capable of conversation," Queen Leaure gave us a look and I
couldn't tell if she was serious. "Although it's not an official test,
there will be many influential people from the Seelie and Unseelie
cities there to meet you. I expect you will all impress. Remember
to keep the conversations simple, light, and make plenty of

connections. You will need all the support you can get for the summer to come."

"What can we expect this summer, Queen Leaure, for our first challenge?" Lilah asked, a little too timidly, but the Queen still heard her.

"Well my dear, I can't give you details. However, it will be a test for you and your protector. It's held in the Unseelie courts, so I suggest when you get a protector, to ensure your bond is strong and you are a good match, or I fear both of you might not make it back."

It sounded odd because her tone was so cheerful, almost as if she didn't want us to make it back.

I smiled at Luxor with pride. We were a strong pair — well, team.

"Speaking of," this time it was Queen Leaure's protector, James, whose booming voice filled the room. "We will have training every morning and night before bed while the protectors are all here together. It will be difficult, but we refuse to lose any more protectors." James looked confidently into Luxor's eyes, then turned to the blonde protector and smiled gently.

"What do you think is causing the deaths of the protectors?" The question slipped out of my mouth before I could think of a more graceful way to ask it.

Jaqueline choked on her food a bit, dropping her dessert fork to her plate with a loud clanking sound, the room went morbidly silent for a moment. It was Queen Leaure herself, who answered.

"Young Adella, we are unsure. Although there are investigations underway. The deaths began when the first candidate turned 16 and continued thereafter. We have a couple of suspicions. The main one being the Dark Creatures group, the very same group that caused issues with the Unseelie kings' trials." This made me uneasy.

I remembered the stories of the uprising my dad had once told me of the Dark Creatures raiding the Seelie kingdom, tearing up homes and tearing apart people. A group that did not want to concede when the veil was raised, and were not happy with the life choices they were forced upon. Some ran to the real world and hid deep in the forests, some went to the Unseelie Kingdom peacefully. The rest rebelled, and eventually went into hiding after the full force of the hunters were set upon them.

"Are you and the Unseelie King to be married?" Jaqueline asked, thankfully changing the topic of conversation.

"No, the Unseelie and Seelie Kingdoms are separate. When, and if, we decide to marry, it may be with whom we choose." Queen Leaure paused for a moment. I couldn't tell if she was deep in thought or waiting for another question. "On that note, we should all retire to our rooms for the night. I expect you to be well-rested for tomorrow."

There was a chorus of thank-yous and goodnights before everyone stood up and slowly left. Luxor stood gracefully. Anna's chair squeaked as she pushed it out. I attempted to be more graceful, but my chair caught on the rug. It rocked back, then when

85

it crashed forward, the front of the seat bumped into the back of my leg, forcing me to brace myself on the table. The tips of my fingers hit my plates, and they crashed onto the floor. I stood in horror, staring at the messy display in front of me. A waiter cleared his throat, and I got the hint and bent down quickly to pick it up.

"No, miss, that's quite alright." His hands guided me gently into a standing position as laughter erupted through the room.

I turned to Anna, who was already attempting to hightail it out after Jaqueline and Lilah. I followed her with my head down. Ungracefully bumping into every single person as we tried to make our way out of the dining hall. As we walked out of the dining hall, I could hear Lilah and Jaqueline gossiping.

"Did you hear that? He's single!" Jaqueline exclaimed.

At least the conversation isn't on me.

"I hear he's unbelievably handsome!"

"I wouldn't know, I've never seen him. I hear he spends most of his days locked away in the Unseelie castle."

Anna couldn't help but let out a giggle and raised her eyebrows at me. As we reached the end of the hall, we split ways with the other two girls, so I couldn't eavesdrop on the conversation between Jaqueline and Lilah anymore. That was okay though, the conversation over dinner was heavy and it was weighing heavily on all of us. I couldn't even imagine losing my protector and my heart ached for Lilah.

Around 10 pm, after it was completely dark outside and the stars glimmered under the evening's moon, someone knocked on my door.

"Come in," I whisper-screamed from my bed. I was not doing much, way too wound up to read or sleep, so I was just lying there quietly. Anna and Luxor came in one at a time and climbed up onto the massive bed.

"Can I sleep with you tonight, Dells? I'm a little freaked out in my room. It's so quiet..." Anna looked sheepish.

"Of course!" I scooted over to make room for Anna, her eyes widened with excitement.

She climbed under the covers and lay her head on the pillow. She looked exhausted.

"Me too, actually," Luxor said. "But I'll sleep on the daybed by the window if it's okay? I'm finding it difficult to sleep in a new place when I know you're by yourself in this room."

It looked like he wanted to say more, but for some reason, he didn't. I broke eye contact with him, so he didn't feel obliged to speak.

I only nodded, blushing crimson. Anna and I made eye contact. I could see her laughing silently. Luxor made his way over to the daybed, grabbed the quilt, and climbed in.

"Those are pretty flowers, who are they from?" Anna asked sleepily.

"I'm not sure, there's no name." I looked over at Luxor and tried to mimic the half-smile he always gave me. I didn't know if it would work, and by the way he looked at me in return, I'd say probably not.

"Less than 24 hours in the Seelie court and already admirers," he shook his head, smiling.

The room became silent. I listened to the patterns of Anna's breathing and Luxor's light snoring for a while before my mind started to shut down and fall asleep.

I woke up late, much later than I meant to. I panicked a little when I noticed that Anna and Luxor were both gone, though they'd probably headed off to breakfast. I rolled over, peeking out of the window over the daybed. The newly risen sun shone on the flowers in the garden, making the colors even more vibrant. I jumped up a bit from the bed too quickly and almost lost my footing, but I caught myself on the nightstand, which hurt. *Today is not the day for another scar.* I stood up, slid the window open, and took a deep breath. A sweet, floral aroma from the roses and lilies filled my room.

I threw on a simple nude dress today and left my hair cascading over my shoulders. I was already running late, much too late to be worried about makeup. Once out the door, I headed towards the grand room where breakfast was being held.

When I walked in, I found Luxor, and Anna already sitting down. The room had been rearranged to hold several different tables today. Next to each of them was a little cart of food. I joined Anna and Luxor, and I saw fresh fruit, pastries, and coffee. I grabbed a small plate and piled the fruit on before taking my seat.

"You should try the pastries," Anna smiled with her face stuffed, a clear contrast to her eating manners last night.

I smiled at my friend. Pastries and coffee with cream — her breakfast of choice. It described her perfectly, very sweet. I glanced over at Luxor, who had just a black coffee, no food. Funny, that also described Luxor, simple and strong. *I wonder what my plate full of fruit says about me.*

"Anna, did you see our plans for today?"

"*Did I?* Of course. A whole day at the spa!"

"Not me, I have to train," Luxor's face was sober. "Speaking of, I have to go, I'll see you two tonight."

"See you later!" Anna waved to him.

"Ya, see you."

Luxor turned to me and winked before leaving the room. My heart leaped, and I had to count my breathing to calm down again.

My eyes were bigger than my stomach for sure. The fruit was amazing but it only took a few bites before I'd had enough. I groaned holding my stomach, looking over at Anna.

"Ready, Dells?"

"As ready as I'll ever be."

I followed Anna down the hall and out the front doors. The spa was on the castle grounds, just past the east side of the garden. She linked arms with me and led the way.

It took the entire day to get me ready for the ball, at least that was what I'd tell my dad when he called tonight. I knew he'd get a good laugh out of it. We were waxed, wrapped, massaged, and bathed in mud. Not to mention got facials, manicures, pedicures, and sugar scrubbed from head to toe. Then our hair was washed, cut, moisturized, and styled. It literally took an entire day to finish. We were just walking out of the showers when MaryAnn came in. Her timing was truly impeccable.

"Ladies it's time to go back to your rooms to get dressed for the ball. I trust you enjoyed yourselves?" She kept such a straight, blank face and I felt a twinge of guilt. MaryAnn could probably use a massage too.

"Yes, thank you," we both mumbled, putting our robes on, and we quickly followed MaryAnn out the service door into the back, and through the back hallways.

As if reading our minds, we stopped by the kitchen. She slipped in and came back out with a couple of pre-made sandwiches. We then headed straight to our rooms, happily shoving our faces. Outside our doors, there was a large cart with two large garment bags. We each grabbed the bags that have our names on it and went into our rooms.

I was slightly surprised to see two women standing next to my bed when I walked in, but also extremely grateful at the same time. My dress would have been next to impossible to put on by myself.

I sat back in the chair and relaxed as they curled my hair and did my makeup before standing me in front of the full-length mirror hung on my bathroom door.

The dress was stunning chiffon, silk, and strapless. Dark blue started at the bottom then slowly became lighter towards the top, with intricate rhinestone designs swirling around the hems. It wasn't a ball gown, but it also didn't lay perfectly flat as it was tight around my waist because of the corset back. I looked around the room for a pair of shoes to compliment this beautiful dress, slightly afraid of what I might find.

A sigh of relief washed through me though, because on my bed weren't heels, but a pair of bottomless sandals, decorated with the same rhinestones as my dress. They were certainly a lot better than heels with the grass in the garden and I was not concerned about my feet getting hurt. Around my neck, I wore a simple silver chain with a single diamond on the end and two stud earrings my mother had given me only a matter of weeks before she passed.

I slipped my sandals on and ran out my door. Anna was already waiting patiently outside. I had to stop and do a double-take. She was perfect. Her dark green dress was floor-length, laid flat, but clung to her, with geometric cutouts accenting her hips. The dress itself looked like silk with a lace overlay, and her fiery red curls were pinned back and tamed so I could see the silver jewelry climbing up her pinched ears in floral designs that complemented the lace.

"You look...wow," I said.

"You too, Dells. Your dress is amazing."

"I know, remind me to thank RayRay if we see him." I did a little spin, admiring the way the jewels glimmered as they moved.

"Oh, I will!" Anna promised, she stopped me mid spin, grabbing my hand and dragged me down the hall and to the ball.

No grand staircase and no fairy tale entrance. *Darn.* However, there was a beautiful flower archway that led to the ball. Not the kind of archway that had been covered in fake flowers, or even carefully-placed live flowers. Instead, it looked natural, like it'd been growing there forever. The sky was black and shined, spotted carefully in an endless amount of stars. There were lanterns and fairy lights lighting the way to the dance floor and around it. Hundreds of flowers expertly laid around, leaving a delicious ambrosial fragrance.

I scanned the dance floor, and that was when I saw him. Luxor's eyes bored into mine. I felt the nervous pressure in my gut decreasing as we made our way towards each other.

"You look amazing," Luxor gave me a half-grin.

"I know, you do too."

"Would you like to dance?" Luxor extended his hand towards me.

Yes, holy crow, yes. Ten thousand times YES.

"Always." He grabbed my hand, and we swayed awkwardly back and forth.

"Have you been in a lot of training sessions?" I had to break the awkward silence somehow. He was stiff. Dancing was not something he was used to.

"Enough to keep me busy. Madeline is kicking my ass so far. If it's not death by Madeline then it's death by PowerPoint. What about you, though? What do you think of the trip so far?" I'd never known Luxor to be one for small talk.

"It's great," I sighed. "I'm having an amazing time seeing you… and Anna." I tacked on, trying not to be too straight forward. "Thank you for the flowers."

"Flowers? What flowers?"

"Didn't you send flowers to my room?"

I looked up at Luxor, trying to read his response. I couldn't tell if he was messing with me or not. He seemed serious and looked deep in thought. He pushed me out for an uncomfortable twirl. It was when I'm mid-twirl that I first saw him. Just a glance, though.

"I didn't send you flowers Dells, but I can find out who did."

But it was too late. I knew. I knew who sent the flowers, who wrote the note.

"*Alike yet distant we stand.*"

It made perfect sense now. I attempted to maneuver Luxor, so I could get a better view of him, although this wasn't a masquerade, no one seemed to pay mind to this masked stranger.

94

His vest was the same colored material as my own, with the same rhinestone accents around the hems. His tux fit him perfectly, accentuating his large muscles. His blonde hair was pulled back into a tight bun, and he was wearing a black mask that showed off his dark blue eyes.

I was so entranced I almost didn't notice him approaching me slowly. He walked tall, shoulders back. His eyes stared intensely into mine.

"May I cut in?" He offered me his hand.

I looked into his eyes and took his hand. Luxor stalled momentarily as if this new advance was unwelcome. Then slowly, he inclined his head and retreated backwards a few steps. Next thing I knew we were twirling. Leaving Luxor behind so quickly, I couldn't spare an apologetic glance. I'd never been much of a dancer, but this masked stranger guided me with confidence. I found myself dipping, leaping, and spinning with ease.

"Good evening, love." He met my eyes. *His accent is hypnotic.*

"Have we met?"

"We have not yet had the pleasure, but everyone has heard about you, and the other two candidates, of course. My name is Alaric."

Blood flooded my cheeks. Our dancing slowed, and we began to sway from side to side. I felt steady on my feet, yet like I could fall over at any moment. The room was spinning, although physically we had stopped.

"Well, it's unfortunate I haven't heard of you." I gave him a steadying look, then he broke eye contact for another twirl.

"You may not have," he said confidently. "I've been away from the Seelie court on business for a while now, and I'm afraid I'm only visiting here to discuss recent attacks on the protectors of the candidates."

"That's too bad. I heard it may have something to do with the Dark Creatures uprising again?" I tried to make my voice sound nonchalant but the curiosity still broke through.

"I'm not certain because there wasn't any evidence. The last time they were attacking, they left a signature. The Dark Creatures wanted to make a statement. The Unseelie King spent a lot of time trying to get the situation under control."

So I was speaking to someone well versed with the histories.

"Well one cannot control their people," I said. "However, the King should be keeping a close eye out and have hunters scattered around — especially with all the deaths, there's no reason to believe the Fay and protectors of the Seelie court are the only ones to be targeted," I added.

"Would it concern you? If the Unseelie people are targeted as well?" He raised an eyebrow at me.

"Of course, we're all one society. One group who utilize two different elements, and yet share those same elements every day." I attempted to mimic his puzzled face. Why wouldn't I care if the Unseelie are also being targeted?

"Some would suggest otherwise, that Fata and Fay cannot be one, dark and light are opposites."

Huh, definitely closed minded.

"That's not what I see," I said, looking directly into Alaric's eyes. "Dark and light are only the energy sources we use, not the good and evil we represent."

Then just as Luxor flashed in my mind, I spotted him over Alaric's shoulder. On his arm was the blonde protector, wearing a short black dress that clung to her curves perfectly. Her hair was up in the high ponytail she always wore. They would be perfect together. He could tell her all his trainer woes and worries, and she could genuinely sympathize.

A pang of jealousy coursed through me. Alaric must have felt me tense. He peeked over his shoulder and let out a chuckle.

"Ah, that's too bad."

Just then, my attention was stolen by a hand gently guiding my chin up. Slowly, holding eye contact, he measured my reaction carefully. He brought his lips to mine. *Whoa.*

This kiss was different, softer, and sweet. He moved with me in a familiar way, that made me feel like we'd done this before. My lips responded easily, naturally. After a short while, he stopped and pulled back a couple of inches.

"I'd like to see you again, Adella Shenning. Soon."

Me too.

With that, he took his leave. He turned and walked gracefully off the dance floor, nodding to Luxor on his way out. Luxor's face was a mix of pure confusion and fury, not that he had a right to be furious, he was the one who told my dad we weren't together, after all.

I froze in place, confused and slightly dazed. I wasn't sure I was processing what just happened. Alaric was sweet, kind, and a total stranger.

With a gorgeous English accent and soft, skilled lips to match. Would I see him again? Would he send more flowers up to my room? Would he give me a way to contact him?

Despite only knowing him briefly, I already craved his presence. The familiarity between us felt like home, but I wasn't sure why.

I made certain to spend the next hour focusing on making connections, allowing Alaric to only take up the deepest, darkest corner in the back of my mind as I moved. I met as many people and shook as many hands as I could; hunters, protectors, Fata, Fay, and creatures from all around. There was no shortage of people to meet. During all of this, I attempted not to watch him. It was absolutely none of my concern, but still, it was nearly impossible not to fixate on Luxor dancing with the other protector. Occasionally, he'd glance my way too. I knew it was immature, but I avoided any direct eye contact.

"So, Adella, have you been active in the discussions of the deaths of the protectors? Are you worried for your own?" The stranger in front of me asked while handing me a drink from behind the small wooden bar.

"I have been following them closely, and while of course, I am also worried for my own, he doesn't appreciate my concern." I tried to laugh it off awkwardly. "Do you live close to the courts?"

"You know the deaths are so frequent, I think -" and that's when the kind stranger lost me.

Everyone seemed to have an opinion or a suggestion as to what was causing the deaths of the protectors, but I carefully diverted the topic every time. Such conversation didn't seem appropriate for a light-hearted party. Instead, I attempted to spend the evening learning about their children, families, and hobbies.

"Alright, my turn to steal the attention of the great Adella Shenning,"

Hearing my full name caught my attention immediately. I didn't recognize the voice but when I turned around, it was quite a surprise to see another candidate.

"My name's Jackie; Jaqueline actually, but everyone calls me Jackie." She grabbed my hand and pulled me into a dance. She took the lead, putting her hand around my waist and smiled at me slyly. I grinned back nervously, I had never danced with another woman before.

"Adella Shenning, but you already knew that?"

I glanced around and no one seemed to be paying us too much attention. Honestly, dancing with her didn't feel wrong, just different.

"Yes, I'm afraid I did. Ever since the word of the candidates meeting at the Seelie kingdom went out, everyone from my hometown started searching for as much information as they could find. I knew everything from where you and Lilah slept to the names of your closest friends before the week was up."

"Huh, well it's nice to meet you properly." I didn't know how I felt about that, it was a bit intrusive, but I couldn't blame her. If I had more connections, I would have probably asked around too.

"I just wanted to let you know that even though we are competitors and going for the same spot, you can trust me." She paused for a moment. "There's not many people here that you're going to be able to talk to. Everyone will have a favorite contestant, even as we mingle through this dance, seeing new faces and meeting new people, we are being watched intensely. They are basing our tests on our weaknesses, and this dance is a perfect chance to see some of these weaknesses."

I didn't know why, but I trusted her immediately. It was hard not to. She was very sincere. Honestly, it was nice to have someone to talk to who was going through the same thing as I was.

"What about Lilah? Is she to be trusted too?"

"I can't speak for anyone, only myself. The only thing I can assure you is whatever you have to say or have questions about, is safe with me."

"You as well. If I hear anything, I'll give you the best heads up I can."

Jackie hugged me and gave me a genuine smile before letting go and taking a step back. *Maybe she could be a real friend.*

"I have to meet more people. The list of attendees is large, and I arrived a tad late. But hopefully, we will get a chance to speak again before we go home."

"I hope so too," I said, and didn't expect to mean it, seeing as we were competitors. But strangely, I did hope to see her soon. I wanted to get to know her better to try to figure out why she was one of the chosen ones, to ask her if she knew why I was one.

I headed back into the sea of attendees, swirling and twirling, shaking hands, and smiling. It was a lot of work having to force it for a prolonged period. The muscles in my cheeks were becoming sore and I wasn't sure how much longer I could hold them up before I released my scowl upon the Seelie courts. *Don't you dare release the resting bitch face.*

Just when I thought my brain couldn't handle one more new name or face, someone grabbed my hands. Energy and excitement radiated from her and I knew who it was before I even turned to see her. Anna. Relief washed through me. No more surprises tonight.

"Who was that guy earlier?" She smiled and wiggled her eyebrows.

I shrugged my shoulders and laughed, because I didn't even know who Alaric really was.

"Tall, mysterious, and handsome stranger. Visiting the castle for business."

"Looked friendlier than a stranger. I wonder if he's a hunter," she suggested.

"I don't know, but I'm getting tired." I looked over; Luxor was dancing with the other protector again, so much for meeting new people. My stomach sunk slightly and my face finally fell from the plastered smile I had forced it into.

Anna's gaze wandered to where mine was, and she smiled in understanding.

"Agreed, let's ditch. No cute guys here anyway. Let's go get some ice cream from the kitchen and head to your room for a movie."

I knew Anna was lying. She'd been flirting all night with a handsome mystery guy. They seemed like a cute match, he was clearly a bit older though, covered in tattoos. I only caught a couple of glimpses while I was in the midst of people. I noticed them walking by the roses for a while.

She crossed our arms together again, tossed her hair over her shoulder. Off we went, leaving her trail of broken hearts, and my broken heart, behind.

9

Every day's a new day. At least that's what I reminded myself when I got up in the morning. Anna was gone again when I arose. Once I was fully awake, I realized that tomorrow was the day we would go home. The fact left me with a bittersweet taste in my mouth. The Seelie court was beautiful, but I missed my dad, and I was ready to return to school. I needed a little more normality in my life again.

I got dressed, tied my hair in a ponytail, and headed out to find Anna. Luxor walked out of his door at the same time. The air thickened. I focused on looking straight ahead, taking one breath at a time as subtly as I could.

"Hey, Dells, I was just about to knock on your door. The Unseelie King and Seelie Queen called for a meeting in the great room. Now."

"Okay, have you seen Anna?"

"She's probably already there. The news went out about 20 minutes ago."

We walked silently to the great room. When we arrived, we quickly found a couple of seats and I scanned the room for Anna.

"Please rise for Queen Leaure," the announcer called.

Everyone in the room jumped to attention, anxiously awaiting the reason we were all called here.

The Queen's entrance was grand, escorted by at least five heavily armed protectors. She began to greet guests, all the while she surveyed the room occasionally; the way her eyes bounced from person to person made me assume she was doing a body count. There was still no sign of the Unseelie King or Anna. The amount of security the Queen had with her was raising my concerns. I had a terrible gut feeling that something bad was going on.

"Thank you for meeting so quickly everybody. I appreciate everyone who helped me spread the message of this emergency meeting," James, the Queen's protector, said. His booming voice halted all whispers and the room fell silent within a matter of seconds. Stepping forward to the Queen's left-hand side, he spoke again. "It seems a few people are missing at this time, and we're currently gathering as many details about the guest count as we can. So far, it's clear that at least four are unaccounted for since the ball last night. If you have any new information as to the whereabouts of the missing individuals or know anyone else who's missing, please let me know immediately."

My heart plummeted. I checked the room one more time before deciding to approach the circle of protectors around the Queen.

As I got closer to the table where the guards sat, at least three stood up, one even appeared to be reaching for his weapon, as if I was a potential threat. Their chairs squealed across the floor as they got up, and one slammed his hand against the table as if to stun me for a moment.

"Adella," the Queen acknowledged me quickly. "The other two contestants' guests and Madeline are all missing. I see Luxor, when was the last time you saw Anna?"

To my relief the guards started to calm down; two sat back down and one tried to play it off, acting like I wasn't the threat at all. He took a few moments to glare at what I supposed could be potential threats in the room, then looked back down to his seat and avoided eye contact with me completely.

"She stayed in my room with me last night, but when I woke up, she was gone."

"In your room? Are you sure?"

"Positive, we watched a movie after the ball, then fell asleep around 2 am."

"Well, that changes things. We assumed everyone was taken from their rooms, but if no one was in your room last night besides you and Anna, then that's not the case." It doesn't sound like a remark that required an answer, so I remained quiet.

With that, the Queen redirected her attention back to the group of hunters. At least I thought they were hunters; it was only an informed guess, since they were all large and in their mid to late 20s.

I took a deep breath and listened in. If Anna was missing, I was going to be involved in finding her.

"We can send hunters out to patrol the courts. Other than that, there's not much we can do. They didn't leave a trail, and no one saw them entering or leaving," one of the burlier hunters said.

"We need to go to the last place the Dark Creatures were seen meeting and question them all."

"There's no proof the Dark Creatures were involved," the hunter pointed out.

The Queen was silent as she considered the information. I didn't personally know anyone in this group, so I stood by quietly in the background, trying to figure out where we were going to start our search. I wasn't a bad fighter. I could help if needed.

"Let's begin by sending patrols down to both courts and review all the footage we have from the castle last night," the Queen ordered firmly.

"Yes. We should also set watches around the gates of the courts."

The thick English accent surprised me. *I know that voice: Alaric.* I stared at him openly as he entered the room. He was dressed like the rest of the hunters were. He approached the group by himself.

"Thank you for joining us. We're going to need permission to walk the grounds of the Unseelie court," the Queen said in a sickly sweet voice as she turned to Alaric.

Alaric nodded, digesting this information. I wasn't sure if he would have to ask higher up before responding.

"Matters are quite urgent, as you can see." Queen Leaure grew impatient quickly.

"You have my full permission as King to patrol and search the grounds. We're going to find the missing people." His stare held me hostage, I couldn't break eye contact.

"Very well." It was James who responded this time.

I couldn't move a muscle, I was still trying to process the information I just learned. King? How could Alaric be a King?

With the beginnings of a plan in place, the group scattered. Only the King and I were left in our spots.

"Good morning, Adella."

"I'm afraid it's not, your majesty. My friend is missing."

I couldn't help but hesitate at 'your majesty.' There was a hint of humor in Alaric's eyes.

"We don't have to pretend that last night didn't happen. You can call me Alaric," he stepped closer and held my hand gently. "I will do everything I can to find your Anna."

I pulled my hand away slowly. The people surrounding us went silent, watching the King's display towards me.

"I will be, too. I just need to find out where I'm needed, and I will begin looking," I said one word at a time, yet the sentence still

107

felt as though it came across unclear, probably because he was giving me a peculiar look.

"Begin looking? Adella, it would be for the best if you would remain on the grounds under the Seelie and Unseelie protection. It's best for the Seelie court trials and because I'd feel better knowing you were safe. I will personally assign you an extra guard, plus your protector will also be with you." Alaric looked over my shoulder as he explained this.

I followed his gaze over to where Luxor was standing, which was almost directly behind me. He gave a nervous wave but maintained eye contact with Alaric. This was the most awkward staring contest of my life. But Luxor nodded in agreement, clearly having overheard the conversation.

"I have to speak to the hunters who'll be searching for the Unseelie court. I will check in with you as soon as I get any news." Alaric bent over and pecked my cheek, then walked away.

I stayed there for a moment, not for my benefit, but the King's. Clearly, I had work to do.

"Well you're not going to let that stop us, are you?" Luxor asked.

I pivoted, grabbed Luxor by the arm, and led him into the corner where nobody else could hear. We needed to make our exit before Alaric had a chance to assign extra guards to me.

"Of course not, I just need to figure out what to do next. Maybe we should visit my grandma. My dad said she lives in a cottage right outside the courts on the Seelie grounds."

"Your grandma?"

"Yes, my grandma. My dad said she was a premonition Fata. Maybe she will be able to see something we haven't already seen."

"That's perfect," Luxor was already handing me his phone. I swiftly dialed my grandma's number.

"Hey, Grandma!"

"I live 20 miles north of the court. I will have Grandpa swing by and pick you up. Wait by the pink tulips in the garden. I can't talk now, I need to concentrate, I'm trying to see. It's been a long time since I've tried to see on purpose darling. Love you, bye."

The phone beeped. I remained where I was, confused. I should have known my grandma would have seen my call. I wasn't sure how much she could see, but it was enough to know what was going on.

"Come on Luxor. Let's go for a walk."

"Adella? Adella Shenning?" My grandpa's eyes were narrow, almost accusing.

"Hey, Grandpa!" I said. I hadn't seen my grandpa since I was little.

"You're so old!" He laughed, a lot from what I could see. The lines around his eyes told me he laughed all the time. I couldn't help but laugh with him. My grandfather had a contagious optimism about him.

I'd never been to my grandpa's house, at least not that I could remember. The thought crossed my mind as I jumped into his car on the south side of the garden.

"Hello sir, I'm Luxor. It's nice to meet you."

My grandpa didn't respond. After we were both in the car, he hit the gas. I couldn't help but peek back at everything we were leaving behind. My new friends, acquaintances, and possibly the competition for the Seelie Queen's crown.

The cottage was only about 20 minutes away from the castle, and it wasn't what I expected at all.

I sensed the magic as we drove up. As I slid out of the car, I had to take a second to adjust to the sight. The cottage was tiny, with a stone chimney, and covered in wildflowers and ivy. I inhaled through my nose, expecting to smell the hundreds of flowers that surrounded me. Instead, the aroma was incredibly sweet, like freshly baked cookies, or a loaf of honey bread.

My grandma threw the door open. She looked amazing. She was tall, with deep laugh lines to match my grandpa's, and a crooked smile. She resembled my mother, so much so that it was uncanny. I stayed where I was for an extra moment and took my surroundings in slowly, everything felt abnormally familiar.

I ran up to my grandma and embraced her. She wasted no time and led Luxor and me inside to a table. Her eyes were stern as she took in a deep breath. She looked at me once more before she closed her eyes. She put on a very serious face and slowly moved her hands to her temple.

"Hmmmmm, Luxor please leave the room," Grandma requested, solemnly. Giving me an odd look, Luxor shrugged and walked out.

I glanced around the room, unsure if I'd been here as a child. The room rang a bell in my head, with bright yellow walls that had floral patterns dancing around the top, but still I couldn't remember ever physically being here. I waited patiently for my grandma to open her eyes, not quite sure where to look. I allowed my eyes to follow the many different flowers that traced the walls.

A huge smile spread across my grandma's face, she peered one eye open and let out a giggle.

"Down to business, Miss Delly. I saw that you met your other half recently."

I let out a nervous chuckle. I didn't know if I would use that term. How could this possibly be more important than finding Anna?

"I don't know Grandma. He's nice but I'm not so sure." She looked confused, startled even.

"Are you sure? My vision is very clear. As clear as they can be I guess, being here in the land of the Seelie."

I felt my cheeks firing up. A change of subject was certainly welcome. I didn't know what my grandma saw but I supposed it explained grandpa's reaction to Luxor.

"Grandma, if you're full Fata, why are you living on the Seelie kingdom grounds?"

"Not every Fata has to live in the Unseelie court. It would help with my premonitions, but when we heard you were going to be blessed with summer, your grandfather and I moved immediately, so we could be here if, and when you need us."

Luxor leaned into the room, only slightly passed the door jam. My grandma instantly stiffened and closed her eyes again. Something about her display told me she wasn't quite comfortable around Luxor.

"Come in Luxor, protector of Adella. Just as I'm telling Delly, I cannot see much, so you two will have to stay overnight, so I have more time. You can sleep on the couch in the guestroom. Adella, you can sleep on the bed."

My grandma got up, hugged me, and left. Her movements were very stiff and abrupt. It was as if she couldn't get away fast enough. A very odd display, considering just moments ago she was laughing and full of life. Watching her leave now, she looked exhausted.

The room to the right of the kitchen was the guest room and was clearly labeled so. I walked in, shrugged my coat off, and hopped into bed. Luxor sat on the edge of the bed, looking at me.

"We should leave soon. Something feels off." His posture was stiff as he gazed out the windows in the room one by one.

"It's my grandma's house. We're fine, she would never let anything happen to us." Annoyance riddled through me. I knew we weren't here for a social visit, but I hadn't seen my grandma since I was little. I followed his gaze out the window, how was it

112

possible an entire day had already passed me by? The sun was just beginning to set, sending off beautiful rays of pinks and golds, reminding me of Anna's aura on our first day of school.

"I know. I could feel the protection spells as we walked up. I don't know though. Something feels wrong, we should be looking for Anna."

"I promise, I hate waiting as much as you do. We can't look if we're tired Luxor. Get some sleep, and we can start again in the morning." My body agreed, although I struggled to hold the emotion back from my voice. My muscles gave up and I fell back into the pillows, wishing Anna was there to jump into the bed with me.

Luxor stood up and walked around the bed. I propped myself up onto my elbows and looked into his eyes. He reached down and cupped his hand around the back of my neck. He pulled my lips to his.

Somehow rougher and more urgent than the first kiss, which I was still convinced happened. This kiss was different, angry almost. He kissed me hard, almost as if he thought it was the last kiss we'd ever share. I reached both arms around his neck and drew him onto the bed. Deepening the kiss, matching his frustration move for move. I trailed my fingertips around his collar bone.

I felt the heat of his body pressed against mine as he rolled slightly onto me. He let out a small moan and tried to pick his head up, but I locked my hands around his neck. I wanted this.

113

He chuckled, kissed me harder, and pressed his body into mine, sliding his hands around the waistband of my pants and up the side of my shirt. My breathing quickened.

I let go of his neck and reached for his jeans, that was when he pulled away from me and rolled off.

"Hey." I mustered up the best glare I could, but it didn't match my half-protest, half pouty exclamation.

"Goodnight, Adella." The corners of his mouth turned up into the half-smile I was so familiar with.

Frustration coursed through me, leaving me puzzled.

Does he like me? Or am I just someone who helps to pass the time?

I put half of the pillow on top of my head and counted my breaths until I fell asleep.

10

His breath was sweet, his laugh soft.

"I wondered when I'd see you again. Where did you go?"

Alaric's eyes were beautiful, but his forehead creased with worry.

I reached out and put both arms around his shoulders to comfort him and looked into his worried face.

"I'm looking for my friend, I couldn't sit at the castle knowing she was gone."

"Well, I couldn't sleep knowing you were gone, Adella. Next time, warn me before you plan on disappearing."

I wanted to be mad. I shouldn't have to tell anyone where I was, especially in a dream. Instead, I sighed, leaned in, and kissed the worried Alaric.

He responded, hesitant at first. He kissed me sweetly, softly. My body yearned for him. I pushed up closer and put my hands in his hair.

"You don't have to worry about me," I whispered to him in between soft kisses. Being with Alaric was different from being with Luxor. It seemed easier, more natural even. I couldn't help but wonder why.

"Of course, I do." He held my shoulders and broke away for a moment, holding my gaze. "I haven't been able to go one minute without thinking about you. I need you to come home to me, so that I may hold and protect you."

"I have Luxor to protect me. I'm safe I promise." I leaned in to kiss Alaric again, but he pulled away; a serious yet sorrowful look flashed across his face.

"You need to be careful around him Adella. You need to think before you let him close to you." He kissed me softly on the forehead.

"Think of me every night before bed, and I can visit your dreams again soon. Right now, it's morning though, time goes quicker in a dream state. You need to go find your friend so that you can come back to me." He pecked my lips softly as a farewell.

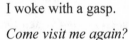

I woke with a gasp.

Come visit me again?

It was a dream, but Alaric was there with me. How was that possible? Was I thinking about him before I went to bed? Luxor sat on the edge of the mattress, staring lazily at me as if he'd been waiting a while for me to wake up.

He slowly reached for my hand but I pulled it away. I couldn't. I was too confused. It was not fair to Luxor or Alaric that I clearly couldn't make up my mind.

I got up and made the bed, avoiding Luxor's accusing eyes as I did so, knowing all too well he wanted to ask me why I woke in such a fright, so I tried to avoid talking at all costs. I pulled my hoody on and went into the kitchen, where my grandma was waiting eagerly at the table with a fresh loaf of bread, homemade jam, and a cup of coffee.

"Sooo?" My grandma smiled from ear to ear.

My cheeks were on fire. She must have heard me and Luxor last night.

"It was great, Grandma, but I don't know if I would say we were meant to be or anything. It was just a kiss."

"Deny it all you want, my Delly. I could feel the connection though. It was beautiful and romantic. Not everyone gets such a special connection, you shouldn't take it for granted." This was beyond the realm of what my grandma should be talking to me about.

Was this what it was like to have a mom?

Guilt racked through me as I thought about my dream with Alaric. *Why was love so complicated?* I was not even sure how

117

Luxor felt about me, or why Alaric gave me butterflies every time I saw him. I didn't know how or why he could show up in my dreams like that. It was all very complicated at the moment.

I snapped out of my thoughts, my grandma was staring at me with her lips pursed.

"Alright, darling, down to business," she sighed heavily and now that I looked at her closely, she still looked exhausted. Dark rings decorated her eyes, and she seemed slightly hunched over. "I saw your friend, Anna, pacing back and forth. She seems confused. I'm not sure of her exact location but it felt like the Unseelie court. That's where you should begin your search."

Luxor marched in, made a coffee, and sat at the table; he didn't even glance at me or my grandmother. He was being outright rude, I couldn't help but wonder if I'd spoken in my sleep.

"How sure are you about the Unseelie courts?" Luxor asked grumpily.

"Delly, you must be careful who you trust. Not everyone is good and honest. Not everyone uses their powers wisely, but you must make these decisions for yourself." My grandmother ignored Luxor completely.

Luxor glanced up, grabbed his coffee, and started sipping. If my grandma thought we were such a great couple, shouldn't they like each other? Maybe it made her uncomfortable to be around both of us in the same room. Or, could it be that she doesn't mean Luxor at all? Did she mean Alaric? But we'd only just met. My own inner monologue had started to give me a headache. I took a few sips of my coffee to try to distract myself from the pain.

"You must start your search within the grounds of the Unseelie court. I'm sure that you will find the truth there, about more than one matter. There's a strong presence drawing my attention there." My grandma took a long breath. "But be careful, Delly. The only thing I can see is a battle waiting. The reason is unknown, and with whom is unknown, so you must be mindful as you pass into the Unseelie kingdom."

Luxor met my eyes and nodded. My grandma closed her eyes, and breathed deeply again as she leaned in to hug me. It was longer than the welcome-home-hug. Saying goodbye was so much harder.

"I'll be back soon Grandma. Will you call dad for me and tell him I'm safe?"

"I know Delly, I will. There's another reason your grandfather and I chose to live in the Seelie courts though. Not only is the power, our fellow Fata draw on, dark, but their hearts are turning dark as well. I will not lie to your father. However, I will inform him I saw you. I love you."

Luxor grabbed my hand and pulled me gently to the door.

"How do we get to the Unseelie courts?"

"Easy, through the changing tree," he said so casually, as if that was all the explanation I needed.

Off into the forest we went. I wish I could say I was keeping up with Luxor, but he moved incredibly fast. We snaked through one

119

of the trails, then to my dismay, we steered away from the path. I ripped my dress up the side to make movement less restricted, and still managed to trip on everything, from roots to small bushes, to air. It was frustrating trying to keep up but I knew moving quickly was important.

The walk had to be at least five to ten miles long. My feet were swollen, and my legs ached. I was pretty sure at some point I was scraped by poison ivy and wish I wore something more travel-friendly.

It felt like an entire day passed before we halted in front of a huge maple tree whose leaves were golden and orange on one side and green on the other. Other than the odd leaf colors, the tree looked ordinary. I walked around the base of the tree, knocking on different spots as I went. It felt solid.

Luxor walked towards the base of the tree. I took mental notes on every movement he made. Taking in a deep breath that he didn't exhale, he walked right through the tree. No explanation, no "Hey Dells, follow me." I was beginning to wonder if I should have chosen a different adventuring partner. I stared at the tree for a moment, trying to understand. When I knocked on the tree it was solid, but Luxor managed to walk right through it.

"Of course! Just like the greenhouse," I told myself, at least I sure hoped it was like the greenhouse.

Why did I bother to say that out loud? I was completely alone. I followed Luxor step by step, walking up to the base of the tree. I held my breath and lunged forward.

It felt like a surprisingly long walk for such a normal-sized tree. When I finally got to the other side, I was gasping for breath. Luxor fell to the ground. .

"I-didn't-actually-think-you-would-hold-your-breath," he was cracking up, so hard that it was taking him a while to form the words.

I shook my head and laughed too. As he stood up, I pushed him back down.

"Jerk," I mumbled under my breath, which only sent him into another wave of laughter.

It took a short while to adjust to the surrounding scenery. It was similar, but there was something off about it. I wouldn't have hesitated to walk into the forest of the Seelie kingdom, but here, in the Unseelie forest, it was like there were a million sets of eyes watching me. The forest was eerie and gave me the impression that I couldn't walk fast enough to escape if I needed to.

The sun started to set. My skin tingled. "We only have 39 minutes until the sun's down," I told Luxor. I didn't know how I knew this, but as I said it, I knew it was right.

"You know, only natural-born Fata, know the exact time the sun goes down. Now that I think of it, you probably didn't know that, since you're so new to this world." He gave me his usual half smile, I couldn't help but roll my eyes. "You would make an intriguing ruler, a natural-born Fata, in charge of the Seelie kingdom."

Now that he mentioned it, he was right. It sounded unbelievable. Although, it made sense that I was a natural-born Fata, as my grandparents were both full Fata.

Stuck in my train of thought, I almost didn't realize that I was walking alone. I looked over and Luxor was a few feet behind me, standing very still. It was almost as if he wasn't breathing.

I walked back and circled him. He was completely still. No breathing and no blinking. The world became silent, no rustling in the trees, no chirping, and no wind whistling.

The world blurred slightly, and I heard a voice.

"What are you doing here Adella?" The voice sounded sweet and hurt at the same time. "It's not safe for you here, everyone will know who you are and where you're from."

Casually leaned up against the tree, was Alaric, not even five feet away from me. I stood there, flustered. Responding was harder than I thought it would be.

"What did you do to Luxor?"

"Don't worry, Adella Shenning, I did not harm your protector boyfriend. You are the one who is currently laying inert. You see, I'm a dream walker; now that you have entered the Unseelie Kingdom my powers are stronger, and I have entered you into a dream-like trance."

"You can't keep me in this state forever. I need to find out where Anna is, I need to figure out where all the missing people went."

"You're right, I can't. I'll be coming to find you though, as will my guards. If you think that finding Anna and the others aren't our priority, you're wrong. Only you made this so much worse by also disappearing, a missing Queen-to-be is causing panic amongst the people. If you're in the Unseelie Kingdom while I'm away, you are not safe." He closed the five-foot distance in three large steps, bent down close to my head, and whispered, *"I will find you."*

Opening my eyes, the world around me moved again. My heart pounded, remembering Alaric's last words. Was that a threat or a promise? Luxor stared down at me with a frantic look in his eyes. He did not seem very happy.

"You fainted!" He accused, and dropped onto the ground next to me in an almost hyperventilating state.

"Not on purpose." My head throbbed. "We have to keep moving."

I slowly got up off the floor, once I was sure I was steady, I continued down the path ahead. If he was going to find me, I wasn't going to make it easy for him. *What did he mean exactly? Did I want to be found? Did I want to be saved?* Now that I knew there was a threat of being taken back to the Seelie Kingdom against my will, I started the next part of my mission with a little more pep in my step.

I could see the gate outside the Unseelie grounds, and the people, elves, and gremlins gathering nearby. The sun was going down. There was a beautiful blue shimmer to the air and everything felt so alive. An enchanting melody played and I sensed a huge amount of excitement in the air. We finally reached the stands and booths outside the kingdom and they did not disappoint.

The second we walked onto the grounds surrounding the gates, the eerie feeling of being followed vanished. I felt myself relax and took in the atmosphere.

"Bread, bread," a small elf shouted, holding a pan of bread, I could smell the fresh sweet aroma.

Next to his shop, was a thoughtfully placed fresh jam shop, with little spoons and samples out front. I reached eagerly for a little spoon but Luxor grabbed my hand.

"Not now," he whispered. "We can't risk anyone seeing you."

My stomach growled and I turned away from the fresh jam, disappointed, using my hair to form a curtain around my face in hopes that no one had seen me already.

Beautiful was the only way to describe the Unseelie Kingdom, lively and full of light — not a physical light, but more internal light. I could somehow smell the ocean and see the rays of light from the moon peeking out from behind the clouds. It was hard to believe anyone could want the Seelie and Unseelie courts separated, or why.

There were no bright street lamps or large lanterns. They used candlelight, but combined with the light from the moon and the stars, it was more than enough to light the little shops on the street.

"Wait right here." Luxor disappeared into a little shop quickly, then came out, handing me a beautiful midnight blue velvet cloak.

"We can't have people figuring out who you are. Not everyone wants a new Seelie Queen."

A shiver ran down my spine as I threw the cloak over my shoulders, and flopped the hood over my head. Luxor began to walk again, and I followed quietly. We came to the Unseelie gates, turned west and walked along them.

"We're not going in?" Disappointment was painted across my face.

"No. If a Dark Creature group took Anna and the others, they wouldn't be waiting inside the gates of the kingdom, they'd be hiding out in the forest nearby. There's a couple of known Dark Creature groups that camp out along the outskirts of the Kingdom, all we can hope is that we find one."

I should have known a group against the courts wouldn't be on court grounds. I couldn't tell where the forest began; the trees slowly multiplied, and we found a distinguished path to follow. We walked for hours on end, climbing through rocks, and crossing short rivers which the moon was shining down upon. The glistening rays of whites and blue hues that were coming off the water was mesmerizing.

Hoooo. Hooo. The noise from a nearby owl startled me slightly.

Luxor grabbed my arm roughly, pushing me to the side.

I tapped him on the shoulder gently, he tensed in response.

Finally, we arrived at a small clearing. It was not significant, but it was big enough that we could set my cloak across the grass, lay down and close our eyes for just a few hours.

12.

I woke up, stiff and out of sorts. I stretched my limbs carefully, Luxor still laid next to me, snoring peacefully. I put my toes in the soft green grass and hoisted myself up, the evening air was cool. *My internal alarm is way off. I was supposed to sleep when it was dark.*

I had no clue where I was. I had no clue where Anna was, and I had no clue where the Dark Creatures' hideout was. I walked to the edge of the small river nearby. Now that I completely understood the gravity of the situation — that I was totally lost, I began to crumble. I sat down and hugged my knees, softly sobbing, listening to the water of the river flow through the rocks. The weight against my chest became almost unbearable. I let myself cry until I didn't have any tears left in me. Hours seemed to pass me by, although I knew it'd only been minutes before I started to feel like I was dehydrating myself.

Now that I'd accomplished that, and I couldn't get or feel any lower, it was time to move on and to shake off the feeling of failure and begin a new day. I got back up, wiped my face, and made my way back towards our little camp.

Luxor reached his arms towards the sky and let out a moan of disapproval. Rubbing his face, he sat up next to me, a little groggy.

"Morning sleepy head. Ready to head out again?" He stood up and straightened out.

"Ya," he yawned. "We need to find one of the castle's safe houses. They have a few around the outsides of the gates. There should be merchants, food, and water."

So, off on our little venture we went. The moon was rising quickly, and my energy skyrocketed. I could feel the light and the stars dancing above me. They added a little skip to my step as I moved along to their flickering rhythm. I breathed in deeply, abnormally calm. The heaviness that was once in my chest began to fade as the cool air replaced the worry.

Clanking sounds were not too far behind us, Luxor must have noticed it too because he grabbed my cloak and threw me into some nearby bushes just off of the trail. I heard a tearing sound as the branches caught my cloak, but only minimal damage was done. I reached out and pulled the bottom part of my cloak into the bushes with us. As the footsteps grew closer, I could hear Luxor's breathing slow. Visitors were an unexpected and unwelcome surprise.

They approached slowly and without hesitation kept walking by, carrying midnight blue shields and leading horses who carried bags and bags of items we couldn't see.

"We should talk to them," I suggested.

"Not a chance. We don't know if they're guards from the kingdom or part of the Dark Creatures' groups. But we can follow them."

We waited until they got a good distance ahead then slowly followed. It wasn't hard since they were going slow. The only problem was they descended deeper and deeper into the Dark Forest.

Going off the trail made it much more difficult to keep up with the group ahead. They formed into a single line and Luxor insisted on walking behind me to make sure I didn't get too far behind.

A few hours in, and we come to a stop. I didn't realize until Luxor put a hand over my mouth that I was breathing heavily. In front of us is a little well-built shack, not much bigger than a one-bedroom house. One of the men began to unpack the satchels and led the horses to the stream nearby. Luxor lowered his hand, and we took this opportunity to approach the small shack.

It didn't look like much at all. We snuck around the back and there were six windows in total around the house, but only one entrance. There was a small chimney, which was currently in use as white smoke billowed out, rising through the dark and covering some stars. *So, someone's already inside.* We looked through one of the windows, but it was too dark to see anything. The next window showed more promise, but it was on the side of the house where we would be too exposed.

So, we waited patiently, crouching down behind the corner of the house, until we heard the men come back with the horses, and then tiptoed around to the lit window.

There was a group of significantly large men, or maybe they were just large in comparison to us. They donned dark blue patches with a crescent moon etched into them. They were the largest group of creatures that I had ever seen. There were all kinds of creatures, from ghostly pale elves, small with pointed ears and imps, who made the elves look like giants in comparison. The imps appeared like they had too much caffeine and were jumping all about. When I noticed the gremlins, my heart faltered momentarily. I could feel the uneven pumping as I stood petrified. I sucked in a deep breath realizing I forgot to breathe. They're scarier in person, yet small in stature, with skin almost a silky tinted shade of gray. One looked directly at me with his bulging, bloodshot eyes, and I ducked behind the below the sill and clutched my chest. Their teeth were even sharper than I could have thought. My nightmares didn't do them justice.

"I don't understand," Luxor said as he glared through the window.

"Well, what are you two doing out here?" A voice boomed from directly behind us.

Panic spread through my veins and adrenaline coursed through me. The emotions pouring out of Luxor-fear, anxiety, bravery-enveloped me. I turned slowly, trying to keep my expression neutral.

I stood and raised my chin to meet the eyes of the man who spoke. He was large and had a dark blue patch with the crescent moon embroidered onto it. Up close, I could see these patches were handmade, beautifully and carefully crafted by expert hands. He was a knight, I guessed, carrying at least four of the many satchels we saw earlier — two in his arms and two slung across his back. We could've probably outran him unless he dropped the satchels. Running would've been less of a risk if we knew how important the satchels were. Luxor remained next to me in complete silence.

"We're looking for the Dark Creatures meeting. We are from the Seelie Kingdom and would like to support the cause," I responded as clearly and strongly as I could, channeling all the emotions that surrounded me, hopefully emotionally charging my statement.

The knight eyed us up for a few seconds. Then relief flooded through him.

"Come on then, this way." He gestured towards the only door leading in or out of the shack.

Luxor stared at me, wide-eyed, and leaned in close.

"How did you do that?"

133

"I don't know," I responded. "I was hoping the guard would trust us, I could feel your emotions and I just poured them back out at him, and he seems to trust us, I think."

"You used my emotions, that you felt, to project the feeling of trust into someone else?" When he said it, I realized how crazy I sounded.

I didn't respond because I couldn't quite put it into words myself. I assumed that was correct, but that was only if it really worked. We stopped at the front door and I couldn't help but stare upward. The door was built much larger than the average door. *Why is that?*

"This way then." The knight swung the door open, which crashed against the wall behind it. "I'm Rupert by the way, second right hand to the Unseelie King."

My stomach churned and my breath caught in my throat. Second right hand to the King? Leading us willingly into a known Dark Creature meeting. What were we about to walk into? Did Alaric know of his hunters' outside activities?

"Freedom is a price!" The voice shouted from the room next door. "The last generation of Dark Creatures is all but gone and we deserve to be welcomed back into the kingdoms arms!"

Hoots and cheers filled the room.

"I hope you're ready," Rupert warned as he pushed the next door open.

I measured myself for a moment, trying to figure out how to tell if I was truly prepared or not. The shack was significantly larger on the inside than it looked from the outside.

The room we walked into was bigger than I expected too. Everyone fit comfortably, all standing in a large circle around one man. There were tables and seating along the outskirts of the room, but no one seemed interested in this option. The powerful speaker was an elf, who was light blue with nothing but what looked like rags on, and was standing on a box. While he was small in stature, he had a voice that filled the room, or two or three of them. Nobody paused to look in our direction, they were completely mesmerized by the words of the speaker. We entered the room unnoticed.

Rupert dropped the satchels; the sound echoed off the walls, significant enough that the children heard and immediately surrounded us. They opened the bags to find bread and fruit inside. The adults stood back until the kids were done, then slowly one by one, they got some food as well. As the gremlins approached Rupert, he opened the satchel and offered them what looked like raw steaks. The entire time, Rupert seemed genuinely happy, as he smiled kindly at everyone who came his way. The attention slowly returned to the speaker who waited until last, when Rupert handed him the last of the food, with a sorrowful look. The only food left was certainly not enough to fill even a small elf's stomach, nothing but pitiful scraps. But the elf was grateful anyhow.

There was no hate in Rupert's soul, no foul looks of disgust as the gremlins gnawed on the meat, no preference for the human children over the elf or gremlin children. I could see in Rupert's eyes that he believed everyone in this room deserved a fighting chance. Coming in here, I was under the impression I was entering a dangerous, potentially lethal situation. Standing here now, I felt remorse, purely for the thoughts that were going through my head. These people were beautiful in their way, just as the Unseelie Kingdom itself. The stories I had heard about the Dark Creature groups were clearly just that, stories.

The speaker's voice softened as he looked at the food in his hands, before handing it to one of the children next to his stool, who took it happily. "We are too tired, and there are few of us who can fight. We are raising the next generations out of the world they should be in. We are sought out and slaughtered for the dark marks etched upon us from birth. But no more, we need to welcome ourselves back into society, we need to get help, and resources. We need peace."

I didn't know what I was expecting, but it wasn't what I saw. I didn't expect tears or families. I didn't expect to see little ones, so starved their skin clung to their bones. My heart wrenched as mothers held to their children in the hope of a new world order.

"We have increased the number of our inside sources to the kingdom in the last few months. People who are willing to help us come back into society peacefully, ones who have been working closely with the Unseelie King to bring us safely back into the

Kingdom. Now it's time for us to move, it is time for us to open the doors and expose ourselves for who we are, not what we were. We can live as society lives, we can function, as can our dark brothers, like the rest of society. Soon, every Dark Creature group will come back into society, soon every life will matter again."

There were quiet grumbles and many silent tears but no one was against the words being spoken. Fear and hope flowed throughout the room. The young minds were curious, ready to explore the open world. But all the emotions I felt were genuine and kind. All except one. The emotions radiating from right next to me. Anger, resentment, and hatred hung stagnant in the air that surrounded me.

I turned to stare anger in the face and Luxor stared back. His maroon aura faded into black and I stepped away from him. I couldn't handle the emotions he was projecting onto me. I closed my eyes and thought of serenity, peace, and understanding. I reached for Luxor's balled up hand.

13

"No!" Luxor pulled away. Everyone in the room went silent, searching for the voice that had spoken out. "I will not calm down. I will not feel bad for these *filthy* creatures!" I fervently hoped he was whispering, but as I looked around the attention shifted to us. His anger escalated at a rampant rate.

Shock and dismay filled the room, including my own. One gremlin mom covered her child's large, pointed ears that protruded from his cute little head and turned him the other way. Rupert clenched his fist, and I could feel the trust that I'd carefully placed into him, was gone. I started backing away from Rupert as slowly as I could, as I saw the realization in his eyes at what I had done.

"We have to go Adella, now!" Luxor grabbed my arm, attempting to pull me from the shack. Instead, he pulled my cloak

138

off and the room filled with mumbles and gasps as my luminescent skin's glow filled the dark room like a nightlight.

"Do you *know* who that is?" One of the little girls gasped.

"This is what we've been waiting for," the speaker announced enthusiastically, trying to pull the attention back in his direction.

"What if she's not here to help, Momma?" But this last comment, the one that stuck with me was drowned out by the conversations that fill the room. I wanted to speak, to give them hope and reassurance, but I was not sure exactly what to say.

The room's atmosphere shifted, and they all looked in my direction. To them, I was the face of hope, one of the trusted kingdom members that were going to help them enter back into society. One of the only people that could help them and their children live healthy and meaningful lives. I wanted nothing more than to be that person.

Luxor gripped my arm roughly and dragged me outside. He shouted at me to sprint and pointed towards the Unseelie Kingdom walls. I didn't know why I ran, but I did. I ran dead sprint in the direction that my protector, the person who was supposed to keep me safe, had told me to go. I turned my head just in time to see him throw something small and round into the shack. I froze in place. I felt the explosion, my ears rung, almost unbearably loud. I changed directions and charged towards the shack. My eyebrows seared and fallen pieces of burning ash burned areas all over my body.

"Noooo!" I was too late. Orange and red flames burst from all corners. The roof crumbled away before my eyes. There was nothing left: no shack, no life.

What if she's not here to help, Momma?

"Nooo, no, no." I choked out the last word. Smoke filled my lungs, making it harder to breathe. Luxor's arms wrapped around me, preventing me from advancing any closer and pulled me violently in the opposite direction, but I fell to my knees. Intense warmth from the explosion pressed on my face and the smell of my burning eyebrows filled my nose.

I inhaled the thick smoke deeply, feeling it scorch my lungs, but I didn't care. The hot tears stung my cheeks as they ran down, mixing with the soot and touching the fresh burn marks that I was sure would leave scars as permanent reminders of this day. I tried to open my eyes wider, to watch the ends of the explosion unfold, to remember what happened, so I could retell the story of the Dark Creature group changing, but my body wasn't obeying.

Luxor put his arms around my shoulders. A feeling of comfort I should have welcomed, but instead detested. For the first time since we met, I didn't want him near me.

"Adella, we have to leave. Adella," I felt him shaking me, but it wasn't working. My body was numb, my mind's too far gone Filled with sorrow for the lost, and despair for the hope that had been yanked forcefully out of me in the final seconds of the lives of those fighting for freedom. "Adella get up we *have* to move." But there was nothing, nothing in me that was willing to respond to these warnings. I had no concern for my own wellbeing or safety.

"What if she's not here to help, Momma?" The child's plea haunted me.

Below me, the world began to move, but not from any movements or decisions I made. All the emotions from before were officially gone. I couldn't feel anyone around me anymore. *Maybe you could have saved them, maybe, you could feel their emotions because they were still alive.*

The taunting of my subconscious pushed me over the edge and the lights went out. And for the first time in the Unseelie Kingdom, my world truly went dark.

14

When I regained consciousness, the room was bright — too bright. I could see the glaring light from the insides of my closed eyelids. The kind of white brightness that couldn't be created by nature. I didn't know what I was waking up to, but the smell of chemicals stung my already tender nose.

I tentatively opened my eyes but the action immediately made my head spin. I shut them and began to breathe slower, trying to slow down the non-existent room from spinning. Flexing my arms and legs was painful. I could feel some kind of cloth covering most of my arms, and up around my shoulders.

I couldn't sense any emotions in the room. Maybe I never really could, maybe there was no one in the room. I heard a sudden rustle as if someone had noticed my breathing pattern change. I

142

held my breath as if to convince them I wasn't awake. I peeked my eyes open and there, on the side of the white linen bed I'm lying in, was my dad, a blinding white light surrounded him.

"Oh, Dad." Tears flowed as I recalled the recent events. I sat up and reached for him, but being slightly dizzy, I fell into him. Searing pain coursed through my body as my freshly-burned arms reached around my dad. My body screamed for me to get back in bed, to relax, and take a moment, but my heart yearned for comfort.

"Easy Dells! You've been out for quite a while, and you've been through a lot. You need to rest." His arms wrapped around me lightly, and he helped me back into a sitting position.

"It was terrible, Dad." I hyperventilated as I remembered all those lives, even the large intake of air felt like it was burning me from the inside out. All the children, the families, the hope — gone in moments. I wasn't sure I could remain together and keep myself from crumbling down into blackness again.

"It's okay. Luxor told us everything. You just need to relax and heal right now, Dells. Luxor is just a couple rooms down."

"*Keep him away from me*," I hissed. "What exactly did Luxor tell you, Dad?"

"He's been up for almost six hours now." I could hear the confusion in my dad's voice at my sudden reaction. He proceeded with caution. "You guys were walking towards the Unseelie Kingdom when you were taken by the Dark Creature group. It doesn't surprise me, Dells, it's not safe for you there." My mind

143

went blank. This didn't sound like what happened, I crushed my eyes closed trying to recall. "You're lucky you and Luxor got out before the building went up in flames. Many lives were lost. Many knights and creatures are gone. The Unseelie Kingdom must have been planning to attack, and you were certainly in the wrong place at the wrong time," Dad said this almost robotically. Something wasn't right.

"Where are we?" I scanned the room, but there were no signs to indicate where I was.

"The Seelie Kingdom Infirmary. They found you and Luxor outside the Unseelie Kingdom gates a little over two days ago."

Two days? I'd been out for two days?

"Now that you're awake, I can call for a meeting with the other two contestants, the Seelie Queen and the Unseelie King. No other persons or protectors are invited to this meeting Dells. It will be tonight at 7 pm in the Queen's main living quarters. Rest up and I will see you soon honey. I love you."

"Wait, Dad, did they find Anna?" Our trip was pointless, lives lost, and nothing seemed to be gained but a better understanding of the injustice that surrounded the courts.

"They did, Dells," he turned around in the doorway. This was good news at least. "They found all the missing contestants' friends and family inside the gates of the Unseelie Kingdom." It sounded more like a question than an answer the way he said it. "I've never seen anything like it. They have no memory of how they got there, or how long they were there for. They didn't see

144

anyone else and all wandered into the merchant's quarters seeking help."

I closed my eyes, in an attempt to process everything that happened, trying to find a reason or answer that maybe I could remember, but my mind was foggy. At least I'd see Anna soon.

"Okay, Dad. I will see you tonight then." I smiled at him as he left the room. "I love you too," I said after him, not knowing if he could hear me or not.

I got up, slowly this time, and stretched. Stiffness held my arms from reaching too high. My legs were sore and trembled as I stood, but I was alive and doing as well as I could be for going through an explosion. I needed to get out, to have fresh air, and find Anna, so I could figure out what's going on. One shaky step at a time, I made it to the pile of clothes on the bench across from me. I could tell my dad brought them. Leggings — not that I could complain at this point — and a concert shirt from the Led Zeppelin concert we saw last summer.

I threw my hair up in a ponytail, went into the small bathroom, and splashed cold water on my face. Finally, I was feeling a bit more human. I didn't dare glance into the mirror. I could feel the flush in my face and the frizz of my hair. I carefully peeled off most of the bandages to let the wounds get some air. I evaluated the damage to my arms. It was nowhere near as bad as it could've been. They were healing, at least. I looked at the small blisters that had formed where the soot hit, second-degree at worst. I flexed my arms a couple of times, the soreness was already fading away. It

145

was only a matter of time before they healed over. I walked out of the bathroom and made my way to the door. I held the door handle for a long time. *In this little room, these four walls, I am safe. Out there, there's no guarantee.* I take a deep breath and push open the door.

Finding my way out of the hallway of the infirmary was simple. I carefully avoided passing by Luxor's room — I was nowhere near ready for that conversation yet. Figuring out where to go next was the impossible part. I decided to go to my room first. I couldn't risk running into anyone, I was not sure I could handle conversations and questions. I would surely have to answer them later, so I didn't want to do it now. Walking to my room, I thought about all the places I could potentially find Anna. I knocked on her room door first. No answer. I should have known better though, considering she never really slept in that room in the first place. I figured that would be too easy. I went to my room, opened the door, and switched on the light.

There, in my bed, upside down on a pillow, was a fiery red, unkempt mess of hair.

"Anna!" I jumped into the bed right on top of her and rolled over next to her. My body protested violently, causing me to wince slightly as the pain shot up my arms, but I didn't care. She moaned and groaned for a minute before she sprung to life.

"Dells, I missed you! Where have you been? Where did you go? There have been rumors, but none I believe!"

"Where have I been? Where have *you* been? Do you not remember anything? How can you just go from lying in bed with me one night to vanishing for days?"

"Listen Dells, there's something you need to know." I instantly sat down, folding my hands carefully into my lap, and prepared myself for the information.

"Alaric came to us, a large group of us. Those who he knew someday would choose Fata. He asked us to disappear for a couple of days, said the contestants needed to see the Unseelie Kingdom, to really see it." She paused for a moment, waiting to see if I had any questions. "He planned to take all the contestants to the Unseelie Kingdom to allow them to look around themselves, to see the creatures in the castle, and become acquainted with the grounds. Then miraculously, we would return safe and unharmed, with a silly story as to how we all went missing. It wasn't the perfect plan, but it was a plan for everyone to see how the Dark Creatures were not all bad. To hopefully spark a change in the heart of the next Seelie Queen."

"I went looking for you Anna, for everyone. Me and Luxor-" I didn't know how to finish that sentence. Clearly, I had ruined a carefully illustrated plan.

"Wait, I'm not done," Anna cut me off with an impatient hand to my face. "That *was* the plan. We were supposed to meet the next morning, but the night before we were due to meet, you were snoring so loudly and I couldn't sleep. So I went to my room to pack a bag for the next day, when I saw a note had been slipped

147

under the door to my room. It stated there was a change in plans and to meet out back immediately. I threw a couple outfits into a bag and ran to the meeting spot. We all piled into the van and the doors were shut, we were all taken, the original group and a few extras.

"The leader of our little group knocked on the wall for Alaric to open the little door, and there was no response. The engine roared to life, and we hit the road, a little too fast. Our leader knocked on it a little louder, and was continuously ignored. That's when we realize it wasn't Alaric who changed the plans at all. After the pure panic and everyone banging on the sides of the van, everything was a total blank, aside from waking up. Someone knew about the plan all along, hijacked it and was one step ahead of us. It seems none of us can remember what happened, it's all somewhat of a blur still." Anna's lips pursed and her eyebrows raised, I could see the confusion coloring her face.

There was a moment of silence as I took this all in. *Someone who was one step ahead.* If my head was spinning any less than when I woke up today, it had officially returned with a vengeance.

"Wait, wait, *wait* a darn minute. You, and *Luxor*?" She interrupted my train of thought, giving me her eyebrow wiggle and a suggestive shoulder shrug.

"No, Anna. It's not like that. I don't think there's any way I could ever be with Luxor, or even allow him to be my protector anymore. Even if my grandma saw us together someday."

148

"Wait? Your grandma saw a vision of you and Luxor?" Anna got up onto her knees, waiting impatiently for the rest of the low down.

"Not exactly. She said she saw that I'd already met the person I'm supposed to be with. She saw mine and Luxor's kiss and said I shouldn't take such a perfect connection for granted. She's a premonition Fata, Anna." I took a deep breath, speaking quickly or for long periods wasn't a talent of mine. Anna remained quiet, so I continued. "So anyways, Luxor and I went to find you. The stories of what happened when we went, between me and Luxor, don't quite match up. There's a meeting tonight and my dad said I can't bring anyone, but I want you to come. I couldn't imagine this meeting without you."

"Of course! Not a chance in hell I'm missing it."

"You can't tell anyone though Anna, not even Luxor."

"You can't tell anyone what happened to us Dells, not even the Queen knows." Anna's face became serious very quickly. "And I promise, as long as you tell the whole story tonight, I want to know what happened."

"Deal. Can we go find something to eat now? I think I'm starving." My grumbling stomach certainly agreed.

We hopped out of the bed, threw some flats on, and headed towards the kitchen.

A few hours later, Anna and I nervously made our way to Queen Leaure's living quarters. Having never been there before, we were nervous. Rows and rows of pictures of previous Kings and Queens lined the neutral-colored halls. Statues of pets, heirlooms, and perfectly preserved wedding dresses stood in cases in the corners. All the halls seemed to go on forever, but finally, they led to a single door at the end of a long, narrow hall.

Knocking was unnecessary as a large man was planted in the way of the door, outside waiting. "Adella Shenning and Anna Gretsome, welcome." He opened the door for us, then shut it the moment we entered.

I leaned into Anna and whispered, "I guess it's okay you're here."

We both shrugged and sat down at the table across from the front door where my dad was waiting.

The Queen entered next, with no protection to be seen and no announcement of her arrival. The other two contestants followed suit, sitting confidently on either side of Queen Leaure, which left me with the only open seat on my right when King Alaric walked in. I stiffened immediately, nervous about what's to come. But he sat down next to me with ease, settled into his chair a little, and cleared his throat.

"Well first things first, anything to be discussed in this room, shall remain in this room, amongst only the people afforded the right to sit at this table. Secondly, I think we need to begin with the truthful story of what happened three days ago. So, my sweet

150

Adella of the Summer, would you please begin with your version of what happened while you were away?" He looked my way, the eyes in the room followed his. Curiosity in some and what appeared to be envy in others.

I was prepared for the spotlight, I knew I was going to have to share the story sooner or later. Maybe I still stood a chance at making Jackie and Lilah see the Dark Creatures differently, if I shared it right.

Off into the story I launched, explaining the trip to my grandma's house, the dream visits (which I think made Alaric turn a slight shade of pink), the trip to the Unseelie Kingdom, and everything thereafter. Explaining the emotional manipulation was the difficult part, but not harder than explaining what Luxor had done to the Dark Creatures soon thereafter. I left no stone unturned, as open as a book could be.

My story ended and I took a shaky breath. I was proud that I could tell the story without too many sidetrack stories or crying. Everyone stared at me, slightly wide-eyed. No one spoke a word.

"Well, I think we can agree that Luxor's sequence of events is false, and he's no longer to be trusted. Queen Leaure, if it's alright with you, I was hoping to request Anna, as the new protector for Adella," my dad said quietly, but sternly.

The Queen pondered the notion for a moment. "I suppose if Anna accepts the position and agrees to attend extra training and courses through the school year, I think that would be a wonderful idea. However, we must consider the fact that Luxor's story could still be true, as there are two sides to every story and Luxor is not known to lie."

"Oh, I will!" Anna squealed, so excited to offer her own life for my protection. I wasn't sure if I liked the idea myself, seeing how quickly we could lose someone.

"Are you insinuating that I may have led on an attack that not only killed dozens of innocents but also my own men?" Alaric's voice was stern, though not quite accusing.

"I'm simply stating that without a second set of eyes, there's no way to be sure," Queen Leaure said.

Her condescending tone made me think that was exactly what she was insinuating. Not that it was my place to question the Queen. My Queen.

"Protector Luxor will not be informed. Instead, he will be kept busy in training and closely monitored for the time being. Some of my best men died in the field two days ago, great men. Men who agreed to help get the Dark Creatures ready to be eased back into society, men who used their spare time to bring food and clothing to those who otherwise wouldn't have had it. Men who were killed carelessly, thanks to *protector* Luxor. And someday, he will pay the price. Until that day we trust no one. We don't know if this was the Seelie people, Unseelie people, a rogue Dark Creatures group plan that was being acted on, or if Luxor was selfishly acting on his own accord." Alaric looked strong and sorrowful at the same time. I reached under the table and put my hand on his own, but he continued to look forward.

152

"This doesn't appear to be a Dark Creature group," my dad said.

"No, however, I think for the safety of those gifted with summer, their friends, and their families, you should all return home until things have some time to settle. Then you will travel back and if it's still not safe, we will set up courses for you next year in the castle. Dan, I was hoping you would lead a group of hunters, and see if you can figure out who took Anna and the others? You can do this from home. There's a base close to your house and this will be a well-compensated position," Queen Leaure said, well, ordered.

"Of course, your majesty, I'd be honored." My dad's face beamed.

The rest of the group besides Alaric, Queen Leaure, and my dad were dismissed. We left without hesitation. The room was stuffy and was suffocating me.

"Easy enough," Anna rambled on. "We go to school and I'll take extra courses. We will have fewer classes together though, but I will make sure to walk you home every day, and if you need to go somewhere, you will call me, so I can escort you."

"Anna, you're about as threatening as a kitten." I tried my hardest to stifle the laugh that threatened to escape my lips.

"But I can fight! And with more training, I could take down anyone bigger than me. The bigger they are, the harder they fall. I know you've heard that before." She picked her arms up and began rapidly chopping the air, flinging a leg forward as if kicking

153

something in front of her. I had heard that saying before, but with the karate moves she currently mimicked, I couldn't do anything but gut laugh in response. My best friend was my protector.

We finally made it back to the room. It wasn't quite dark yet. *Now Anna is in just as much danger as the last protectors. Luxor is a bad guy, and now Anna is in danger.* My brain played these thoughts on repeat over and over again as Anna ran to the bathroom to get ready to sleep. So, bed sounded like the safest option at this point. Anna stepped back out of the bathroom in pajamas and smiled at me. *I wonder if she'd still be smiling at me if she really knew that her life was on the line.* I faked a smile back.

I was too tired to change so the leggings and a t-shirt were good enough for me. We crawled into bed and snuggled close, for the feeling of safety and because I never thought I'd see her again. Soon enough, we went to sleep. Deep, dark sleep.

15

"Of course," I said, eye to eye with Alaric.

He stood there, motionless. He didn't say anything, nor did he need to. The burden of losing his men, and many people of his kingdom, was written all over his face. Alaric was defeated. I walked over to him slowly, not wanting to startle him, but to console him. I held him and we sank to the ground. It felt like we were there for hours, just lying there, arm in arm, confused and melancholy about the world around us.

"You'll have to learn to control what you know. Not everyone wants to feel happy all the time," Alaric looked at me soberly.

"Control what?"

"You can't always change people's emotions, Adella. Some people want to feel the pain, they want to grieve."

"I wasn't trying to take your pain. I'm trying to share in it. I'm also deeply affected by what happened to the families, children, and soldiers. I, too, am grieving."

"Hmm, we will need to further work on your emotional manipulation skills then, as I'm certainly getting a calming effect from you. Not that I don't appreciate the effect you have on me, but the families and soldiers lost deserve to be grieved." Alaric leaned over and kissed me.

"You should have told me," I said, pulling away. His lips were salty from the tears. But I was just moments late. The effect his kiss had on me was overpowering.

My insides crushed uncomfortably, constricting my heart and squeezing until it felt like it was going to pop, making my knees weak, and my thoughts jumbled from lack of blood flow. Alaric's grief was overtaking my own. It ate its way inside my emotions and spilled tears onto my cheeks. The closer he held me, the harder it was to push away. I could feel his devotion to me acting as inner cords or magnets that pulled us in tight together, threatening to merge us into one. I understood the lengths he was going through to keep me safe and how protective he felt over me. I put my hands on his chest and pushed him back for a moment, and met his eyes. "I, I," I gasped for air, the constriction made it hard to breathe, and I was unable to complete my sentence. His proximity made it hard for me to put my thoughts together.

In response, he pulled me back into the kiss, this time more fiercely, needing more of me than I had to offer at this moment. I carefully stopped the kiss and rested my head on his chest.

"If the Queen of Summer and the King of Winter fall in love, what is to become of the Kingdoms?"

I felt the hope and worry for the future coursing through Alaric's being as he spoke. "The plan had a few unexpected twists, but in the end, I could see you truly understood. Your story was moving and powerful. And the hearts of Jackie and Lilah are also beginning to sway."

"Yes but the Queen-" I said, he cut me off crushing his lips to my own.

I set my hands on his chest and pushed him away, just enough to try to gain control of the situation. Annoyance now filled the small void between us. His and my own.

"-didn't want to understand. Her priority is to her kingdom and hers alone," he said.

"Does my father know?"

"About the fact that I planned to steal the people? Indeed. We will be using the time he's taking with the hunters wisely; however, and preparing the hunters for a potential war. Inviting the Dark Creatures back is going to be more serious than I thought. Judging by Luxor's reaction, we have much more to prepare for than we originally anticipated."

I flinched at the mention of his name.

"Maybe someday, the beauty of both courts will be seen for what they're truly worth, for the souls of their people rather than the cost of their abilities." I met his eyes and stared into them, not ready to say goodbye, even if it was only a dream visit.

He stroked my hair until I lost consciousness of the dreamland and woke up in my bed.

Going home wasn't on my priority list. Packing my bags and saying goodbye to half of the Seelie Kingdom (most of which I knew the names of, some of which I still must learn), was the hardest thing I'd done since I got here. I belonged here, I could feel it in my blood. I desired to be amongst the people, to rule. For the first time since I was told of my calling, I truly realized I was a competitor.

Packing felt too real, but my suitcase was light. I hunted around the room for a minute, but my clothes barely filled half the suitcase.

"Adellaaaaaa," Anna sang as she marched into my room, using a little rectangular piece of paper to fan herself. "You know, I don't remember mail delivery being part of a protector's job. Yet, here we stand, you locked away, hiding in the room and me delivering secret sexy messages." She casually waved the rectangle a little slower.

"Where did you get that?" I reached for it, but she hid it behind her back.

"Alaric's guard handed it to me about ten minutes ago and told me to deliver it immediately. But if I give it to you, I wanna read it." Her bargaining skills were unbelievable.

"Please, you know I'd let you read it anyway!" I couldn't help but roll my eyes.

"Just checking!" She tossed the letter in my direction; I'm a little nervous and almost didn't catch it.

I was expecting a formal letter, instead, I held a piece of paper that'd been physically folded into the shape of an envelope. I carefully unfolded it so that I wouldn't damage any of the writing inside.

My sweet Adella,

I don't know the next time I will get to see your face; I would like to spend an evening with you in the Seelie gardens starting tonight at 5 pm.

I hope you will see me,

Alaric.

My heart skipped a beat as I read his words. Anna's jaw dropped.

"You know I have to go right?" Anna stared at me intensely.

"No. Anna, I need you to stay in my room and cover for me in case my dad comes up. Besides, you *know* I'll be surrounded by guards if I'm with Alaric."

"*Fine*, but you *owe* me, Dells! I want to know everything *and* I want the number to the cute bodyguard who gave me the letter today."

"Deal!" That was easier than I thought. Now, to get ready. *What do you even wear to a meeting with a king?*

I stared at him in disbelief. Jeans and a t-shirt; casual and completely unexpected. He took my hand and led me toward the gardens. He didn't say a word, but then again, there was no need to. We went to a small canopy in the tulip fields, where there was a checkered blanket and nothing else. He laid down and pulled me to his chest. I breathed in his sweet aroma and closed my eyes.

The night was calm, not even the trees were swaying. The mild breeze raised tiny goosebumps on my arms.

"You know," he whispered. "Courting someone is much more difficult than I originally anticipated."

I smiled up at him. "Well, you seem to be doing a fine job so far."

"Oh good," he sighed a little in relief. "I wasn't sure if Jackie was even noticing me." I detected a hint of sarcasm in his voice.

"Hey!" I sat up, and he pulled me back down against him.

"Oh please, you know I'm only kidding." I could hear his teasing tone, but I sensed some worry in him, like maybe he wasn't sure if I knew he was kidding.

I laughed easily, his chest rumbled as he chuckled along with me.

He seemed to be in thought, so I didn't dare interrupt. His eyes focused on some of the candles lighting up the canopy above, his hand traced circles around my lower back. He looked slimmer laying here like this, I slid my hand under his shirt and allowed my fingers to follow the contour of his abs.

I looked at him expectantly. If he wasn't talking, maybe there were other activities we could do. He stared back at me for a long moment, before leaning in slowly.

He whispered so quietly I barely heard him. "Now to figure out how to win you this crown."

It was easier to adjust to being at home than I thought it would be. Anna was training night and day to be the best protector possible, and Luxor had been kept busy as promised with errands for my dad, assignments from the Seelie Queen that involved traveling to the kingdom often, and the frequent (and slightly obsessive) paragraph text messages he sent to me throughout his day.

7:00 am

Adella, I'm traveling to the Seelie Kingdom again, today for training, the Queen has assured me you would be sent a protector.

9:21 am

Adella, I miss you. We should plan time for just us this weekend, go see a movie, or even just stay in and get pizza at my place. Could be fun?

11:47 am
Adella, you're probably busy with school today. It's fine just get back to me when you get the chance. We are running obstacle courses again today. Forever repetitive work.

I read and reread the texts, but I couldn't seem to come up with the right words to say to him. We hadn't had a real conversation since…that night. *Do I break up with him? Were we even together in the first place?*

Somehow, I managed to keep myself busy with reading History and Mystics passages from my textbooks. Since I was graduating a year ahead of time so I could study at the Seelie court this year, my education had been fast-tracked. I found myself in my little corner on my pillows in my room often studying.

Truth be told, I was not busy with school today, at least not too busy to text Luxor back. I decided to do most of my studies from home. Without Anna in my classes, they became abnormally slow and boring.

Our table in the lunchroom wasn't much anymore either. Since Anna was too busy for a relationship, Dustin and Devon had been keeping their distance, and since Luxor didn't make any appearances at school, Rachael no longer sat at the table. Some of

162

her posse stayed behind, I assumed, to spy. But as I kept my nose in a book during the whole lunch hour, I imagined they were pretty bored.

She spent most of her time outside of training with me, studying, so she didn't fall behind or miss a single breath I took. When she walked into the room, I gave her an approving look up and down.

"Do you like it? Really? I know you don't like her, but Madeline knows the best stores for durable clothes that don't get ruined in training."

I rolled my eyes. Anna looked stunning. She'd taken to Madeline's love for black clothes. They were almost identical, only Anna kept her wild mane in a bun on top of her head and sported a daring red lipstick. Today's ensemble was tight black leather pants and a simple black tank top. I would almost guess she was going for a night on the town if I didn't know she'd been training all day. Her jewelry still lined her face and arms and her clothes were still skin-tight, so at least everything didn't change.

"You look amazing. The red lipstick is a nice touch." Anna smiled, looking pleased with herself. "Hey, Anna?" I pondered out loud.

"Yes?" She answered.

"What do you do at training? Is it hard?"

"Well, protectors are trained by other protectors and sometimes hunters depending on what they deem is their "special talents."

163

Mine is my size, so i'm taught a lot of hand to hand combat and camouflaging, and we work a lot on shooting from a distance."

"So you're like a sniper?"

"No, just working on my aim. Snipers have way more skill than I do," she laughed and rolled her eyes at me.

"So there *are* snipers?" I pushed.

"Dells that is so not important were all trained to shoot. Some of us are just better than others. I need you to focus, though. Protectors were given a message today. Do you wanna hear it?" Anna pulled out a small piece of paper from her pocket.

"Of course, I wanna hear it. Was that a letter for me Anna?" Well, she managed to get my full attention now; I even put my book down.

"Shh, no time for debating who should have opened the mail now, Dells, this is important." She held her finger up to her lips. I pretended to zip mine. "Adella Shenning. Contestant to the Seelie Queen trials." Anna paused for effect, but I was going crazy. "Your first assignment is to find the *Tenebris Librir,* before your return to the Seelie courts on Christmas break. If you do not find the object, do not return."

My eyes widened. My first assignment: find the Tenebris Librir. *Whatever that was.*

"I looked it up and it means dark book, in Latin. I was about to go to our library to see if I could find any more information on it."

"Dark book like Unseelie? Or dark book like evil book?" I asked her.

Anna shrugged, clearly as in the dark as I was. "I don't know, but I'm going to head to the library and see what I can find out."

"Thanks, I'm going to get some sleep, Anna. I'm not feeling too well today."

"Oh!" Anna's protector mode triggered right to life. "I can stay here with you or get you some soup. I can sleep over if you would like."

"No Anna, it would be really helpful if you could go to the library and come back tomorrow."

"Okay. I will text you if I find anything worth mentioning." Anna turned and left, clearly pleased with herself and her new mission.

However, I knew the truth. She wouldn't find anything in our small library; they wouldn't have made the challenge that easy. I had so many questions. Did everyone get the same assignment? Is this a race to see who could get to the book faster? One thing was for sure. I needed to call Alaric. No, I needed to see Alaric.

16

It had been months since our little date in the Seelie gardens, Alaric has been busy ruling his kingdom and I on my studies. An understanding of priorities we both had. I missed him though, and I wasn't sure how this mind thing worked. "*Alaric!*" I screamed in my head. "*Alaric, I need to speak to you.*" I was not sure if I needed to yell it in my head for him to hear me, but it was certainly worth a try. Jumping into bed I lowered myself under the covers, all I could think about was how there was no one I'd been missing more than Alaric. When I closed my eyes, it was almost like I was with him again on our last night together. I could smell him, and almost feel his chest under my fingertips, I could even hear his heartbeat. I focused on the fake heartbeat my mind was making up to comfort me, and counted the heartbeats to keep myself from bawling until I finally drifted to sleep.

Apparently, Alaric didn't hear my calls, because there were no dreams at all that night, just endless blackness. Every time the blackness came, panic raced through me, and I remembered the last time my world went completely dark.

My eyes were extra heavy in the morning; rolling over and pushing myself out of bed took all the energy I had. I stumbled into the bathroom and washed my face, at least I felt a little more human. I threw on my slippers and robe. I needed a cup of coffee. Heading out of my room and into the kitchen, I poured the coffee and heard my dad talking.

"There's nothing to report." My dad must have been on the phone with protector James again.

"I'm not here for a report, I'd just like to see Adella." The familiar voice rang through the house. *Alaric.*

My coffee dropped out of my hand and burning hot liquid splashed all over my shirt. The cup fell to the floor with a loud crash. I looked back up and peered around the corner into the living room. There were about eight bodies, but only the closest three turned to see what was going on. I put a finger to my lips, signaling with them not to say anything, and they all turned their attention back to the conversation at hand.

"May I ask what this pertains to?" My dad pried.

I fell to my knees and started to crawl down the hall, leaving the shattered mug and contents to clean later. I did my best to keep my shirt away from my skin as I crawled, the wet fabric was quickly getting very cold.

167

Since I announced what happened between Alaric and me to everyone, my dad had been extremely cautious around both Luxor and Alaric. He didn't seem upset, but he certainly wasn't ready to let me have free rein. Since then, Alaric had been calling and trying to win my dad's favor and throwing a dream visit or two in for me now and again.

"You may not." I didn't stay to listen to the rest of Alaric's response, knowing my dad would bring him down the hall to my room at any moment. I got to my feet as soon as I knew I'd be out of sight and sprinted down the hall to my door.

There was no time to get dressed up, leggings, and a long simple blouse would have to do. There was a quick knock at my door while I was running a brush through my hair.

"Dells, you have a visitor."

"Thanks, Dad, be out in a minute." I didn't want to keep the King waiting after all.

I slipped on my flats and waited until I could hear my dad's footsteps down the hall, before slipping out my door and following closely behind.

Clearly, my mental call to Alaric worked, even if not in the way I expected. Excited and nervous, I paused in the doorway and my cheeks flushed; the room was full of people, at least 12, all of whom stared at me expectantly.

"Good morning Alaric." My voice sounded odd, almost too formal.

"Good morning Adella, I trust you slept soundly?"

The twinkle in his eye told me he knew I didn't sleep very soundly. My cheeks reddening made my dad look at me suspiciously.

"I was wondering if you would care to join me for a cup of coffee?"

"I would love to, when do we leave?"

"Now would be best, if you don't mind."

"I don't mind at all. Dad, I will be home in a bit, I love you." I hugged my dad, this was such an odd display to do in front of so many people at one time.

"That's fine Dells," Dad glanced at Alaric and bit his bottom lip. He looked like he was trying to decide if he should say more or not. "Don't leave down without calling. If you're past ten, you need to call every hour."

"Promise, dad."

"And Dells, I know you guys have a *thing*, but no staying the night with him, and he certainly cannot stay the night here."

"I will, Dad," a lump formed in my throat. I couldn't believe my dad was choosing now to set so many limitations.

I gave my dad the most genuine smile I could and he gave me a satisfactory one back. *How embarrassing.* I looked to Alaric who had his eyebrow raised and lips pursed, amusement smeared across his face. Alaric gestured for me to exit first, he followed and then all 10 of his bodyguards stayed close by.

"This feels a bit extreme. Do you always have this many protectors with you?"

169

"Only when I travel outside the Kingdoms. Only one is my personal protector, the rest are hunters and are going to assist your father at work shortly."

We ended up at the little café down the road, the only café really. We didn't have many places to go out here in town. The windows and doors were all closed. The second we stepped inside, the front door also closed and was locked by one of the hunters. There was a small intimate table set up and no other person in the café, not that it appeared they would be letting anyone else enter.

"Hunters, you may leave now, to the location you were previously given this morning. Do not make any additional stops and make sure you mention the code word."

One by one the Hunters exited the room until there was only one remaining. His salt and pepper beard was indication that he was quite older, and the gray tux he wore complimented him. But the worry lines on his face were concerning.

"Adella, this is my protector. He doesn't like to give his name out but I thought you should know it. His name is Abel, and he doesn't say much, but I assure you he is the best protector there is."

The older man nodded and left the room without a word, walking back into the kitchen. The barista brought out two lattes and set them in front of us, then he exited swiftly without saying anything to us. I picked up my drink and took a sip. It was perfect. I let the hot coffee surround my tongue and sit for a second to take in the vanilla accents in the coffee itself.

"So, my dear Adella. I received your... not-so-subtle call last night. When I attempted to enter your dreams, however, it was blocked. I couldn't get in. Do you know why this may have happened? Have you visited any sprites, other Fay or Fata recently?"

"I slept rough and woke up a lot. Could it have just been hard for you to get through because I was waking up a lot?"

"Yes, that could certainly add complications. Check your room for any unrecognized stones or dream catchers though, just in case, someone might be blocking me on purpose."

"I will, Alaric. There's something I need to speak with you about though. I got my first assignment."

Alaric took a moment to respond. Bringing the coffee to his lips, he let it slowly seep in. I'd never seen someone drink attractively, or maybe I was thinking that because I missed him terribly. Either way, he looked as tasty as the coffee was. He put his cup down. His lips were slightly red and swollen from the heat. I just wanted to lean in and...

"Alright love, well, what is it?"

I took out the little piece of paper I'd written it down on, so I wouldn't forget what it was called.

"Well," I take a second to clear my throat and my thoughts. "I needed to find the Teneeeeebbrrissss Liiibrir," I pronounced it the best I could. It didn't sound quite like Anna's, but I think I had gotten the point across.

Alaric's eyes widened considerably. He started spewing out part of his drink he seemed to inhale by mistake. He cleared his throat and composed himself quickly.

"Are you quite sure that's what you're supposed to be looking for?"

I handed Alaric my little piece of paper.

"I'm sure. Anna told me today. What is it?"

"Tenebris Librir is a Latin term for 'dark book.' To be exact, it's the original book to help Fata, of all sorts, practice their powers and use dark energy. Only one person is allowed to have a book like this in their possession."

"And that would be..."

"Me, Adella. This is my book. To be more specific, it's a book passed on from Unseelie ruler to Unseelie ruler. I haven't the slightest clue on why you'd need to find it. There are two books in which only the rulers are supposed to hold. The dark book, and the book of light. The Seelie Queen holds one book, and I hold the other."

I didn't realize I was fidgeting with my napkin until Alaric reached across the table and grabbed my hand. He took in a deep breath and I squeezed his hand. It had been months since I'd seen him, and I didn't know how long he would be staying.

"What do you think the Seelie Queen would want with the dark book?"

"I haven't the slightest clue, Adella. When a Fay or Fata pick their side or are chosen, the element they decide is the only element they may practice. If a Fay attempts to practice dark elements, they may be denied powers from the light altogether and be banned from practicing any magic. If I hand you the dark book, I would be handing the dark secrets to you, and possibly to the Seelie Queen herself."

Something in his body language told me that wasn't about to happen. Maybe it was his red-knuckled death grip on my hand, stiff posture, or stern glare as he finished his sentence. I leaned towards him and smiled at him sweetly.

Glancing at our hands I gave mine a little wiggle and he loosened up immediately.

"Why do you think the Queen wants me specifically to get the book? Couldn't she have given this trial to Jackie or Lilah?"

"Honestly, curiosity, or to test our relationship. To see what draws us to the dark or how our energy source works. It could be several things. What I do know, is that I will not put it in the Queen's hands willingly. The dark book says everything about dark magic, including weaknesses and downfalls to all the Dark Creatures."

Test our relationship. That gave me an abnormal amount of butterflies.

"Maybe you're right, maybe the Queen does want to test our relationship, maybe she wants to dabble in dark magic. Either way, it was my first assignment to get my hands on that book. And I will not fail the first assignment. I'm not ready to give up the throne so soon." I tried to sound sure, confident even, but I could see in Alaric's eyes that taking this book from him willingly was not an option. No matter how sweet my smile was.

"I wish I could be of more assistance, but you see, I gave the book to my protector to hide. I needed it hidden, somewhere so well, that not even I could find it if someone hunted around my thoughts. I told him to hide it somewhere I will never find it, and to uncover the location only to the next Unseelie King who takes my place."

Alaric shifted in his seat and I gave his hand a few short squeezes.

"Don't leave yet, I don't know the next time I will get to see you," as I said it, I could hear the panic in my voice.

"I wasn't going anywhere Adella, at least not yet. I'm here for a progress update as well. I'm here to check in on Anna and Luxor." Something flashed across his face, but before I could put my finger on it, it was gone. Pride maybe?

"Oh, Luxor might not be back for a few days, he's in the Seelie Kingdom. Anna is in training most days and nights, but she's doing well. Sometimes she's so sore from training, she collapses and doesn't move all day or night."

"I see. Anna will be tested while I'm here. Honestly, I am glad Luxor has other…things keeping him busy."

Alaric stretched across the table and kissed me gently. His kiss in real life was so much better than dream Alaric's kiss. Warmth and pressure told me that he was real, and he was here. I took in his scent. It was somehow sweeter than my latte's, with the same cinnamon kick. He was intoxicating.

Alaric pulled away too soon. It was probably for the best. If I got too carried away, I would have become oblivious to the rest of the world. Just that small peck had my heart racing, Alaric knew this though; he had a confidence in him, almost verging on arrogance that only grew after he made me flush crimson red.

"I'll probably be staying somewhere in the town nearby. I will stop by daily with reports and updates."

"I'm sure Dad will love that."

"Isn't your 18th birthday soon?"

"I wouldn't say soon per se, but still, birthday or no birthday it doesn't matter. As my dad says, his house, his rules. And I don't plan on leaving his house unless I'm going back to the Seelie courts, so, please don't pick any fights."

"I won't. I feel your dad is starting to warm up to me, actually."

"I think so, too." I only said this for Alaric's benefit, as the truth was, my dad would probably never warm up to Alaric. "So, how old are you?"

"I'm 18. Aging works a little differently in the courts. Fay and Fata, who live in the courts and practice their elements, age a lot slower than those who live, say, in the regular world or the wrong court. Practicing our element gives us power and keeps us youthful. You could practice your element on your own, but that wouldn't give you quite as much strength. There is power in numbers. I didn't go through quite the same process as you to take the Unseelie crown Mine was passed on to me. There will still be trials with three competitors and me. But that won't be for a few more years. Some of the competitors are not of age just yet."

"So, you only held the crown temporarily? How much does aging slow in the courts?"

"Well, yes, unless I marry before the trials, win the trials, or the competitors recede the crown. I am only the temporary crown holder; I'm okay with this, though. I have met Fay and Fata centuries old, who still look twenty because they have only lived on the grounds. Aging on the grounds pretty much comes to a halt at 18, but can pick back up the second you leave the court."

"Why are you okay with only being a temporary King?" When I saw Alaric with his people, he seemed so…confident and in charge. I couldn't imagine a better or more caring ruler.

He raised his eyebrows at me. I didn't know if he was surprised I asked why, or hadn't thought about the answer himself.

"It's a lot. I feel I could do better, do more, get to work with the people instead of ruling them. I want to make a change but change takes time. I want to make strides in welcoming Dark Creatures back before the crown gets passed on. I want to be able to focus on our people and make the kingdom whole again. However, as the King, I must focus on everything — taxation, teaching or mentoring powers, hunter and protector assignments, and rules and laws for our kingdom. I would like to take the time to focus on our people and solely on our people." His response startled me for a moment. *Alaric might not want to be king?* Alaric leaned back and folded his hands together. Finally, he seemed to be relaxing.

"Do you ever worry that the Dark Creatures won't be welcomed back?"

"There will always be groups who oppose their return, but I find the Unseelie Kingdom to be extremely open."

"What about the Seelie Kingdom?"

"What about them?"

"Well...if you welcome back the Dark Creatures, couldn't it cause an uprising in the Seelie courts? They were affected by the attacks and defiance as well. Homes were burnt down; people were injured, and lives were lost on both sides of the courts." I finished slowly, because Alaric's face slowly turned deeper and deeper shades of red. *Why is he reacting this way?* As he thought, his face flipped through different emotions. Anger, rage, annoyance, and maybe finally it appeared he may be at understanding.

"No," he responded. "While the Seelie Kingdom has many wonderful people, my loyalties lie with the Unseelie Kingdom. The Queen is aware of my efforts and plans. It's her job to prepare or warn her people the best she can."

"Okay, back to the age thing," I giggled furiously and tried to cover them. "You're not in the Unseelie Kingdom right now? Does that mean you're going to be an old man soon?"

"No," he rolled his eyes at me. "We age at a normal progression in the real world," he said as he laughed with me.

Our laughter was abruptly stopped when there was a small rap at the door, and the King's protector raced to it, pulling out his small black gun from his side.

"Did you invite anyone?" Alaric whispered.

"No, I haven't even had my phone on."

The protector clutched the knob of the door, keeping the weapon in his right hand and swung the door open. However, the second it flew open a foot came upward and kicked the weapon out of the protector's hand.

"*Get down!*" Alarm rang in Alaric's tone. I began to crawl under the table; Alaric ran in front of me, taking a defensive stance.

17

"Don't get down! Tell him it's just me, Dells!"

"Anna, you *scared* us!"

The two protectors struggled to subdue one another. Alaric straightened up. Anna was losing but still put up one hell of a fight.

Anna's fists shot fiercely at Abel's face, but as he ducked, he caught her under her arm with his left hand and pushed her roughly against the door frame. Anna's whole body writhed and wriggled against him. But his weight was on her and she was pinned.

"You may stop now," Alaric spoke calmly and his protector immediately dropped his hold on Anna, and walked away.

"That was quite impressive, protector Anna, tell me. How did you find us?" Alaric closed the distance between himself and

Anna, the height difference was noticeably large when they were face to face.

"It's my job to find Dells and keep track of where she is. I certainly wasn't about to let someone hold a gun to my face!" Anna wiped the sweat from her dark red forehead. There was a line across her face where she was pushed up against the door jamb. She was breathing as if she'd just been on a five-mile run.

"I'm impressed, Anna. It must have been difficult."

"Not really. Dan said you were going to a coffee shop." Anna relaxed a bit. Alaric's tone of voice went from defensive to calm and so did Anna's demeanor. "So, unless you were going to drive two or more hours for coffee, this was the nearest option." Anna gave us a sly smile. Clothes from Madeline and facial expressions from Luxor, Anna was becoming quite the prodigy.

"Was there something you needed, Anna?"

"Yes, I needed to speak to Dells about the assignment."

"Okay, I needed to head out anyway. Adella, are you okay walking home with Anna?"

"Of course. Thanks for taking me for coffee." Alaric grabbed my hand and kissed it, then escorted me out of the coffee shop and back onto the bright road. As soon as I knew Alaric and his protector were out of earshot, I slowed my walking pace.

"What'd you find Anna?"

"That's just it, Dells, I found nothing. Not online, not at the library, have you heard anything?"

"Alaric said the book belonged to him."

"Well, what would the Queen want with Alaric's book?"

"I don't know... Alaric doesn't know the book's location either, he said his protector hid it for him, and get this, the book holds a lot of the Unseelie kingdom's power secrets and weaknesses."

"Whoa," was all Anna could manage to get out.

"Exactly, his protector wasn't one for talking, and is probably guarding the books hiding place with his life."

"That's *it*!" Anna jumped in front of me and we both halted.

"What's *it*?"

"In training, we as protectors are taught to guard you with our lives. If we're given the options, we're always to stay with you and to be prepared to sacrifice everything in a moment if we must."

"I'm not following your logic here Anna."

"If you need to protect something that's entrusted to you and only you, promising to guard it with your life..." That's when it clicked.

"It has to be on you, or at least near you," I finished Anna's sentence.

There was a moment of silence. Even if we had a general location (which we didn't), the Unseelie King's protector, as he said himself, was "the best." He was certainly not going to hand it over willingly.

"We're going to have to break into his living quarters." I looked at Anna solemnly. This wasn't part of her job description.

"We'll have to make it appear as if it was ransacked, Dells. No one could ever know it was us, trespassing and theft are things we could be arrested for."

My stomach felt queasy. Not only were we going to break into Alaric's home, but we would also be destroying it and quite possibly betraying any trust that I held with him. I looked at Anna, who seemed at ease, I didn't know exactly what protector training she had been through, but it appeared one had helped her learn how to handle guilt.

"It's for your people and your future kingdom Dells," Anna whispered softly.

I nodded, it was for my people. My future kingdom that deserved a strong enough leader to do whatever it took to rule them.

"Doing it while they're going to be gone for a prolonged period would be easier than having to get in and out quickly. I will check my dad's meeting schedule over the next month and see when the next meeting is held. I don't want to bring my dad into this though if we don't have to."

"I know, but Dells...we need outside help, someone willing to do anything for you," Anna gave me a leveled look. I hoped she wasn't suggesting who I thought she was suggesting. "Another person who took a vow to protect you with their life, someone so into you, that breaking the law won't seem like such a huge request."

Anna met my eyes. She didn't want to say the name any more than I wanted to hear it.

"Luxor." We both stated at once, the name was bitter on my tongue.

There was no more debating and no further planning we could do until we got some help. Alaric made it clear he couldn't be the one to do it. So, I picked up my phone and scrolled through the dozens of unanswered texts, before hitting the call button.

The phone rang only once before I heard the familiar and slightly worried voice.

"Dells? Is everything okay?"

"Not exactly, Luxor. I need you to come home."

18

The plan came together quickly. Luxor was willing to come all the way home at a moment's notice and on top of that, willing to break the law for me. I couldn't help but wonder when he would get the news that he was no longer my protector and I would have to say goodbye. Would they tell him the truth? Or Would they simply reassign him, and I'd never see him again?

I put all of my questions and feelings to the side. There was nothing more important than Mission Librir.

"Mission Librir? Really, Anna?" Luxor wasn't a fan of tacky mission names or over-the-top plans. If Luxor was the sole leader, this would have been a two-step mission. Step one: get in undetected. Step two: leave without a trace, as if we were never there.

However, if this protector was as good as Alaric said, step two wouldn't have been possible. He was going to notice that we were there. I was positive the book was well hidden, meaning we would have had to tear the living quarters apart to find it, which was what led us to Anna's abnormally complicated and over-the-top plan.

Phase one was easy enough. At least that was what I kept telling myself as I walked right into my dad's study. It was unlocked, of course. He trusted me. No reason to lock things up when the only one home was his trustworthy daughter. His laptop was gone. I figured as much. The computer was probably with him now in his new office the Queen leased for him. I ran over to his desk and started pulling the drawers. The first one was locked, that was the one his firearm was probably in. The second drawer was full of files, none even remotely resembled a calendar. The third and fourth were full of office supplies. I decided to head out, feeling like I had failed, when right by the door, straight ahead of me, was a wall calendar.

Meeting with Alaric. 26th at 4 pm.

The 26th gave us two full days until we had to have all our preparation phases done. That left no time to waste. I turned to leave and the door flew open, hitting me in the face.

Oomph was more or less the sound I made.

"Dells, is that you?" The light flickered on and my dad closed the door a little to get it out of my face.

"Ya Dad, I was just peeking at your calendar to see if you had any more meetings today. I was going to order takeout." Lying shouldn't have come so easily with my father.

"Takeout sounds great honey, however, the Kin—errr, Alaric, invited us all to dinner tonight."

"Who is, 'us all'?"

"Me, you, Anna, and he heard Luxor was back in town. He was wondering if you would extend the invitation." I sensed the hesitation in my dad's voice. He wasn't pleased Luxor was back.

"Absolutely, Dad. What time and where?"

"206 24th ave. 5 pm."

"Thanks, Dad. I'll send them a message right now." My dad walked away. I flipped my phone open and sent Luxor and Anna the details. This made phase two a breeze; find a way to scout Alaric's house for the most probable protector living headquarters.

I went to my room and picked out a dress for dinner. I was 3:30 pm already and Anna was on her way, so I knew I needed to be quick. I decided on a simple, knee-length black dress.

I heard the front door open and shut. Anna arrived. She didn't bother to knock anymore, not that I minded since she was going to be with me all the time soon.

"Dells?" Anna called.

"In my room."

I heard her footsteps as she came down the hall.

"Will you braid my hair?" I asked Anna as she entered the room.

"Sure how would you like it?"

"Two braids on top, leading to a twisted bun?"

That was Anna's new hairstyle of choice, and I was becoming quite fond of it. Anna wore her typical black leather pants and tank but dressed it up a little with bright red flats and an arm full of bangles that matched her lipstick. I kind of wished she would have fully dressed up with me, but her outfit did make braiding my hair much easier. She made her way to the edge of my bed and sat down. I dragged a pillow over to the edge of her feet and sat on it. She got to work swiftly.

"You managed to get phase two set up pretty quickly," Anna said.

"I didn't. Alaric invited everyone and sent my dad to tell me. He caught me in his office."

"Was he mad?"

"No, I told him I was checking to see if he was going to be home for dinner tonight." Anna stopped the braiding for a second.

"So, Alaric set up phase two and almost foiled phase one?"

I nodded my head slightly under her hands.

"You know, I don't believe in coincidence Dells. Do you think Alaric knows somehow?"

"I mean, I'm sure he knows I'm not going to just stop looking because he doesn't want it found. He's probably trying to distract us."

"That's true. I have an Uber waiting outside. We need to get Luxor, then we can go." Anna finished twisting the rest of my hair

187

then pinned it tightly into a bun. We left my apartment and knocked on Luxor's door.

Luxor answered without saying a word. He looked amazing in dark wash jeans and a tight v-neck t-shirt. He was definitely gaining a lot of muscle from all the training he'd been doing.

"Ready?" Anna seemed impatient, or maybe it was her nerves.

"As ready as I can be for this ridiculous plan." Luxor certainly didn't sound excited.

"Good, let's do this. Phase two here we come."

19

The Uber drive was uneventful. The driver did like to sing though, which made Anna roll her big green eyes and bite her tongue. I was surprised she could. Before she became "protector Anna" she wouldn't have been able to help herself to a sarcastic comment, or at least a giggle.

Walking up to Alaric's front door, phase two became slightly more intimidating. Plotting out the house and bedrooms was going to be quite a chore, as this wasn't just a house. It was more of a mansion, or close to it.

Alaric's protector opened the front door and waited patiently for us to enter. "Luxor, Adella, Anna," he stated as we walked by. Once we were all through, he shut the door and secured the three industrial-sized locks on the inside. Luxor turned to face him and held out his hand.

"It's nice to meet you. I didn't catch your name?"

The protector just stared. The look on his face made it seem like breaking Luxor's hand might have been more pleasant for him, rather than reaching out and shaking it. A laugh almost escaped my throat. I covered my mouth and sent myself into a coughing frenzy.

Luxor dropped his hand and the older protector walked right past. We followed him through an elegant room, into a large dining area with what looked to be family portraits hanging around the walls. We found our seats, and surprisingly, the protector sat at the head of the table where I assumed Alaric would be sitting. I sat on his left-hand side, with Anna directly next to me. Luxor claimed his place on the opposite side of Anna. There was no small talk. Anna's impatience got the best of her, and she began tapping her foot.

My dad entered next, and following him were two unfamiliar faces. Alaric was almost directly behind. He sat directly across from me.

"Everything in the center of the table is edible and for grazing; dinner will be out shortly," Alaric announced.

The food in the center of the table looked too good to eat. An elegant display of cheeses, fruits, and pieces of bread. Everyone began digging in, except for me. Alaric's eyes bored into mine and although nothing happened yet, suspicion clouded his face. I averted my gaze, so I wouldn't give anything away. Suddenly the grapes looked too good not to eat.

"I brought you all here to get to know you all a little better, also, hopefully, to allow you all to get to know me." Alaric beamed at my dad, of all people, and oddly enough, my dad smiled back. At least that relationship was going well.

Dinner came out and Anna excused herself for a bathroom break. When she came back, the next one to leave for the bathroom was Luxor. They both disappeared for exactly three to five minutes so as not to raise suspicions. My turn was up. I took out my phone and slid it on my lap. I opened it and dialed Anna's number. It rang loudly and obnoxiously.

"I'm so sorry I need to take this." She stood up and put the phone to her ear and started talking as if someone apart from my lap was on the phone and scurried out of the room.

Alaric raised his eyebrows at me and only seemed to grow more suspicious as dinner went on. I glanced at my phone often, impatiently waiting for Anna to return to the table. My phone said seven minutes and forty seconds when Anna finally returned. Luxor and my dad were discussing the latest information linked to the protector's murders. For the first time this evening, Alaric's attention was completely elsewhere and zoned in on their conversation.

"We have three hunters patrolling each contestant at all times, sending back any word of abnormal activity or new people in town." Funny, you'd think I'd have noticed three extra people following me. Thankfully, the look on Anna's face said she did notice and had a plan for that when it was time to enact the final phase. "Lilah has been assigned a new protector, one that is already finished with his training and is helping keep an eye out." My dad finished his update and took a sip of his wine.

He made a face and swirled his glass a couple of times. I'd never known my father to be much of a wine drinker and I wondered if he knew swirling his glass wouldn't change the flavor. The look on his face after the second sip made me giggle.

"It has been brought to my attention also," Luxor began. "That all three of the contestants have been given their assignments. All three are different but all are based in the Unseelie Kingdom." Luxor and Alaric locked eyes.

The tension in the air was thick. I peeked at Anna. She looked at ease, I sure hoped I looked the same.

"Probably to see how resourceful the contestants are no doubt," Luxor said calmly. He seemed to keep his cool in the worst of situations.

Luxor and Alaric locked eyes again. Not a word was being said, not verbally at least. I didn't know how long this silence went on for, but it felt like forever.

"Anything we should be worried about Dells?" My dad asked.

"No Dad, nothing unmanageable," I retorted quickly. That got Alaric's attention. He broke eye contact with Luxor and gave me a tired look.

"On that note," Alaric looked directly at me. "I have something I would like to say." Alaric stood up, took a deep breath, and moved swiftly around the table. He reached his hand out for mine expectantly. I accepted it and he assisted me in standing. The second I was on my feet, Alaric got on one knee.

The room went silent. The cliches of time slowing and being able to hear your heart pound in your ears was extremely accurate. I shut my eyes softly, took in a deep breath and tried to focus on something else. I zoned in on my dad's breathing, nice and even. When I heard Anna gasp suddenly I opened my eyes and gave Alaric my undivided attention.

"Adella Shenning, Fata-hearted, and Summer-represented. Getting to know you these last couple of months has been amazing. I don't need any more time to realize that losing you would be the biggest mistake of my life. You are the one I would like to have ruling by my side for the rest of my life." He pulled out a little box and opened it to reveal the most beautiful sun-inspired diamond engagement ring I had ever seen. "Adella Shenning, will you do me the honor of becoming my wife?"

Marry him? I can't marry him? I barely know him! Has he lost his mind? Or maybe this is just a joke, an over the top, hilarious, haha joke. Ha, Ha.

The expectant faces of my family and friends bored into mine. *Maybe it's not a joke.* Anna's mouth gaped at me in shock. The pit of my stomach was queasy and I struggled to hold it back. I turned ever so slightly to my dad, hoping for any silent advice he could give me, but he just smiled, and shook his head, yes. What a traitor.

Alaric cleared his throat and looked up at me. I had so many questions now, that needed answering first.

"I...I...I...I—" I struggled to find the words. I heard Luxor storm out of the room. I did the only thing I could think to do at that exact moment. I pretended to faint.

20

I fell hard. Part of me was hoping that at least someone was close enough to catch me if I fell. But it must have been a convincing faint because no one saw it coming. I fell backwards, my head hit the edge of the chair and I was pretty sure the lights went out for a few moments because when I came to again, my dad was carrying me up a flight of stairs.

"Shhh, be still," he whispered.

I closed my eyes and returned to my limp state.

"She just needs some rest. I'm sure she will be awake soon. I will notify everyone when she is." My dad set me on a bed, shooed everyone out, and locked the door behind them. I peeked at him to make sure the coast was clear. He put his hands to his temples as if I just created the worst headache he'd ever had. He turned around slowly and approached the bedside.

"Dells," he whispered.

"Dad." I started opening both eyes fully.

"I have to give you props. That was one of the most convincing faints I've ever seen. You almost had me. Right before you hit your head, you scrunched your forehead just a bit. Then you managed to knock yourself out cold. Do you even know what you probably did to Alaric's self-esteem?"

"Thanks, Dad. I'll take notes for the next time I have to pretend to faint to get out of an awkward situation. I'm hardly concerned about Alaric's self-esteem." I probably shouldn't have laid the sarcasm on so thick. It wasn't my dad's fault. "My head is regretting that fall at this moment."

"I bet it is Dells," he sighed, defeated. "You have to accept the King's proposal."

There was something in my dad's expression I didn't quite comprehend.

"I don't understand Dad, why would I accept it? Aren't I too young? Don't I have too much going on right now? Haven't we known each other for far too short of a time?" These all felt like questions my dad should be asking.

"There are things you don't know."

"So, tell me."

"Okay Dells," my dad took a deep breath. "When a contestant fails an assignment, the magic is physically drained from their bodies, along with their representative colors. Contestants typically aren't forewarned because the experience can be quite painful

196

mentally and adds extra unneeded anxieties. The more magic you have, the harder it is on your bodies. Some contestants don't survive the withdrawal process."

"Oh." The only word I managed to speak.

"When Alaric told me your gift for emotional influence I began to worry. You have so many gifts and talents. You represent summer but were born to be winter. When the moon comes out, you just glow honey. You get more energetic, happy, and excited on nights of full moons and find comfort in large groups of people, almost like you feed on their energy. That's a lot of magic Dells. Being fluent in both summer and winter is not a talent that's been seen for a very long time, on top of your green thumb and emotional influences. It is…amazing that you have all of these gifts, and I'm sure you'll have more to come. These great gifts could come with a hefty price."

"So, what then Dad? I marry Alaric, then even if I fail the trials, can I keep my gifts and be okay?"

"Well no, we've been searching for a loophole for a while now. This seems to be the only option we can come up with thus far. If you accept this proposal, you will hopefully transform from summer to winter. It's never been done before. We aren't positive it will work exactly like we think it will. When Alaric informed me about your assignment—"

"—he told you?" I cut him off.

"Yeah, he told me. I'm a little disappointed it wasn't you. This challenge, I don't know why, but it seems like it was created for you to fail." My dad's face said it all. The same face he gave me every time I took a risk as a child. The first time I rode my bike and told him to let go, my first day of school when I wanted to walk alone, and the day I found out I was going to be a Queen.

He was worried, scared for my life — scared enough to agree to allow Alaric to marry me in an attempt to bail me out of my responsibilities and maybe save my life.

"Well I know I don't want to give up Dad. I don't want to step aside and hide from ruling the people I was foreseen and chosen to rule."

"So, you're going to say no to the King's proposal?"

"I'm going to discuss this with the King, Dad."

"You sound just like your mother when you start getting stern with me. Alaric genuinely
  loves you, you know?"

"I think I know that. This is something he and I need to talk about though."

My dad nodded. He kissed my head and whispered, "You're growing up so fast. I love you, honey."

"I love you too." I felt the tears welling up in my eyes, I sniffed them back the best I could. I don't want anyone to see me crying.

"I will go get Alaric, then tell everyone you survived the faint."

Dad went to the door and opened it. He didn't have to go far; Alaric was standing right outside the room, looking defeated — maybe even a bit mopey. There was no telling how much of that conversation he might have heard. He sat on the window seat next

198

to the bed, his eyes were rimmed red as if he'd been fighting or holding back tears.

"You're going to die," he said.

"You can't know that."

"I don't want to know, but I have a feeling."

"So then help me."

"Marry me."

"You know that's not what I meant."

"You don't think we noticed?" He became really frustrated, almost angry. "You and your friends conveniently take turns to get up and disappear throughout dinner. You don't think we're taking extra precautions this very second to stop whatever plan you think you guys have formed." He paused for a second, not waiting for an answer though. They were rhetorical questions for sure. "I love you Adella Shenning. But I also have a duty to my Kingdom. I will not allow you to find the Tenebris Librir. There's too much at stake for my people."

"I too, will have a responsibility to my Kingdom soon, maybe to both of the Kingdoms."

I got up slowly, steadying myself carefully before sauntering over to him and setting my hand lightly on his flustered cheek.

I saw a flicker of hope in his eyes, but it was gone as soon as it appeared.

"You can't help any Kingdoms if you're dead."

I gasped, dropping my hand and stepped back. His demeanor didn't change. I looked at him, I mean, really looked at him. Worry lines creased his forehead and dark circles rimmed his eyes, appearing as if he hadn't slept in days. I wasn't going to lie, the comment hurt. The air around us was thick. Just arguing like this made my stomach churn.

"You don't have to help me but I do need you to trust me."

"I trust you will go home, stop this attempt to steal from me and move on."

"It wasn't an attempt Alaric," I said, almost sadly. I knew at this very moment Luxor was on his way to the Seelie Kingdom to turn in my first assignment.

It wasn't in the plans to take the book today. We were going to wait for an opportune time when Alaric was gone, to come back and take the book. The second Luxor stormed out of the room I knew. Alaric had created the perfect moment for Luxor to go unnoticed. Alaric had created the perfect moment, for Luxor to sneak away yet again, into the most likely room, and ransack it while the attention was focused on me.

I looked Alaric in the eyes, as I watched the understanding sink in. At first, he seemed calm, then in an instant, his eyes went wild as his face turned a deep shade of purple. He looked like he had something he wanted to say to me, but couldn't find the words. So instead, he acted like I didn't exist.

"Lock the house and find Luxor," Alaric yelled, no longer staring at me. Instead, it seemed he was looking right through me. As if I was no longer in front of him.

Immediately things changed, he transformed from the Alaric I knew, to a powerful King ruling his people. The guards ran frantically, the metal sheets slid down the windows and I heard the doors around the house locking.

"Sorry Miss, I have to escort everyone to the living quarters."

The guard sounded somewhat apologetic but grabbed my arm roughly. I wasn't offended, I knew his job was to escort everyone to the safe zone by force. I spared a glance in Alaric's way. He was busy speaking urgently to a guard. Too busy to even look at me.

What had I done?

21

I hadn't heard from Alaric or Luxor in days. I was not sure if it was due to them not wanting to talk to me or my dad prohibiting contact. Normally, the silence would have killed me. However, wallowing in my own self-pity seemed to be the best way to solve all of my problems lately. I'd gained a comfortable routine over the last couple of days. Bed, coffee, bed, and repeat. It provided an easy-to-follow, no-thinking-needed type of pattern.

Luckily, my dad was too engrossed with re-finding the Tenebris Librir to be mad at me too. I heard him getting ready in the mornings and peeking into my room before leaving for the day. He didn't return until late in the night, where it was the same routine. He put his things by the door, rummaged through the fridge, then peeked into my room to make sure I was still in bed.

Not that I left bed at any point. I think he too, was finding comfort in the safety of my new self-pity routine.

"Adella?" My dad's voice broke the silence of my inner monologue.

His eyes were tired as he leaned in my bedroom door, he hesitated slightly before stepping into the room.

"Yes, Dad?"

"Get up, we need to go to Alaric's to discuss the events of the other night," he said this carefully as if one wrong word could fracture my spirit more than it already was.

I knew it was coming. My breath caught in my chest. I sat up straight so my dad could see I wasn't broken. I dreaded the thought of leaving my comfortable bed. I knew I owed everyone an explanation — or did I? They wanted me to succeed, but at what cost was I willing to pay to do it? Apparently, the price of Alaric's love.

"Adella, tell the group exactly what your plan was, exactly how you planned to implement it and what you did from the moment you got here on." Alaric's face was expectant, no hint of anger, but also no hint that he was still my Alaric. He waited patiently for an answer I wasn't sure I could give him.

Anna was sitting across the table. From the amount of sweat on her upper brow, I would say she had already been questioned, maybe even multiple times. Probably from my dad, judging by the way she was leaning away from him. My dad looked tired, probably from being the interrogator no doubt. His eyes were drooping, and he hunched forward slightly.

"Nothing was supposed to happen, not that day at least. The only goal was to scout the home and figure out which ones were the most likely to be your protector's living quarters." I made eye contact with my dad, looking for comfort and silently begging him to maintain eye contact, but he glanced away, disappointed in me no doubt.

"And who was in on this plan?" Alaric's face was stern. I felt as if I was being shamed.

"Just me, Anna, and Luxor." Alaric's face flinched just at the mention of his name. As if the crime itself was involving Luxor rather than entering and raiding his home and stealing.

"Call Luxor and get him to return immediately for questioning."

I picked up my phone and dial his number, but it went directly to voicemail.

"No answer," I said. Guilt racked through me. He brought me here to try to save my life and in return, I betrayed him, stole from him, and perhaps put the whole Unseelie Kingdom in danger. I just wanted to go back to the comfort of my bed.

I wrapped my arms around myself, trying to hide as much of me as I could. Everyone was staring at me from around the table and it felt very intrusive. However, none of the looks were as violating as the look on Alaric's face. Every time I tried to make eye contact, his face was pure pain, like he was trying to mentally ask me questions, ones he'd probably never speak out loud.

How could you betray me? How could you lie and not tell me? How could you violate my home, trust, and betray the entire Unseelie Kingdom?

The feelings were overwhelming. I began to hyperventilate quietly.

I knew I was doing it to myself, Alaric hadn't said one unkind word. The guilt and silence were eating me alive. He just kept pacing back and forth. Anna's eyes were wide with fear. I could only imagine the inner monologue she was giving herself right now. I couldn't believe I had dragged her into this. The only saving grace for me right now was my dad. I focused on his face, it was relaxed and kind. He was not looking at me, but it was still comforting all the same.

"I'm so sorry, Dad." I began my apology, which was supposed to be long-winded, but I lost the words.

"No one's mad at you Dells, we're mad at the situation you were put into. You were only trying to complete your assignment."

I hung my head in shame. If what I did was to be expected, then why did it feel so dirty?

"Everyone may return to their homes. I may visit later with follow-up questions. Adella, you must stay behind. I still have a few more questions for you." Alaric's voice was softer now. I didn't raise my eyes to meet his, I didn't deserve pity.

People started leaving one by one. My dad hugged me.

"I'll see you at home," he said.

Anna refused to leave. She settled for waiting for me on the couch in the great room. Alaric shut the dining room doors. There were two hunters, him and me, all standing awkwardly.

"When and why did Luxor come back to town?" Alaric began the line of questions.

"I called him the day before dinner and asked him to return. I knew I wouldn't be able to complete the assignment without some extra help."

"Luxor dropped everything to come back? Just like that?" I heard the jealousy in his voice. It was starting to sound more like accusations and less like questions.

"Well yes, as far as he's concerned, he is still my protector."

"What did Luxor say when you told him the plan?" Alaric asked.

"He was ready and willing to help like always."

"What was Luxor's part in the plan that night?"

"He was supposed to look at the bedrooms on the second floor, draw a quick sketch of the hall, mark which ones were bedrooms and star the ones that were most likely the protector's living quarters."

"Did he get the blueprints first?"

"Blueprints?" Now he'd lost me.

"Yes, as protectors, people like Luxor are shown where to get and how to use resources that are openly available. He wouldn't have come into this situation blind. He would have gotten lost just looking for the staircase."

"No, he did not. Not that I know of at least." My head was spinning, I could feel the guards' judgment, and Alaric's anger. It was enough to make the hairs on the back of my neck stand up.

"Adella, I'm going to be very blunt with you. I hope that's all right. I believe Luxor might be using you."

That couldn't be right. There was a connection between Luxor and me, no matter how small, that had been there since day one. If he was using me, I would have known it, wouldn't I? His dropping everything and coming back to see me seemed like something Luxor would do. We'd been through a lot. Storming out of the room made sense. I could see why he wouldn't have wanted to stand around and watch another man propose to me. Him not calling me though, and no word of the trials yet, that was the part that had me concerned.

"What makes you say that?" I asked through clenched teeth.

"He can't just get up and leave from training whenever he wants, and he certainly wouldn't have come into this situation unprepared." Now his tone was accusing.

"What exactly are you saying?"

"I am trying not to say or assume anything about him, but I'm curious if maybe he has ulterior motives or orders from another source."

There was a long pause. I didn't know how to respond or what to say. I couldn't honestly answer that question because I didn't know if it was true or not. I couldn't come to terms with the fact that I may have been used this entire time. Alaric slid the box with the ring to me from across the table.

His hopeful eyes waited patiently for a reaction. I looked down at the tiny box, surprised and overwhelmed that Alaric would still be interested in marrying me.

I grabbed the box and opened it slowly. Surely he wouldn't want to marry the woman who just betrayed his whole kingdom?

"I know your answer is not yet, but I want you to hold onto the ring until you have a solid answer. I will never lie to you Adella, never use you, never hurt you, and never run from you."

"I will." I got up and put the ring into my pocket, trying to fight back the tears.

Alaric walked around the table. I could sense hesitation in his movements. There was understanding in his eyes, though, as he approached me, and I held onto that. Maybe it wasn't over, somehow I didn't ruin everything. He embraced me and I folded into him. I needed him to hold me, I needed validation that I was not a horrible person. For once in my life, I needed someone else to be the strong one because at that moment it felt like my world was crumbling apart.

The next day I hid in my bed almost all day clutching the little box that held the beautiful ring I didn't deserve. I didn't know what else to do or where else to go. *Should I give the ring back? Would Alaric even want me to have it? Should I marry Alaric? Would*

doing so make Anna and Luxor, my protectors, safe? I could be
safe. They could have been safe. I ruined that.

The more I considered the proposal the more I saw the potential advantages. There were so many things going through my head. The lights were dimmed in my room and I remained under my covers, only leaving the safety of my bed to utilize the bathroom.

"Is she okay?" Anna asked my dad for the 15th time today.

"I'm sure she will be fine Anna, she just needs rest," he said calmly.

That was how he responded to everyone who came through the door, including a couple of random hunters, Alaric, Alaric's protector (although he didn't say a word when he was here, my dad just assumed the reason and answered the silence), and Anna, who asked every time she turned around.

Our front door became a revolving door, while I laid silently and listened to each person come and go. Wallowing in self-pity wasn't my strong suit, but coming to terms with just how bad I messed up was difficult. I hazed in and out of sleep, my body was emotionally tired from the stress and physically tired from trying to hold back tears.

"Alright Dells, I hope you're decent!" Anna knocked once, then barged right in. She flipped the light switch and opened the curtains. "That's enough sadness for one day. I have news."

I pulled the covers over my head. One day of wallowing didn't seem like too much to ask for.

"Seriously Dells, it's big news." She motioned with her arms re-enacting a huge explosion.

I peeked an eye out of the blanket. I knew she wasn't going to leave until I talked. I threw the blankets off my face and sat up, feeling a little groggy. My hair was surely a haystack.

"That's better," she said. "I got the news today that two competitors completed their assignments."

"How did they finish so soon?" This news wasn't making me feel any better. I didn't even have a plan now that Plan A had failed. Plan B was to make another plan.

"Have you checked your phone recently?" Anna asked.

"No, it's over there plugged in. Why?" I pointed to the top of my dresser across the room.

"Well, when I heard two competitors were finished, I began asking around. The rumors aren't good Dells. So, that leaves me with good news, and some not-so-good news. Which would you like first?"

"Good news. I need good news."

"You are one of the competitors that completed their assignments. The Tenebris Librir was turned in late on the night of the dinner at Alaric's, just hours before the second competitor."

Luxor, it had to be him. Why though? Why wouldn't he text me back or tell me he'd turned it in already?

"Alright Dells. Seriously, prepare yourself for the bad news." Anna paused for a second to steady herself. "There are a lot of rumors going around that you have something against the Unseelie Kingdom. Apparently, you caused the Dark Creature bombing, stole the Tenebris Librir, and are the leader of a rogue Seelie cult, bent on causing the downfall of the Unseelie Kingdom."

My mouth dropped open. That was simply not true. I loved the Unseelie people.

"That's not all," she warned. "The word got out that King Alaric proposed to you last night, now there's violent rioting at the Unseelie gates. People trying to burn the trees lining the outskirts, and painting violent messages onto the gates, thinking Alaric is a traitor for proposing to you."

I waited to make sure she was done. I wasn't sure if that bit of good news could make up for any of the bad news she had just told me. None of it was right. I didn't feel like a winner; knowing I would've been welcomed back to the Seelie Kingdom this summer as a winner of my first assignment, then shunned by the Unseelie people for completing the same assignment was a losing scenario, no matter how I looked at it.

Anna stayed the night. She was unsure if it was safe for me with everything going on right now to be alone. Especially now that I was officially considered a traitor. I needed to get in touch with Alaric tonight, so I scoured my room for stones or dream catchers of any sort. Anna was nice enough to assist in my mad hunt. Together we tore my room apart bit by bit, but we found nothing.

"Are you sure Alaric said stones or a dream catcher?" Anna asked.

"Positive."

"Eh-hem." I heard my dad clear his throat; he leaned up against the door jam with his arms crossed, simply observing our madness.

"Looking for something?" he asked.

"Dad," I pleaded. "You know the only contact I have with Alaric is through my dreams right now."

"Well, you won't find whatever it is you're looking for, I had the protection spell placed against the whole bedroom. Not a single object." The pride in his voice was clear. He won this parenting battle. He said it so matter-of-fact like, of course, he'd still try to protect me from boys. He was my dad after all, but now that he was ready for me to accept Alaric's proposal, why not let me see him?

"The spell will wear off in about a month. Until then, you'll have to sleep on the couch if you want to see him." That was all my dad said before smiling and walking away, the clear winner of this conversation.

"Slumber party in the living room?" Anna asked.

"Absolutely."

We grabbed some pillows and blankets and made ourselves a bed on the floor in the living room, turned on *27 Dresses* and mindlessly watched romantic comedies until we cried and laughed ourselves to sleep.

"Hello, Adella."

"Hi, Alaric."

I stood up off the floor-bed I made.

"I wanted to apologize for how I spoke to you the other night."

"You're sorry? Alaric have you heard the rumors? The Unseelie Kingdom hates me." I was utterly shocked that somehow, he was the one apologizing right now.

"I don't know how the news got back to you so quickly, but I can tell you it's not as bad as it seems. The riots are few and far between. They were worse when I banned practicing magic without registering powers first. As for the rumors, they are all different and hard to keep up with. New ones are starting every hour, but they're nothing I would take to heart."

That did make me feel a little better. I walked over and sat on the couch. Alaric sat down too, I scooted over and leaned on him.

"I did hear one rumor that interested me though," he said as he tucked a piece of hair behind my ear.

"And what was that?"

"I heard you were going to say yes. A lot of the Kingdom would like for you to say yes."

I just looked at him.

"Kidding! Only kidding," he laughed. "Seriously though, there are plenty of people in the courts that would celebrate our union."

"Also, plenty that wouldn't mind seeing both of us burn to the ground." I pointed out to him.

"If you could only see it, Adella. I think it would be a different story."

"I know where the book is Alaric."

He sighed. This was clearly not a welcome change of topic.

214

"I know too, we are making plans now on how to send our hunters over to raid the Kingdom without starting an all-out war."

"Let me help. I know where the Queen's quarters are." I also desperately wanted to make things right with the Fata. If they only knew I meant them no harm, maybe things would be okay again.

"I want you to come to the Unseelie Kingdom to stay for a while. You can make an appearance and help plan with us. However, getting you here is an impossible task. We cannot officially announce your involvement in our plans until you're no longer a contestant in the Seelie trials."

"What happens if I win, Alaric? What happens if I pass all my trials and I'm the last one standing and I'm named the new Seelie Queen?"

"Then there will be nothing stopping you from becoming my wife. It has never been done before but there are no laws against the marriage of the Seelie and Unseelie rulers."

"Why hasn't it been done before then?"

"Well, genders are simply a matter of chance. There have been Unseelie Queens and vice versa. The gender depends on what premonition Fay and Fata see when they see it and if whomever they pick is suited to compete." That was a good answer. If I somehow won the trials, he would still want me. Alaric continued, breaking me out of my thoughts. "Can we stop thinking of the trials for a short while? I have other things I would like to speak with you about, things of the utmost importance." The expression on his face became serious.

"Sure, what's on your mind?"

"Well for starters, what's your favorite color?" I didn't expect this.

"It's green, yours?"

"Also, green." His face broke into a smile.

"What is your favorite food?"

"I don't have a favorite food, dinner at your house the other night was really good."

"Oh, I made that, but it's not my house," he said, proudly.

"Whose house is it?"

"It is my father's house."

"What is your father's name? Why didn't he join us? I would like to have met him."

"He did, you sat right next to him."

"Your father is your protector? Abel?"

I should have realized it was the protector's home when he sat at the head of the table.

"Yes, my father felt like my current protector wasn't doing an adequate job of keeping me safe and challenged him to a fight. It was a dirty one, challenging a protector means a fight to the death. If my father won, which he did, he would get to be my new protector. I knew he would win, my protector was too caught up in the fame and glory of being the King's protector. He wanted to make my father's defeat slow so that no one else would challenge him. He put on a show, so to speak."

"That must have been terrible to watch."

216

"It was, but it didn't last long though. My father was in it for the win. He's been by my side ever since. He doesn't like to tell people his name, or where he's from. Very few people know the truth. He's afraid people will see it as a weakness."

"Caring for others, especially your family, is always a huge weakness in the eyes of some people." I nodded in understanding.

"It can also be a great strength, though. My father likes you. It was his idea to test Anna while we were here. So far he is pleasantly surprised by her progress."

"So, does he speak more when there are fewer people around?" I couldn't help but ask. I'd barely heard him put a sentence together.

"Yes," Alaric laughed. "He speaks a lot more. He has a very heavy say on hunter selections, protector assignments, and other such decisions."

I looked up at Alaric and no other hint or word was needed. Alaric brought his lips to mine. I responded with urgency. He kissed me desperately, deeply. I wrapped my arms around his neck. His hands felt like they were everywhere, traveling up my back, down my sides, touching the hair at the nape of my neck.

He pulled back slightly and grinned at me.

"In a perfect world, I imagined getting down on one knee, proposing with a heartfelt speech, then you, full of joy, saying yes and then kissing me like that. A kiss so open and so passionate, everyone in the room would know you loved me too." There was a sadness in his eyes I didn't quite understand.

217

"I do love you too, Alaric." As I said it his eyes lit up, though I could see he was trying to mask the excitement.

I'd never told him out loud I loved him before. I thought we'd have plenty of time for the first steps in the years to come. How was I to know we would skip right to marriage?

"So, then maybe the other day, your sadness and fainting, wasn't due to Luxor storming out of the room?"

"You know, for a King, you're pretty self-conscious."

"It's not that," he said too quickly. "I just knew he was courting you first and I wasn't sure if there was maybe something still there."

"Honestly, I didn't know either. We never discussed it. But I knew I could never be with him after what he did that night—" My throat tightened up a bit. It was hard thinking about that night still, let alone talking about it. "That night he murdered all of those families and children."

"Do you see them that way? The Dark Creatures? Do you see them as families and children?" He watched me intently, waiting for my answer.

"I felt it. Their hope, love, and emotions. I didn't know for sure what I was going into, or how I would feel seeing the Dark Creatures gathered together. Then Luxor tore it out of me in a matter of minutes and left a gaping hole in my chest that I thought he had filled at first. Instead, I realized it was a spot for the Seelie and Unseelie people."

I didn't get a chance to say anything else before Alaric started kissing me again, eagerly this time.

"I... Love... You..." He said between kisses. My heart was racing as I climbed onto his lap.

"I -." As I tried to say it back though, he started to fade. The light and colors in the dream were dimming.

"I will speak to you soon Adella."

Just like that, I jerked awake. Tapping on my shoulder caused my eyes to fly open. Leaning over me was Anna, making kissy faces.

"Gonna kiss me too, Dells?" She hooted with laughter.

Even my dad was cracking up from the dining room table.

"No, but Anna, there's a plan."

I sprung out of bed and headed straight to the kitchen to get Anna and me some coffee. Grinding the coffee beans seemed to take an eternity, but it wasn't long before I was setting the cups down on the table. Anna snatched hers up and sipped it, a content smile spreading across her face. Holding my mug of coffee, I began my story, trying to make sure I didn't leave anything out.

"I don't know if Luxor can be trusted or if he's working for someone else, but we need to travel to the Unseelie Kingdom soon to help them plan. Alaric wasn't making our involvement public, but he does think it will play a part in helping me win back the people of the Unseelie Kingdom."

219

"The Unseelie courts? Are you sure that's safe?" Surprisingly it was Anna asking, not my dad.

"Alaric said the riots are few and far between, that the rumor's bark is worse than its bite."

"Won't the Seelie Queen be upset?" My dad chimed in.

"People visit the Unseelie courts all the time, dad."

"Dells, I hate to remind you—" my dad started.

"—but you're not just any person," Anna finished.

I looked at them both incredulously. I was starting to feel like they were ganging up on me.

"Then we will just have to find a cover story, a reason for us to go without raising the Queen's suspicions."

"I have an idea. But I'll have to tell you about it later, though. I have a meeting with Alaric and the hunters tomorrow and I have to prepare." My dad rose from his chair.

"Okay, dad. I love you."

"Good luck Dan."

"Thanks, girls. Love you too." With that, he was gone.

The second he left, Anna made kissing faces at me again.

"Was it that bad?"

"Worse," she giggled. "Your dad wanted to wake you up but I convinced him you might be getting important information."

"You should have let him wake me up."

"I know, but it was funny."

"Maybe for you." I rolled my eyes and abruptly stood up. "I'll be right back. By the way, we have errands to run today."

"Like what?" Anna raised an eyebrow, leisurely drinking her coffee.

"Well, for one, we're going to visit my grandma."

23

I called my grandma, who was more than happy to send Grandpa to come and get us. I was surprised he agreed to come. I knew he hadn't driven outside the kingdom for a long time. A little over an hour later, we heard his car engine as he pulled up in front of the apartment and honked. Anna raced out calling shotgun and jumped into the front.

"Hey, little ladies! Ready?"

"We are soooooo ready," Anna responded. She was excited to get out of the house. She didn't like to stay cooped up for long.

The car ride was the easy part. We passed the time with an hour of I spy, ABC find it, and loud and obnoxious sing-along songs. Before we knew it, grandad was pulling up to the familiar little cottage. I saw grandma waiting patiently at the door.

"Anna!" My grandma reached for Anna first and embraced her. "It's nice to finally meet you!" She kept one arm around Anna and led her inside. After sitting her on the couch, she turned to embrace me.

"I know what you're here for Delly; it's no small task, but luckily for you, it's a full moon. Out the back, down by the river, I have a moonstone circle in place. We will burn sage and meditate to see if we can find your answer."

"Thanks, Grandma."

"Don't thank me yet." She pulled away from the hug, her face full of sorrow, making her look older. I wished I could've visited on better terms. *I would have to visit soon without needing something in return.*

Grandpa entered the room and put his arms around my grandma's waist. They were silent for a moment.

"Come on ladies, let's go to the garden and see what's ripe enough to eat for dinner!" My grandpa rubbed his hands together in excitement. Grandma started taking out cutting boards and Anna and I followed my grandpa out back and into a small gated area.

On the outside of the gates, it didn't look like much. My grandpa unlocked the little hasp and let us both inside. On the inside, it was enormous. There were seemingly endless rows of vegetables and herbs.

"I don't understand Grandpa, on the outside, it looks so small…"

"Ahh yes, well. Your grandmother has quite the knack for enchantments." He handed us both a basket. "And lucky for us, cooking too. Find whatever sounds good to you and she can whip something up."

That wasn't hard, we went up and down the rows, awestruck at the various vegetables and herbs. When I filled my basket up, it looked like a rainbow. I had a large purple eggplant, green fresh zucchini, ripe orange peppers, and big red tomatoes. I grabbed some herb sprigs and a purple onion too. Everything looked so good, I'm not even sure it needed to be cooked.

Apparently, Anna agreed, since her basket was also filled quickly, we met by the front. I peeked at her basket, which was full of spinach, mixes of lettuce, carrots, beets, and radishes. I was a little curious about how Grandma planned to incorporate all of this into a meal.

Anna and I walked back to the house arm in arm. I loved these moments, when life seemed simple and we were just normal teenage girls helping with dinner. My grandma took the baskets and scurried away to the kitchen, excited to cook.

"Do you need a hand?" Anna called after her.

"No thanks, dear. Dinner won't be long, so go get some rest, we're going to have a very long night." My grandma turned and gestured towards the hall and I knew she meant the guest room. I showed Anna to her room. She immediately leaped on the bed and buried her face in the pillow.

I laid on the bed next to her, in comfortable silence, listening to my grandparents circle about the kitchen in perfect unison.

"Do you think you and Luxor could have had that?" Anna asked, she was clearly listening to them in the kitchen too.

"I don't know Anna. With Luxor, things were hard work. I never quite felt good enough. It was like I needed to work to be with him in every way. Yet, with Alaric, things are easy, almost too easy." I sighed, saying it out loud made me feel pathetic.

"Easy is good," Anna replied, but I could hear the question in her voice.

"Easy is weird. I feel like I should feel different, I feel like I should want to say no, or choose my people over my feelings for Alaric. Would it really be good for the kingdoms when they're at war, to try to force them together?"

"You can't help how you feel, only how you act."

"When did you get so wise?" I asked Anna, elbowing her playfully.

"Well, I have enough boy problems myself. It only makes sense I can help you with yours," she laughed and I joined in.

After the giggles subsided, I said, "We are a mess, aren't we?"

"Dinner!" My grandma called from the kitchen.

"Chubby messes if your grandma's cooking is as good as it smells," Anna closed her eyes, inhaling deeply. We got up in unison and raced to the table.

Dinner was nothing short of amazing, vegetable stew with a large side salad and freshly baked sweet dinner rolls. I looked

225

outside as I ate because it was peaceful. Hard to believe we'd already lost a full day. As we ate, the sun started setting slowly.

"We better get walking before the sun sets completely," my grandpa said, looking out of the window too.

"Yes, I suppose. It's better than trying to find our way through the dark." my grandma agreed.

After cleaning up, we wasted no time heading towards the trail that led out back of my grandma's garden. We traveled down a simple path that looked like it had been used often. We reached the river as the moon started to show. My grandma led us to spots in the circle and began burning sage.

"I'm going to need you guys to close your eyes and focus on the Tenebris Librir, Luxor, the Queen, or her guard — whatever is easiest for you to link together in your head. I need very clear pictures."

We closed our eyes; I tried thinking of the book but I didn't know it well. I didn't know the Queen or her guard very well either, sadly. My mind drifted to Luxor, I knew him pretty well. My mind couldn't help but wonder, thinking back to a simpler time.

The moment that I met Luxor, him opening the office door for me on the first day of school. I tried to focus on how I felt during that moment. But suddenly, the image in my head shifted, and I was taken back to that moment in the Unseelie grounds.

I relived it. The burning building, the flames licking the walls, the intense heat in my face as I hear children screaming. My body trembled.

As swiftly as it came, the memory faded and changed again. Only this time, the images were not my own. It was as if I was watching a movie. I saw and heard people moving, but it couldn't have been a memory because I'd never seen it before.

"Patience, patience," the Queen said simply. "Dropping the veil will be no easy task, we must make sure the hunters are prepared and I must have the power I need to perform the ritual first."

She was speaking to a room of people. I couldn't quite make them out, their faces not quite as clear as hers.

The picture soon disappeared too, just a short snippet of what seemed like a different world. I looked at my grandma, who was rooted to the spot, her wide eyes stared back at me in fear. I'd never seen her like this before. Clearly whatever the veil was, losing it was not good news. My grandpa, on the other hand, jumped up.

"Well, that's enough for one day. We need to live a bit more in the moment," he said hastily as he half-jogged toward the group of sprites dancing around the edge of the forest.

"What are you waiting for?" My grandma asked us, appearing to shake off her concern, for the moment at least. "Let's have some fun!"

Anna and I exchanged odd looks, then chased my grandma straight into the center of the sprite-filled meadow. The sprites hummed little songs of joy. Smiling, my grandma took off her shoes and started dancing barefoot in the grass with them. We twirled with her, feeling airy and light for the first time in a long time. We let our heads hang back and laughed.

I heard a splash and my head whipped around to see my grandpa kicking around the river water, throwing rocks into random directions for no reason, just to see how far he could throw, I guessed. He too, had a happy carefree smile on his face.

The sprites acted as a euphoric drug. I was not sure I would remember much, but I knew that I was jerked out of the trance-like feeling by my grandma shouting at me.

"Run, Delly! Run!" My grandma shook me violently.

Immediately coming to my senses, I took off toward the house, barefoot. Before long, Anna was by my side, running so fast for such a small person. I glanced behind me to see figures in black chasing us. I didn't know why but I didn't want to stay to find out. My grandma and grandpa were trying to hold off a small group. I'd never imagined them to be fighters, but they were certainly holding their own and buying us time. The sprites also seemed to be on our side as they fluttered around some of the figures in black, they caused a few to veer off into random directions. That left only three chasing us. I whipped my head back around and concentrated on running.

I knew I couldn't keep up running much longer; Seelie Queen training did not involve endurance or stamina-based trials. I started climbing the nearest tree; even if I could've somehow continued running, I would have just got lost. Someone grabbed my ankle, trying to pull me down but I kicked out wildly. As I did so, I looked over at Anna, who was already up a tree.

"Adella Shenning and—"

My foot connected with his face, feeling the crunch as his nose broke. It forced him to release his grip on my ankle and clutch at his nose. He lost it. "Goddammit, Adella Shenning you're under arrest by order of the Unseelie King!"

I froze and peeked at him from between the branches. "What did you just say?"

"You are under arrest. The King said we wouldn't need many people, that you would come quietly," he spoke as blood trickled down his face.

Suddenly it all clicked. I made eye contact with Anna, and she was in clear agreement. We slid down the trees, ashamed at what we'd done. As if it wasn't humiliating enough, they cuffed us and hoisted us over their shoulders.

"This wasn't necessary," I tried to say while I was being bumped up and down as the guy marched on through the trails.

"It is. You run fast by the way. It was impressive," he admitted. "Come on guys, we gotta go!" He called out to his team.

My grandparents stopped fighting, staring at the men as they hauled us away. My grandpa's eyebrows knit together as he glared at them. Tears clouded my grandma's eyes, threatening to spill down onto her cheeks.

"If I knew the grandma was going to bite me, I would have taken chase duty." One of the biggest guys held his arm as he limped alongside the rest of them. Clearly, they were losing the fight to my grandparents before they realized the guards had finally caught us. Part of me was strangely proud of them for putting up such a fight.

"Don't worry," the guard carrying me whispered. "Someone will come back and talk to your grandparents."

That was comforting, at least, to know my grandma and grandpa wouldn't think of me like a fugitive. I didn't respond, being hauled away in cuffs wasn't exactly how I wanted to spend my morning with my grandmother. The second we were out front, he put me into the back of a van and jumped in behind me.

"Hurry up!" he commanded. The other guy set Anna down, and she scooted over next to me. Once everyone piled in, they shut the doors and sped away.

"We're not going to make it," the man who carried Anna spoke. The guards began taking off their masks.

The van jerked to the left and I hit my head against Anna's. We picked up even more speed, which made the trip feel that much more dangerous.

"Well, getting caught wasn't an option."

"Caught?" Anna asked, raising an eyebrow.

Her guard looked at her. "Yes, caught. Much like I caught you, the Seelie guards are trying to catch us. We're not supposed to be here, especially arresting the future Queen." This guard's ego and personality matched Anna's. I couldn't tell if they were going to go into an all-out brawl or if they were going to start making out in front of everyone.

"You didn't catch me," Anna said smugly.

"Oh, really? Well, maybe we can play another game of catch later and see who wins?" the guard suggested, grinning.

Her face turned a lighter shade of red, but that didn't stop her from winking at him. I couldn't believe she was flirting right now. Of all moments, right now.

"Hold on!" My guard yelled.

I tried to look around but my arms were still cuffed behind my back. The next turn threw me off the bench I was on which caused me to hit my cheek on the edge of the bench across from us.

"Grab her!" The only female guard screamed.

Gentle hands swiftly lifted me off the floor. My cheek pulsated as the aroma of iron filled my nostrils. Warm blood slowly meandered down my face.

"Great, now we're all going to get chewed out," my guard sighed. "I'm Aeries, by the way, head of the Unseelie Hunters." He produced a small med kit out of nowhere, extracting a piece of cotton from it, he went to wipe away the blood. "Well, I was the head. I'm as good as fired now." The corners of his mouth turned down; he looked so upset.

"I'm sure it'll be okay." I didn't know why I was comforting him when my face was the one that had blood smeared all over it. "It was an accident."

"Good luck explaining that to *him*," Anna's guard said. "Henry by the way." He unmistakably nodded in Anna's direction. "We were under direct order for a peaceful pick up. We didn't know you would be in the middle of the forest or put up a fight." He rolled his eyes.

"What did you expect, coming at us like that?" Anna retorted.

The rest of the ride was fairly calm, we must have passed through
the barrier because the guards visibly relaxed, and the rest of them took their masks off. I wished I could've seen outside. The trip seemed to last forever and my cheek was still throbbing.

24

The van screeched to a halt, the back doors were thrown wide open, and Alaric's face came into view, eyebrows scrunched and eyes narrowed. The fury radiating from him hit me like a heatwave, and I could feel the sweat start to drop down my back.

"Uncuff them and get me a medic at once," he barked at someone.

Avoiding eye contact with Alaric, Aeries got up and started to undo our cuffs. Stretching my arms out felt good, they were stiff from being behind my back for so long. The red marks around my wrist bruised. I ran my fingers around the welts, trying to get the blood to circulate through them quicker. I looked up to see Alaric's eyes were set on me. I could hear his teeth grinding as he watched me anxiously.

He reached his hand out and helped me out of the van. "Well, that took long enough." He directed the comment to Aeries.

"She put up a fight, sir." Aeries hung his head in shame. Alaric raised his eyebrows at me, a smirk crossed his face. "I expected nothing less. Sorry, we didn't have time to explain beforehand. We needed it to be as believable as it could be."

"Where are we?" I asked, looking around.

"The back entrance of the castle." My dad's voice rang out as he approached. I stepped away from Alaric and embraced my father. "Alaric has arrangements for all of us to stay for a while. But as far as the Queen knows, you're undergoing trial for stealing from the Unseelie courts. It won't take long before the Queen can order you back to the Seelie grounds, but it will give us some time. For now, Anna will train with me and the other hunters and you will brush up on the histories of the courts."

"I will train Anna," Henry volunteered as he stepped out of the van. "If she can keep up."

His smirk was met by Anna's daring glare. Now in the light, I saw Henry properly. Tattoos decorated his skin from his collarbone up to his neck and his entire left arm. He looked much more dangerous in the light than he did inside the dimly lit van. *Would Anna be able to keep up with these people?*

"Try me," was her cheeky response.

"Anna, Henry is second in command of the hunters here in the Unseelie courts and will make a fine trainer. Aeries, I'm putting Dan in charge of the strategizing for the return of the Tenebris

234

Librir. He was a hunter for many years and there is much you can learn from him." Hearing Alaric mention my dad's name so casually was odd.

"It would be my pleasure," Aeries stated, nodding to my father.

Alaric turned his attention to me. "Adella, you will be in meetings with me and my father most of the day. He would also like a private audience with you to tell you a bit more about the history of the courts."

Thinking about spending more time with Alaric's dad was nerve-wracking. He'd been through so much, so the fact that he was making time to give me private lessons was a bit intimidating. I nodded confidently at Alaric, ready for my meetings to begin. My first taste of true royalty.

My eyes flicked to where I saw movement. People were leaving, but I hadn't noticed until now. Alaric held his arm out and I carefully linked mine in his. He led me through the unfamiliar castle doors.

Although the castle was somewhat less grand than the Seelie castle, it was more elegant. Instead of marble, the castle was built of carefully carved stone with dark, beautifully aged wooden beams running along the ceiling. The castle itself was smaller than the one in the Seelie courts, but it didn't take away from the beauty it held.

The walls were warm to the touch in the great room, as the large, handmade, granite fireplace was alive with flickering flames that reflected beautifully on the smooth, dark stone.

I looked over to find Alaric staring at me, smiling. "Admiring the view?"

"You can tell this castle was made by people who cared." I looked at him curiously, hoping for a quick history lesson.

"It was made by the Unseelie people themselves, grateful for the opportunity we were given to practice on our own terms." My jaw dropped as the realization hit me.

"She's going to drop the veil," I whispered to Alaric.

"Who?" Alaric asked, wide-eyed, and alert.

"The Queen. Queen Leaure is using the Tenebris Librir to drop the veil."

Alaric grabbed my arm and yanked me into the nearest meeting room. Once he closed the door, he began pacing. Deep in thought, his brows furrowed slightly. His hand rested over his mouth while his eyes darted back and forth as if he was fighting with himself, but he stayed silent. I honestly didn't know just how bad dropping the veil was, but I couldn't help but think by Alaric's reaction that it was really bad. And maybe even my fault.

"Dad, can I get you to meet me in the small conference room please?" He talked into his radio. Hearing Alaric addressing his dad as 'dad' sounded strange. Maybe it was a normal thing here in the Unseelie courts — a less formal and more familial approach.

Two minutes later, there was a sharp rap at the door, and a pause before Abel opened the door and walked in. He stood there silently for a moment, hands folded across his chest, not as if he was waiting but as if he expected to be called sooner.

"I need you to give Adella her history lessons sooner rather than later," Alaric stated.

"Of course, son." He pressed his lips into a tight line as Alaric started leaving the room. "Adella, would you mind taking a seat? I would like to tell you a story of how the Unseelie Kingdom came to be."

I didn't say a word, speaking didn't feel necessary. I took a seat at the only table in the room and Abel walked slowly around the table sitting across from me. He had gray short hair and a salt and pepper beard, but he carried himself like he was still in his 30s.

"Young at heart," he commented, as if answering my question, however; I hadn't realized I'd asked it out loud. "And you didn't," he responded again.

"Let me explain," he said, pausing to wait for the slight nod I gave him before carrying on. "You see, my son can walk in dreams, and I can read thoughts. Not minds, just thoughts. A question or statement that runs through your head comes to me as clearly as if you've spoken the words." He looked at me for a moment. "No," he said calmly. "This is not a common gift, and I cannot see every secret you have. It's as if you're speaking to me, you just don't have to use your words. But we're not here to speak about me, we're here so you can learn the histories of the courts — the kind of things you won't find in your history book, because you see, the histories were not as peaceful as you might think."

There was a long pause. I'd never read anything in my history books that may have hinted that there was a rough or unfriendly

237

start to the courts. Everything was magical, like it all just fell into place.

"Sadly that's not the case, Adella. You see, the Unseelie Kingdom used to be nothing but a broken village of starving Dark Creatures and confused Fata trying to figure out where they belong.

"Aurthor Dames, the original author of the Tenebris Librir, started studying worship of the moon at a very young age and wrote his findings down in the dark book. It wasn't long before people took notice of his odd sleeping habits and late-night trips to the river, and wanted to get involved. Before Aurthor knew it, he had hundreds of followers who were interested in learning more about what they called 'Dark Magic.'"

Abel sat back a bit farther in his seat. The excitement that danced in his eyes told me he was really getting into the story, I was too.

"He married at the ripe age of 20 to a beautiful lady who followed his practices with him, and they had a son named Jonathan. Together they raised their son; however, they didn't have much money as they both worked low wage jobs to keep a roof over their heads. Soon they planned to petition the courts to give them a larger space to practice their gifts.

"Unfortunately, the courts received word that dark magic was being practiced in the Seelie Kingdom, and before they had the chance to plead their case, the small village was raided. Homes were burned and Dark Creatures ran into the forest. A select few stayed and what started was the first and only war written in the histories of the Seelie courts. War is a light term, for it was a slaughter of our people and many families. Children were taken from their parents and placed with what they considered suitable fosters. Parents were put on trial and sentenced to death. During this time is when Dark Creatures truly darkened; Fata hid who they were or stopped practicing altogether and, sadly, Aurthor Dames and his wife were both killed publicly, leaving their son Jonathan with the Tenebris Librir to be raised by a group of dark magic worshipers who took him in."

They killed them publicly? I hope Jonathan wasn't there to witness it. Abel gave me a stern look, and I froze for a minute. Only my leg that I hadn't realized was shaking the entire table was still bouncing. I paused the bouncing and gave Abel an apologetic nod. He smiled back kindly. His face was warm and kind when he smiled like that. I wish he did it more often.

"Jonathan is the one who raised the veil. When he was 15, he began preaching as his father did before him, only he did it in private. When the family who took him in learned of his practicing, they cast him out in fear of a second war. He knew he needed a way that he could practice safely without worrying of being attacked as his father was. So he brought the Tenebris Librir to the acting Seelie King at the time and pleaded his case. He went alone so they wouldn't think he was threatening an attack, and was granted much more than expected.

"The King bestowed upon him the title of Unseelie King. While he didn't know it at the time, it was a title that would grow with a kingdom. It was a gift Jonathan would never forget. To ensure no more violence happened on the Seelie lands, the King banished him from the Seelie courts. For some, this would be a punishment, but the King was kind and gave Jonathan one more gift, companionship. He told Jonathan where he could find a small village outside the Seelie grounds, with a group of very powerful Fay who also practiced in other elements.

"No one knows how long Jonathan searched for. He was gone for almost two years before the veil was raised, and when it was, there was panic in the Seelie courts. The premonition Fay saw the change coming and the Seelie King gave his people a choice: go to the Unseelie King and worship the Winter, the darkness, the moon, or stay in the Seelie Kingdom and worship Summer, the light and the sun.

"This caused much confusion throughout the Seelie Kingdom; it tore apart many families and caused many rifts between friends."

Abel's voice lowered slightly and there was a sadness in his eyes that made me wonder if he was there during this time. *How old was Abel?*

"Simultaneously, it also brought peace to both Kingdoms, for when they split, the Dark Creatures no longer felt like outcasts. They no longer lived on the streets or struggled to survive in the land of the sun. Instead, they went to worship the dark and spent their time, energy, and love building their new Kingdom right here on this very ground.

"The Seelie King grew old and was aware that he would need to present a new ruler to the Kingdoms soon. The fear of war between the courts pushed him to set a meeting with the Unseelie King to set rules and limitations between the courts. They both offered three premonition Fay and Fata, and three of their best hunters to begin a court together, who would come up with laws and regulations for all to abide by as one system, in two different elements."

Abel paused, breaking eye contact with me to walk to the window. He observed the people on the ground. "I hate to say it, but I fear the peace that was created between the lands may come to an end if the veil is lowered. We are not ready to enter into one kingdom together, not yet anyway. Dark creatures are grossly misunderstood and would be led to their deaths. Fata are thought of as dark people because of their choice of energy source." He looked at me solemnly. "We cannot let that veil be dropped."

Maybe the Seelie and Unseelie people were less alike than I thought. I nodded in agreement.

25

The weeks seemed to drag on. I attended endless meetings, had
no time alone with Alaric, and only saw Anna at bedtime — even
then she was asleep, exhausted from her extensive training. Dad
was busy plotting the next step in our plan, not in a hurry to move
too quickly, for the courts would be expecting it.

Worst of all was waiting to be called back to the Seelie courts.
News of my arrest didn't seem to startle the Queen, and she was in
no hurry to send a notice for me to return home. I couldn't help but
wonder if, in her eyes, my role had been served and my services
were no longer requested, or if she was simply denying that my
arrest had anything to do with the trials she'd sent me on.

I knew the mission to recover the Tenebris Librir was coming
up soon, and I couldn't help but worry about the safety of everyone
involved with the plan. Alaric assured me they had men on the

inside and the job was already half done, but from the number of meetings they had that I wasn't allowed to attend, 'half done' was certainly an understatement.

Anna and I were informed that before we could make the retrieval, we had to return to the Seelie courts so that we weren't associated with the crime. I was sure it would only be a matter of time anyway before we were called back to learn of our next trial. Somehow, it still felt like we were leaving home.

Anna walked into the room as I was packing my belongings. I glanced at her, and then I did a double-take. Instead of her typical workout ensemble, she sported a pair of tight black mini skirt, a tight black tank with a sequin overlay, and to my surprise, no jewelry. She was certainly dressed up for some kind of occasion, I couldn't tell if that occasion was leaving, or going on a hot date.

"Soooooooo…what do you think?" she asked, twirling for me.

"Whoa." I stood up and walked over to her, saying, "Sit still." I pulled out the pins in her ultra-tight bun; her hair cascaded over her shoulders and bounced back into the wild mane that I knew and loved. "The hair is your thing. You should keep it."

Her face split into a broad smile. "I probably should, it just gets in the way of being a badass killing machine sometimes." She laughed, but it was short-lived when she glanced around at our belongings scattered on the floor. Her face fell. "I can't believe we're leaving."

"We will be back." Even as I said it, I sounded unsure. Would we be welcomed back into the Unseelie Kingdom? Hopefully, we would be guests instead of fugitives.

Anna helped me pack the rest of our stuff. Somehow, even all of her simple black clothes had their own unique style, and she had almost twice as much as I did. It wasn't long after we finished packing that there were men at the door taking our bags and escorting us to a van. It was similar to the one we came in. Thankfully, we didn't have to wear cuffs this time.

"Just one more minute, please?" I asked the guard as he reached to shut the doors.

I waited patiently for Alaric, my dad, or for just someone to say goodbye, but no one came. My mind raced, trying to figure out why no one would take the time to see us off, but I came up blank. Clearly, there were more important meetings to be done today. The guard (whom I'd never seen before) bowed his head as if he understood and closed the doors slowly. He knocked the side of the van, a signal to indicate to the driver that we were ready to go. And so we did.

Unlike last time, when we entered into the Seelie Kingdom they were ready. We were stopped just after passing through. The Seelie guards searched the entire van and tried to get the driver to switch vans, but our guards vehemently refused. This took about an hour before the Seelie guards agreed to follow the van to the courts, then escorted the van back to the changeover area.

When we were finally let out of the van, it was very much like when we first got into it that morning. There was not a soul in sight, so we walked up to the castle doors and let ourselves in. Inside, alone in the large room, was MaryAnn.

"Leave your things here and go straight to your rooms, dinner will be brought up shortly." Her appearance wasn't as immaculate as it usually was and her behavior was erratic, almost frantic as she tried to hurry us along to our rooms.

So much for a welcome back from our friends here in the Seelie courts. We hurried up the familiar corridor, both of us went straight into my room. Not that I expected any less, sharing a room felt familiar, safe even.

"What do you think is going on?" Anna asked as she began searching the room.

"I'm not sure. Clearly, they weren't expecting us yet, or maybe they just didn't have an agenda made for us." I watched her flutter around, picking up random items here and there, and studying them carefully. "Uhm... Anna? What are you looking for?"

"Any items that are out of the ordinary or weren't here the last time." She carefully set a few items in a small pile.

"Do you think we've been bugged?" I whispered — *would whispering make a difference?*

"Being bugged would be the least of our concerns, I'm checking to make sure we aren't jinxed or hexed." She stared at her small pile of items, clearly content, and carried them next door to the room she never used. As she came back into the room, she set up a small radio. "If we were bugged," she explained, "this little contraption I carry in my bag blocks frequencies, so their bugs won't work."

"Why do you think no one came to say goodbye to us?" I asked her.

"Wasn't it obvious? We were rushed out, they sent novice hunters to transfer us, the stop at the gate took over an hour. We are the distraction."

"You think they're enacting their plan?"

"I think they've already completed it, and the Seelie courts are either on lockdown, and we didn't get it, or they got it and the Seelie courts are in panic mode trying to figure out what went wrong. They clear our names while they're at it by having us in their sight during the whole thing." Hearing Anna rattle through the possibilities of what happened was almost intrusive — like I could hear her inner monologue.

"Well, what happens next?" I looked at her. She didn't bother to unpack her things, I wondered if she knew something I didn't about how long we'd be here.

"Now we wait. I'm sure there'll be an announcement of some sort, maybe some questioning of all persons involved, or who might have seen something."

There was a rap at the door. Anna jumped up and cracked it open to see a guard standing there.

"Adella Shenning and her protector are requested in the great hall in one hour," was all the guy said. He handed Anna a tray that

246

held two drinks, silverware, and two meals covered with silver bowls before leaving. It smelled divine.

Anna turned and set the tray on the bed; it was almost the size of her. I walked over and uncovered one of the meals. A whole glazed quail on a bed of mashed sweet potatoes with a side of steamed vegetables. I picked up my silverware and, ignoring the etiquette I'd learned since visiting the courts, I dug in. Anna followed suit.

"What do you think they're going to say in the meeting?" I asked Anna, not sure if she'd understand as I used one hand to cover my full mouth.

"Probably just an update, letting us know that Seelie court property was stolen and giving us a briefing on what they're going to do as a repercussion."

"That's odd seeing as it wasn't Seelie property to begin with."

"No, but I'm sure they follow more of a 'finders keepers' approach when it comes to this kind of thing. I mean, the Queen gave you the assignment knowing you would have to steal it. Not to mention, half the court has heard about Alaric's proposal to you; however, I highly doubt she'd mention it. Considering you stole from him immediately after, I suppose she would no longer consider an engagement a viable option."

I was a little taken aback by how frank Anna was, but she was right. Although, technically, she was wrong as Alaric still expected an answer from me. Her assumption that the Queen probably believed the engagement was reconsidered was probably correct. At least I hoped it was. I didn't want to be singled out tonight.

There was another knock at the door, only this visitor didn't wait for an invitation. In walked Jackie, with a fresh new bob-length haircut, and Lilah followed closely behind.

Jackie studied my face for a moment. "You sly dog, you!" she exclaimed. "Tell me *everything*. When did your romance with the King begin? Were there secret rendezvous? *Did. You. Say. Yes?*" She sat by me, impatient for my answer. I felt as if she was staring into my soul.

"Of course she didn't say yes," Anna said. "And throw away her right to rule as a single, strong Queen? She has other obligations to uphold."

"That's not what we heard," Jackie gave Anna a smug look.

"Well, what did you hear?" I asked, curious.

"That the King rescinded his proposal and arrested you on the same day." Jackie flipped her hair and looked back at me.

"Well, you're not wrong. We were arrested, it was terrible." I knew I was not a good liar, so sticking as close to the truth as I could was my best bet.

"Did he really arrest you for stealing the book? We all had assignments to steal something of value, but you're the only one who was arrested." It was only Jackie who spoke. Poor Lilah stayed silent, apart from the odd sniffle.

"Yep, cuffs, and all." I turned my wrists upright for her, so she could see the fading bruises the cuffs left. "Is everything alright Lilah?"

"She's fine," Jackie spoke for her. "She technically finished her assignment, only the object she returned was just a replica of the real item. So they have to decide if she passed or failed. They'll probably tell her tonight. I'm pretty sure they are going to pass her, I mean, how was she supposed to know?"

Lilah held her face up slowly, tears streamed down her cheeks. She certainly didn't look fine, she looked scared beyond reason. I wondered if she already knew what happened if we didn't pass the tests.

"We should probably head down to the meeting," Anna said in a less-than-enthusiastic voice. While it should've been good news that there might've been less competition, the air in my lungs had been knocked out of me. Things dwindling so soon was an unexpected turn.

We followed Anna down the halls, where there was much more movement since others were leaving their rooms to attend the meeting as well. I glanced at this person and that person, wondering where Luxor was. I wasn't sure why I cared but I had a bad feeling in the pit of my stomach. My body seemed to be feeding off the nervous energy of those around me. I felt sick to my stomach.

Entering the great room wasn't any better, the emotions in the room ranged from nervous and anxious to excited and impatient. It

249

was overwhelming. I squeezed myself in between two unimpressed guards who didn't seem to be bothered about the whole situation. Breathing slowly, I attempted to calm my senses and nerves.

The lights dimmed and there was complete silence as the Queen ambled into the room. The world had slowed, as we patiently waited for her to speak. She took her time, pacing the front of the audience twice, nodding hello to a couple of people, and made direct eye contact with me for far too long.

"Today, our castle was raided and our people were put at risk." Every word felt directed at me, but she broke eye contact and scanned the room. "One of the contestants in the Seelie trials went to grave lengths to retrieve an item, and was arrested. Even then, she did not surrender easily." The room stirred uneasily. "In the past, the Unseelie and Seelie Kingdom did their best to work together, to choose a new ascendant to the throne together, for the better of the kingdoms. I fear that this may no longer be the case."

Whispers spread like wildfire amongst the audience, fear washed through them in waves.

"King Alaric has not only tried to sway one of our Seelie Queen contenders into leaving the trials by way of matrimony, but he has also sent a traitor to our courts to spy and plot against our people," The Queen said serenely as if it wasn't a big deal to her. To the people though, this was a huge deal.

Anger and confusion spread through the group like wildfire. It lit one mind at first, then quickly swept through the room. Emotions changed rapidly as the tension escalated, starting with revulsion in the left-hand corner as two guards entered the room, followed by a weird jangling sound. I immediately recognized the sound of chains. They must have been bringing the traitor into the room.

I tried to see who it was but I stood too far back. I assumed they were bringing the traitor in because in the corner, people's moods changed rapidly to disgust, anger, and for a select few, pity. Finally, the prisoner came into view.

He was mangled, covered in purple and blue bruises and lashes that showed the red flesh from beneath his torn shirt. He barely had the strength to lift his head. His face so contorted he was almost unrecognizable. As we came eye to eye though, I felt a recognizable pull, drawing me closer to the front of the room. A pull that took me straight to the man bound in chains. He used the last of his energy to pull me closer and attract my attention. A man who hung his head in fear and shame. *Luxor.*

26

Panic racked my body as I pushed my way to the front of the room. Unsure of what I was going to do, of what I could do, I moved closer until someone grabbed my arm. I whipped round to see Anna's wide eyes warning me. I tried to jerk my arm from her hand but her grip was solid. She shook her head slightly, mouthing, "Don't."

But when I looked back to the front the Queen was making direct eye contact with me again, holding a sly smile, as if to punish me for getting too close to Alaric, or maybe she knew we were involved in the raiding of the kingdom. Either way, it worked. I was shaken to the core. I couldn't feel anyone around me anymore. My rage filled my body and radiated out of me. Anna stiffened as the unrest in the room escalated and others became rowdy.

"Dells, stop," she whispered urgently, but it was too late. I couldn't control the red heat pouring out of me. People around me began to yell as the anger spread out from me in a circle, infecting others. People screamed for peace, others screamed for the death of the traitor, the latter only serving to fuel the rage my body was feeding the room.

The Queen called for guards to subdue those who were out of control, but every guard who came into range of my pulsating rage found themselves filled with fury too. The first fist was thrown from a civilian at a guard, the catalyst of the fighting. The whole room broke out in violence. Anna started to drag me to the outskirts of the room but I resisted, feeling at home in the heart of the hate. Arms outstretched, I belonged in the middle of the chaos.

Madeline turned and helped Anna drag me out. Reluctant to leave, I kicked and yelled the whole way. When we got away, we were down four or five different halls before the anger and the effects of the room faded.

"What was *that*?" Anna screamed at me.

"They have him, Anna! They have Luxor and we *have* to get him out. Tonight." Madeline and Anna made eye contact for a second, as if having a silent conversation.

"We know," Madeline said. "That was always the plan, Adella. Luxor was always going to be the scapegoat. He sacrificed himself to make sure you had a clear name. We knew the Queen wouldn't believe you had no involvement unless there was someone else to hang out to dry. He figured he owed you as much, after what happened in the clearing."

"He doesn't owe me *anything*. Especially his life. Why didn't anyone tell me? Warn me? Why did you not *prepare me* for what I just saw?" I was screaming now. They pulled me into another room, I assumed to hide us from those running toward the great hall to help break up the riot still happening.

"You had to believe that Luxor was aiding the Queen, or the Queen wouldn't have believed it herself, Dells." Anna was speaking in a tone I didn't recognize, and for the first time, I noticed fear was radiating from her. Anna was afraid, afraid of what was happening — maybe even afraid of me.

I stepped backwards and shook my head. "We have to get him out."

"We are working on a plan now," Madeline tried to reassure me.

"No, we need to get him out *now*," I said, staring at Anna. "While the guards are stopping the riot, they will have to move him because there aren't enough eyes to watch him. We need to get him *now*."

"You're right," Madeline conceded, shaking her head. "It sounds crazy because, of course, they're going to be expecting it, but you can still hear the chaos happening. We have to do it now. I'm calling Alaric to send a van."

"*No*," I almost shouted at her. Of course, Alaric was involved. hHe was probably all too happy to get rid of Luxor permanently.

"Call my grandma. She's already on the grounds so there won't be any passing through the main gates. She could take Luxor to the changing tree through a longer route and get him out safely. They won't be expecting it."

Anna nodded and pulled her phone out. We started walking back towards the great room, only this time, we took the service hallways that go all the way around the room, and listened quietly through the walls.

"Leave him, he passed out. We have to calm the room," I heard one guard say.

"Absolutely not. You two will take him down to the cells. Along with that one." We heard a familiar whimper but I couldn't put my finger on the voice. "Return after they're locked away safely. These are the orders of the Queen." James's voice was filled with authority. It was unmistakable. I heard a moan as the men lifted the chains off the floor and dragged Luxor's lifeless body down the hall.

Staying as silently as we could, we trailed the men to the end of the hall. When we were sure they'd turned to go down the staircase to the cells, we slipped out the door of the service hallway and waited patiently.

"Are there any cameras down there?"

"No, they don't want proof of what they do to the prisoners. The only cameras in the castle are through main hallways, which we managed to avoid."

"So, what now?" I whispered to Madeline.

"This," she whispered back. Closing her eyes and mouthing the numbers I saw her count back a few more seconds before she swung her foot into the doorway, kicking the hunter who was almost to the top, square in the jaw, which knocked him back into the guy behind him. Both of them tumbled down the stairs.

Anna and Madeline chased down the stairs after them, but they weren't down for long. By the time everyone was at the bottom, the fighting had begun. The hunters kept trying to reach for their guns but Anna and Madeline prevented them from doing so. Madeline fought like a damn Viking, throwing brute punches and kicks mainly to the midsection of the large men in front of her repeatedly. I followed cautiously down the stairs, trying to stay out of the way. I walked to the edge of the room and ducked down to watch the rest of Madeline's fight quietly.

He got a couple of good hits in, but he didn't swing fast enough. Madeline ducked and pounded his chest with her fists until, slowly but surely, he fell to his knees; she gave him one last kick to the face and knocked him out cold.

Anna, on the other hand, was struggling. She fought like a lioness attacking its prey, aiming at the knees and lower gut to try to bring him down to her size. She had an easier time blocking his blows than Madeline had, but she wasn't quite winning. Brazenly, she fought her way onto his shoulders, she attempted to strangle him with her legs, but that was when he stopped clutching his neck and reached for his gun.

256

It all happened so fast it sent me into a mad panic. My eyes blurred as I heard shots fired. I looked around, trying to process what was happening. I didn't know what to do, or if I could do it fast enough. Anna and the hunter crashed to the ground. I ran over, but Anna was already standing up and dusting herself off. We both looked over at Madeline.

Madeline was visibly shaken, the gun plastered in her hands, eyes wide open. Tears streamed down her strong face as Anna walked over to her and took the gun from her hands gently and silently. Still in shock and in an almost zombified state, Madeline walked up to the guard to check his pockets for keys. Anna did the same, but in one swift movement, Anna put a bullet into the other guard's skull, killing both guards and leaving no witnesses. Anna's hands jingled the set of keys. We followed her as she unlocked and went through the main door.

Cells lined the walls but judging from how quickly the guards left and came back, Luxor had to be close. We scanned the cells which were mostly empty until about halfway down.

"Lilah?" Madeline asked. Lilah looked over at us, clearly terrified of what was to come.

"No, don't. I'll be fine, take him." Lilah said to us. I could feel the fear in her; I knew she was lying. This meant Lilah had failed her trial and was now awaiting the ceremony to be drained of her representation. She pointed to a couple of cells across from her and to the left, and Anna ran to the door to begin unlocking it.

"I will be fine, I promise," Lilah insisted. "I have nowhere else to go if not the Seelie courts. Just leave me. I will be okay." Leaving her felt wrong, but I knew I had to help Anna carry Luxor. I ran to the open cell. Luxor was hunched over on the floor, conscious but weak.

Anna grabbed one arm, I grabbed the other, and we dragged him out, there was no time to waste. Madeline dragged the guards into the corner and left the keys with them. Anna and I barely reached the top of the stairs when Madeline caught back up and sneaked ahead of us.

"I will go check the hallways quickly."

Anna and I waited for what felt like an eternity, but it was only a moment before Madeline looked around the corner and waved to us.

We went through approximately twenty deserted service halls before Madeline shook her head and took my place at Luxor's side.

"I will take him out back, your grandma is already there. I'll put him in the car and see him off, Adella. You can't afford to be seen."

"You can't lift him alone," I said.

"She isn't alone, I'll help her." A whisper came from behind us, sending chills up my spine.

Jackie reached her arm out to take Anna's place. Saying goodbye to Luxor would've felt too permanent, at least now I knew that as long as he got out in time, he would still be alive.

258

"It would be just as bad for you if you were caught Jackie," I insisted.

"Yes, but no one would believe I had any reason to help Luxor, I barely know him, you need to go into the common halls and be seen, you need people to be able to give you an alibi."

I turned before she could see the tears stream down my cheek. I stepped back reluctantly and walked away. I didn't know why Jackie would want to help me, but I was forever grateful for her in that moment. *Maybe we really are friends.* Anna followed me quietly down the walkways, no words could fill the emptiness I had. No words could fix what we all went through. Madeline, even though she saved a life, killed someone today. Anna committed a crime against the Seelie courts and me, a Queen-to-be, was now a traitor to my own people.

27

A chill filled the air, and I couldn't shake this eerie feeling. Greed and hunger mixed with excitement, which was weird considering what was going on. I decided to follow the feeling. I couldn't possibly be in more trouble, I doubted anyone would notice me or Anna were missing at this point with all the fighting.

A scream pierced through the air, loud enough to hear through the service hallways, but too quiet to hear from the main areas. We walked up to a set of double doors that led to a medical office, and we looked inside the little windows.

Strapped to a bed in the room, was Lilah, pale, and sweating. She was drained of her representative color, but something was still very wrong. She appeared to be moving her lips but I couldn't make out what she was saying. The Queen loomed over her.

The Queen took a deep breath and tilted her head back, before reaching out and touching Lilah once more. "Please, please, please," Lilah screeched in pain, unable to form any other words. Lilah was shaking her head, her body writhed, rising off the table but the Queen prevented her from getting up. Lilah turned a sick shade of white, while the Queen's colors darkened.

James stood on the side, still smiling. He was waiting for something, or maybe just enjoying the view. We ducked our heads down and exchanged looks. Anna gave me a wide-eyed, scared look. Lilah's screaming faded, and I no longer sensed her emotions. I grabbed Anna's arm and began running her down the service halls until I knew we were clear. I came to a halt. Dusting myself off, I stood up straight and made my way through a door to the main halls.

I walked Anna around the halls, although it was past curfew they were still filled with people. I said hello to a few people, nodded to a couple others when words evaded me, I was emotionally and physically exhausted. *Time to call it a day, at least for the night.*

"She's dead, Anna," I whispered as I closed the door behind us.

Anna sat unmoving. "That wasn't supposed to be how it happened," Anna explained. "There was supposed to be a ceremony where you and Jackie laid your hands upon Lilah and drained her together. It's done publicly and has never been known to be painful. Exhausting yes, and rarely, someone dies. But it's never painful." Anna took a deep breath. "After the final contestant

261

drains the last contestant, she gets the prior representation from both of her competitors. This makes her more powerful, more resilient."

"Then why did the Queen kill her, Anna?"

"To get enough power to drop the veil."

"Would draining Lilah give her enough power to do that?"

"No," Anna said soberly. "But draining all three of you would be enough. We have to make sure you and Jackie pass your next two trials, Dells."

28

"What do you mean we have to go home?" Anna insisted while dragging her already-packed luggage to the trunk of the car belonging to the hunter Alaric had sent to collect us.

"The Queen gives her greatest condolences and believes everyone should return home to mourn," MaryAnn said, rushing us out of the castle. "Everyone is to return home immediately."

"More like to hide the evidence of murder," Anna hissed into my ear, out of MaryAnn's earshot.

"Maybe Alaric will know what to do about all of this," I whispered back calmly, no reason to fight now, our bags were packed and by the doors before we got back from breakfast. There was no argument on staying.

The hunter grabbed one of my bags and started loading them into the trunk.

A car hurtled up the road toward us, hitting the brakes so hard, black smoke erupted out of the exhaust as it screeched to a halt, temporarily deafening me. It narrowly missed the hunter's car, only gently tapping the bumper; the hunter jumped to avoid being squished. My dad got out, slamming the door behind him, his face red.

"Absolutely not," he exclaimed and marched toward the poor hunter to take my luggage from him. "We are going home, dammit."

Although the hunter appeared as if he was going to put up a fight, Anna and I were not prepared to go to war with my father; we both jumped eagerly into the backseat of his waiting car. Dad raised an eyebrow at the hunter as he went to retrieve Anna's bags. The hunter handed them to him sheepishly. After the bags were loaded he climbed into the car, nodding in satisfaction.

"Well, now that that matter is settled, I propose a no-boy summer," my dad announced, making direct eye contact with me through the rearview mirror.

My mouth gaped open, not necessarily to protest but in shock. A whole summer without Luxor or Alaric? My dad held up a curt finger.

"I won't hear any arguments. Your safety is what matters most, especially since the Queen may come after you as she did with Lilah."

"You told him?" I rage whispered at Anna, jabbing her in the ribs with my elbow.

She grabbed her side, and death glared back at me. "Of course I did," she hissed back. "There is a fine line between being your protector and your friend, and I needed to be your protector."

"That's right, Dells, this was something I needed to know." Dad interrupted our whisper argument and continued. "They're covering up what happened for a reason. I'm not going to sit here and let you go off this summer when we don't know what the Queen is planning. I need you safe, Addy." He sighed, running a hand through his hair. "I can't afford to lose you. Alaric's men and I are doing everything we can to uncover her plans. All I need you to do is stay put and do your schoolwork — I know you're behind on it as is."

My breath caught in my throat and I closed my mouth. Now that he'd said it all out loud, I realized I hadn't been taking it seriously enough. He was already worried about me anyway, so maybe he was right, a no-boy summer was what I needed.

I reached a new level of boredom over the summer as I remained home and had no contact with both Luxor and Alaric. It made for an uneventful summer, but it enabled me to complete my studies for what was left of my sophomore and junior year. I was still worried about what the Queen wanted with us, and despite not knowing her that well, I grieved for Lilah too.

Given everything that happened, the school board allowed me to use my real-life experiences for my electives, physical education, history, and mystics courses. So, all I had to worry about over the summer were the courses for my senior years, English and Math.

I went into the school for my bi-weekly tests, but apart from that, I studied at home — a perk of being a queen-in-training. Or was it? Considering I wasn't allowed out, I was stuck in these four walls. My tests didn't always consist of written exams. Sometimes, they would send in a representative from the Seelie Kingdom to talk to me, a lady, to check if my learning "in such an abstract way" as she would say, was satisfactory.

The rather large lady had a slight mustache and her face permanently wore a sour expression.

She would ask me questions such as, "If you are to quote the law, section 3, subsection AA, what would you use as an example to show the rule in place in our society today?" Or questions like, "Who won the 42nd Seelie King or Queen trials, and what were the names of the failures?"

The first time I was tested, I sweated buckets, but learning throughout my day-to-day activities helped me retain the information I was learning, now it was just another part of my routine.

Dad helped teach me mystics, Abel carried on with teaching me history, and Aeries told me I was going to attend a hunter boot camp soon — I didn't know if he was kidding, or if this was their extreme idea of homeschool physical education.

266

Anna studied with me, but the school board wasn't as lenient with her school requirements. The only class they excused her from was physical education, so she still spent the majority of her time studying. On top of that, she had detention for a week because she rolled her eyes at the school board — I didn't know what she was thinking. It wasn't going to be subtle with her large eyes.

Lately, though, she'd been at the apartment a lot — and I mean, much more than usual. My birthday was coming up soon, and she'd been not-so-slyly trying to glean information from me for a surprise party she was organizing. I probably wouldn't have guessed what she was doing by the questions alone, but the fact that she scribbled in capital letters: 'Make no plans! Dell's surprise party!' on my dad's calendar in his office, kind of gave it away. According to the calendar, it was organized for tomorrow night.

Seeing as this was where she spent most of her time now, Anna was going to arrive soon. Her parents were proud that she'd been chosen to be a protector before she turned 18 — it was an incredible achievement and honor. They were more than happy to support her training and job duties whenever they could, which meant, to keep me safe, Anna unofficially moved in. She vehemently denied this, but her large pile of clothes in the corner of my room begged to differ. I was glad she was there. She was a welcome distraction and someone to talk to, considering I couldn't talk to Luxor or Alaric. Speaking of which, the latter had sent many men and flowers to the house attempting to persuade my dad and me, to change our minds about my break from boys — he even

267

sent a case of beer for my dad with the last flower bouquet. Although my dad was impressed with his efforts, his resolve never wavered. His decision was final and there was no swaying it. Not only did he block all calls coming from Luxor, Alaric, and half of Alaric's guard, he also called in reinforcements — Grandma — to lay enchantments around the house to keep Alaric out of my dreams. However, the enchantments would stop working once I turned 18.

She was hesitant to come at first, though my dad persevered and managed to persuade her. At first, I thought it was because she was reluctant to separate me from the outside world, but I realized she hadn't left the Seelie grounds in a very long time. Grandma stated that she needed to stay the whole weekend to "ensure it worked appropriately." I was sure that was just an excuse to visit because the enchantment only took about ten minutes of her chanting and walking around with burning sage and sweet grass.

She managed to talk Dad into changing the decor in the guestroom to make her feel more at home, as well as new bedding. She even talked Grandpa around, and he stayed for one night. She cooked while she was here too, though she made discouraging faces at the crockery, so she bought new ones as well as the store-bought groceries. She was not impressed with what the stores had to offer, but her cooking was as amazing as I had remembered. I thought she was going to stay longer after redecorating the guest room and rearranging the kitchen cupboards, but when Sunday night arrived, she packed her suitcase and left, probably hoping Dad would invite her back again soon.

"Dells, I'm home," Anna yelled from the doorway. I suspected Anna was half-expecting me to meet her at the door and put away her suitcase.. Anna had no such luck.

"In here!" I yelled from my room. There was no way that I was moving.

Anna bounced into the room, hair flying everywhere. "Do anything fun today?"

"Nope, just locked myself in my room and completed another half a month's worth of math. Oh, look what else I did," I said as I jumped up from the bed and pulled open my closet doors.

"Want to finish half a month of my math too?" She joked as she followed me.

"Only if you wanna take my exam at school next week?" I returned.

"Not a chance. One meeting with that lady was enough. I'm happy taking my tests the normal way." Anna and my examiner didn't see eye to eye.

I pointed to the new pins I'd carefully placed on the inside of my closet door. I'd made a messy spider web of everyone linked to the Queen. While Dad and the hunters searched for the answers, I was here doing an investigation into it by myself. So far, the Queen's name was in the center, with a red string linking it to the names of James, Lilah, and Jackie, the latter having a question mark next to the name. I wasn't sure how involved she was in everything.

Anna gave me a skeptical look as she closed the closet door.

"You know your dad said to let him handle it, Dells. We aren't equipped to take this on. We need to focus on what we can deal with: school, the trials, and frankly, your mess of a love life."

I didn't say anything. Anna flopped onto my bed.

"Are you seeing Luxor or Alaric after your 18th birthday?"

This was the last thing I wanted to talk about.

"I don't know. I haven't thought about what I'm going to say to either of them yet," I sighed.

It was the truth. The last time I saw Luxor was when Madeline carted him away after the rescue. Since then, the only thing he did was publicly announce he lived in the Unseelie castle. It was probably so he was safe and protected and for everyone to know he wasn't a prisoner. Since the Queen's announcement as a traitor, he had become somewhat of a hero in the Unseelie courts, who were aware of his attempts to return their dark book to them, even though he was the one who took it in the first place. It was no small accomplishment in the eyes of the people. It helped that he was publicly welcomed back by King Alaric himself. They made a grand entrance into the court, then a long trip to the medic's quarters to be checked over.

Alaric, on the other hand, had fallen silent. Other than the occasional messengers and flowers that arrived from him, I had heard nothing from him. I couldn't help but wonder if he was doing this on purpose, and it kept me guessing. Just thinking about him frustrated me. I casually felt my pocket. The little box with the beautiful diamond engagement ring still sat there, waiting for me to decide.

"You know you'll have to answer him eventually," Anna called over her shoulder without looking at me. She had moved from the bed and was staring into my closet, disappointedly flipping through my dresses and blouses, as if something was missing.

"I don't know how you do that," I responded.

"You're predictable Dells. You're thinking about Luxor and Alaric. I know this because when you're stressed, your breathing increases. Then you reach down and touch the ring for comfort as if the ring itself means Alaric hasn't forgotten you and moved on." She fully turned around and jumped on the bed. "But I can assure you he hasn't. You're not forgettable Dells."

I rolled my eyes and took a deep breath. I couldn't even fathom giving Alaric a solid answer until after the trials were over. He had quite the waiting time, but luckily, he was a patient person. I think deep down, it was hurting his ego to not have an answer, but I really didn't mind the extra attention and courting attempts in the meantime.

We heard the front door being opened, then slammed shut.

"Hey, Dad," Anna and I called out. Anna had gotten much more comfortable around my dad in the last couple of months. It felt like she belonged here. She no longer waited for an invitation to join us

271

on trips to the store, and she never asked for keys anymore before checking (and reading, might I add) my mail. Not that I minded, it was nice having another girl in the house, especially my protector and best friend.

"Dells, Anna, I need you both to come into the dining room, please," my dad's voice was deep and authoritative. It felt like we'd done something wrong.

Anna raised an eyebrow at me, clearly concerned. As was I. There was something in my dad's voice that I couldn't quite place. Reluctantly, we made our way to the dining room to find we weren't in trouble.

We found my dad, fists clenched, red-faced, and not alone. Next to him was Queen Leaure of the Seelie Kingdom and her full royal guard, right here in our little dining room.

We froze in the doorway, Anna ahead of me.

"Ahhh, Anna," the Queen's voice was sickly sweet. Anna's body tensed up. "It's so good to see you taking your job as a protector so seriously." She mocked her.

I saw Anna's hand twitch slightly, but she only nodded her head slowly once and remained silent. She didn't give the Queen the satisfaction of getting under her skin. We moved into the room and out of the doorway.

"I really can't stay long. You see, there are many preparations to make for your second trial, and we're close to finishing it. Once we are finished, you will receive a letter with the details. Usually, we would have you all in the great hall to make the announcement in person, but this time we have to keep you at home, for obvious reasons." The Queen gestured to a small present on the table with a small envelope on top and smiled, but there was no warmth in her eyes. "You don't have to open the present now, you can wait until your surprise party tomorrow. I hope you have a happy birthday, Adella Shenning."

Anna's face grew cherry-tomato red as she grimaced in annoyance at the queen. Who, without waiting for a response, nodded to her guard and walked out of the dining room, her hunters following behind. Closing the front door behind them, they left Anna, my father, and I where we were, speechless.

Anna threw her hands up. "Welp, that sure as hell ruined the surprise," she muttered.

"She already knew Anna," my dad said lightly, trying to defuse the tension.

I tilted my head to the side and looked at my dad.

How did he know?

"You left the drawer in my office out of order when you returned the pens you borrowed, blue goes before purple," he said as if it was obvious. Of course, they were organized by color. I should have known.

Anna threw her head back dramatically and sat at the table. "Well, are you going to open the gift?" Anna inquired.

"Uhm, I don't know." I walked over, picked up the extravagantly wrapped box, and gave it a slight shake. It was light, despite it being the size of a microwave.

Why would the Queen give me a gift?

Setting the box down I picked up the small envelope and ripped it open.

Dearest Adella,

Search and search and you will find, it's not only a gift I leave behind, solve it quickly and you will see a Seelie queen you are meant to be.

Happiest of Birthdays,

Queen Wyvette Leaure

I read the note in my head again. Anna stood up from her seat and read aloud to my dad from over my shoulder. *Uhm, what?*

"I have no clue what that means Dells, but I'm not going to lie to you. If you don't open the gift, I will." My dad was seriously worried. "We need to know it is."

"Okay," I agreed and put the letter to one side.

I grabbed the corner of the present and ripped the paper; underneath was just a plain lidded box. I methodically unwrapped the rest of it, removed the cover, and reached for what was inside cautiously. Dad and Anna waited with bated breath to see what it was. Confusion coursed through me as I grasped soft material. Eyebrows furrowed, I looked up at Dad and Anna before pulling it out of the box. It was a blouse, wrapped in crumpled paper. I hadn't expected such an elegantly wrapped gift to then contain random paper to fill the box.

"Oh my god, Dells," Anna gasped. She snatched the blouse out of my hand and unfolded it.

It was dirty as if it had been worn. It wouldn't fit me, it was far too long, but there was something familiar about it.

"It's Lilah's blouse from the night she died." Even to me, my voice sounded eerily calm.

My dad picked up the papers and started unfolding them one by one and laying them out on the table.

"We need to call Alaric."

I saw the pattern to the order he was laying the papers out. It appeared to be copied pages of a book.

29

Adrenaline coursed through my veins, causing my fingers to shake as I dialed Alaric's number. I hadn't spoken to him in months, and now I finally could. I pressed call, heart thumping to the phone ringing. *Answer, answer, answer.*

Usually, Alaric picked up on the second ring, so I counted them mentally as the phone rang. "1...2...3...4...5...6...7...BEEP." I reached his voicemail. I rolled my eyes impatiently and let out a deep breath of air I'd been holding in. *Crap.* I deliberated on hanging up, my finger hovered over the red button but ultimately decided this was too important and left a message.

"Hey, uhh, Alaric." I don't know why, but this felt awkward and ridiculous. "So, listen, we need you to come to town tonight if you can. I mean, I know about the party tomorrow, and I don't know if you knew, or if you knew and were planning on coming — or not coming." Smooth, real smooth Dells. I cringe at my awkwardness. "Just call me back," I said as I went to press the red button. "Oh uh, it's Dells," I added hurriedly. I hung up before I could make a fool of myself more than I already had. That was awful. Not a single line of that message came out smoothly.

In fact, that couldn't have gone any worse. I looked over at Anna, who was staring at me, incredulously. It was just us two in the room. She didn't say a word, but turned her back on me and sat on the couch. Clearly, she had overheard that disaster unfolding. I heard a phone ring and swiped my screen, quickly holding it to my ear.

"Hello? Hello?" Nothing. I looked at the screen, but there wasn't a call. All I'd done was unlock the screen.

"Hey, Alaric," my dad called out dramatically from the other room. "Just the man I needed to speak to." My dad grinned at me, shutting the door to his office before he continued the conversation.

"Seriously?" I exclaimed.

Anna chuckled from the couch. "Don't you see Dells? He's trying to play your game." She turned to look at me. "You ignored him for months. Now, he's ignoring you."

"That's ridiculous," I protested. "I was ignoring Alaric because my dad wanted me to. So, wouldn't he need to ignore my dad?" *And I'm not playing a game. Am I?*

"No, because it's not your dad's attention he wants. Besides, he needs to stay on Dan's good side." As she explained, it made more sense.

He was ignoring me so that I would be thinking about him, and it was working. Clearly, it was working because he was all I had been thinking about since we had left the Seelie Kingdom.

"Was he invited to my birthday party?" I asked Anna.

"Absolutely. Half the kingdom was." She gave me a broad, toothy grin.

I know she was joking about inviting half the kingdom, but I was still excited to see people. "Even Jackie?"

"Everyone," Anna responded simply, turning back to the TV to let me mull over the information.

I grabbed a banana and headed back to my room to see if I could eavesdrop on the conversation between Alaric and dad through the wall. I shut the door and put my ear up to the wall, holding my breath just in case it made a big difference. It was no use. I couldn't hear anything.

I sat down and flipped my math book open to start the next chapter. The words on the page were blurry. My mind couldn't focus on the numbers. I threw myself onto my bed, face down into my pillow, and groaned.

Pointless as it was, it did get some of my pent-up frustration out. *Hopefully, I would see Alaric at the party tomorrow. I mean, if he comes, he must want to see me, right?*

I didn't know exactly what time it was, but I managed to drift off, but it wasn't pleasant. Even in my sleep, I felt conscious. I couldn't escape my thoughts. Swirls of colors and patterns traced behind my eyelids. They kept my mind semi-conscious. The blackness didn't arrive to rescue me.

A shaking sensation woke me, I opened my groggy eyes to Anna's face nose to nose with my own.

"Jeez, Dells! Did you sleep at all?" She sounded annoyed.

"I think I did. I don't know." Sitting up felt like a lot of work. Exhausted, I propped myself up on one elbow and looked at Anna.

"I'll make coffee. You get dressed," she ordered.

The moment she left, I fell back into the safety of my sheets, once again closing my eyes and watching the patterns dance behind them. All too soon, I heard her footsteps approaching.

"Dells," she exclaimed. "Seriously, you need to get up. We need to go to the mall and get you something to wear for your party." She sat on the bed and waved the cup in front of my face. The smell of warm, bitter, black coffee wafted in front of me, zoning in my attention for a moment.

"I already know what I'm going to wear," I told her. "Jeans."

"Over my dead, fabulously-dressed body." She left the bed and rummaged through my dresser. After a few moments, she threw a pair of dark, distressed jeans and a t-shirt at me. "Get dressed. We have errands today, and Alaric can't be seen courting a plain Jane."

My eyes flew open. Anna was right. It'd been months since we'd seen each other, the least I could do was make an effort with

279

my outfit. I sat up in bed. Anna handed me my coffee. She left the room so I could get dressed. It took longer than usual to get ready. My legs felt like they were made of lead. Each limb felt a thousand pounds heavier than it actually was. By the time I had my shirt and pants thrown on, I had no energy left to do my hair, so I slipped it into a messy bun, grabbed my mug, and headed out the door.

Anna clapped her hands, mocking me. "She lives!"

I shrugged my shoulders slightly and took a sip of my deliciously scalding coffee, before setting it on the counter.

I grabbed my dad's car keys. Luckily one of my birthday gifts was no longer needing to ask to borrow his second car. I called it the turtle. It was a slug bug and was two odd shades of green. It wasn't not pretty and it got us to where we needed to go. Anna stood up from the table, slipped her shoes on, and followed me out.

The drive to the mall was uneventful. The scenery in Tombstone was pretty amazing though. I wasn't sure I liked it at first, but it was growing on me like vines on a trellis. I liked to peek out the window on drives through town and admire the brown, desert land. The city itself only had about 1,300 people, which meant all the stores were locally owned. The shopping in town was limited to antique malls and essential stores, but it was a 45-minute drive away. I could've gone to the mall in Sierra Vista, which was far enough away so there were no crowds, but it was still close enough to be convenient.

Luckily the mall wasn't too busy today and it was easy to find a parking space. The mall's front door was enormous. They left them open all the time — the perfect invitation to spend all of our money here today.

Inside was surprisingly busy despite the lack of cars in the lot. Anna dragged me through shop after shop, making me try on at least 50 outfits before giving me an approving look. We took the approved dress to the register to pay. My favorite part about the mall though was the food court, where I could get an iced coffee, lunch, and dessert in the same area, and I was still supporting local businesses.

I ordered my coffee, and as I watched the barista's expert hands craft my caramel macchiato, someone caught my attention. He towered over the rest of the crowd, his face oddly familiar. Then it hit me.

"Uncle David?" I called out.

The barista handed me my drink, I tipped and looked back up, hoping he stopped. He was gone.

"Uncle David!" I called again as I ran into the crowd of people. I abandoned Anna, who was still waiting for her coffee and looked for his familiar face among the large group. I weaved in and out, faces staring at me because of my odd behavior. It was no use. He was gone. Maybe it wasn't even him in the first place. Defeated, I made my way to Anna when a scream pierced my eardrums.

It came from where I left Anna. The crowd had already started to congregate toward the barista stand. Bile rose in my throat as I pushed through the thickening crowd. It seemed endless. More people had gathered to see what was going on. It was starting to get claustrophobic. I was lost in this sea of people. I kept pushing through until I broke through the final barrier and saw what they were gaping at.

Anna was writhing on the ground, foaming from the mouth. Her body was convulsing as if she was having a fit. The barista hovered near her, arms wrapped around herself, wide-eyed and on the verge of tears.

The group shifted once again. I heard small protests as people were roughly shoved aside. Someone else was pushing their way through. I knelt by Anna and hurriedly put her in the recovery position. The endless foam was now pouring out of her mouth on the floor. Her eyes rolled into the back of her head, and a gurgling sound escaped her throat.

The person who pushed through the ground knelt by me and shoved something into Anna's mouth. I grabbed their wrist, preparing myself for a fight.

I turned to look into the face of the assailant. It was my grandmother. She gave me a reassuring nod. I hesitated, but let go of her wrist. She thrust the unknown substance into Anna's mouth, turned Anna onto her back, and moved her jaw in a chewing motion. Anna stopped foaming almost immediately. Her eyes rolled back and began to close. Her body relaxed, no longer convulsing. To my relief, I heard sirens approaching.

"We need to get her out of here Delly. Help me stand her up," my grandma said, cheeks flustered. She looked alarmed as we grabbed Anna's arms and lifted her. Maybe the person who did this was still here. I thought we were going to take her to the medics who had just arrived, but we ran through the crowd in the opposite direction. The people parted but were perplexed at our actions. We placed Anna into the backseat of Grandma's car but I paused at the door, looking back to see if anyone had followed us.

"Stop dawdling Delly, and get in," Grandma yelled, snapping me back to the here and now.

I jumped into the passenger seat. Grandma didn't wait for me to put my seatbelt on, she revved the engine and sped off. I frantically clicked the buckle in place as she accelerated more. She had to be driving between 90 and 110 mph. The trees and buildings were just blurred as we sped past them at dangerously high speed. I clutched the handle on the side of the car, feeling nauseous.

"I don't understand Grandma, what just happened?" I couldn't keep the panic out of my voice. My heartbeat deafened me.

"This morning, I had a vision that someone was going to try to hurt Anna. I didn't see much, besides her writhing on the floor and foaming. I called your dad, but he didn't pick up, so I mixed all the herbs to soak up or treat poisoning as fast as I could — hoping one would help — and headed out the door."

She kept her eyes on the road as she spoke. For that, I was grateful, because she was accelerating more each time I looked at the speedometer.

"I didn't bring my phone today," I said to no one in particular. I was too tired this morning, just trying to get up and get out for the day. I didn't think to grab my phone.

"I know," Grandma responded flatly. "I got into town and realized you weren't home. Your dad finally called me back and told me you two went shopping. Anna was going to fall soon, I felt it, so I followed my gut and went to the closest mall I could find. Thank goodness I did. If I'd have left in a couple more minutes, Anna would be dead."

I looked back at Anna; her eyes were still closed, though her breathing was too ragged for her to be asleep, her whole body twitching slightly. We were fast approaching the town. Grandma looked at me.

"She's going to be okay now," she said softly.

"We were so careless, Grandma." Shame consumed me, taking on a swirling blue and gray aura. I could physically see the colors surrounding me. I clenched my teeth. I felt my heart thumping out of my chest, but no longer because of Grandma's speeding.

"Stop that right now. I don't have time to save you from yourself too," she scolded. Her hands tightened on the steering wheel as she felt the effect of my emotions pouring out.

I closed my eyes, took a few calming breaths, and told myself over and over again that Anna was okay. My grandma took one hand off the wheel and rested it lightly on my knee. The effects grounded me. I slowly opened my eyes. The colors were gone, and we were officially in town again. I attempted to calm myself as Grandma arrived outside the private cafe Alaric had once taken me to. We climbed out of the car and opened up the back door. At the door's creaking, Anna's eyes fluttered, and she held her hands up.

"No," Anna's voice was feeble but insistent. "Don't you dare carry me again." Her eyes flitted to me. "I am the protector, and I will walk." She stood up and raised her hand as if she was going to swat at us. She used the side of the car for support and closed her eyes. Her body rocked back and forth on her feet as she shakily tried to regain her balance. Once she steadied herself, she opened her eyes, let go of the car, and walked towards the café.

The café blinds were drawn over the two small windows, so we couldn't see if anyone was inside. Grandma stepped ahead of us and knocked on the door in the dum-dum dum dum dum, pattern. She listened carefully to the door. Dum dum, someone knocked back before unlocking the door. It was my dad.

"Seriously?" Anna says. "That's the top-secret code to get into the building."

Wordlessly, he embraced her the moment she stepped in. He pulled away, held her at arm's length to check if she was hurt, then pulled her back in for a hug.

"We were short on time," he laughed, which was a soothing sound. "But I'm so glad you're okay." My dad reached his arm out, so I joined the hug. My grandma joined in too, and we stood there for a moment, thankful that Anna was still here with us.

"Eh-hem." Someone from behind Dad cleared their throat obnoxiously. We released each other and went into the café. I was prepared to give the intruder a taste of my mind, but it was James, the Queen's right-hand protector and lead hunter of her guard —

and I certainly wasn't about to tell him off. Next to him stood Alaric, waiting patiently with his hands resting silently by his side.

I averted eye contact immediately, stepping back and straightening out a bit, wiping the tears forming in my eyes. Alaric didn't care. He didn't even bother to call me back. Someone tried to hurt Anna, and there was nothing I could do to stop it. On top of that, I left her alone. Fresh tears of frustration formed. I piled all the guilt onto myself at once, hoping to get it out of my mind just as fast. I turned my head to wipe the tears from my face again, take in an exaggerated breath, and spun around to face Alaric and James.

"I don't know what you've heard, but today someone tried to kill Anna. I thought I saw a familiar face, so I left her side, for just a few moments. When I returned, she was writhing on the floor, foaming from the mouth." I paused and looked at Anna. She stood by my father. Some color had returned to her cheeks. "My grandma and I got her out of there quickly. Luckily, she showed up just in time to help, or Anna would be dead right now."

"Anna, do you remember what happened?" James looked at her as if he was bored. It was clear to me he wasn't bothered in the slightest.

"I remember taking a sip out of the coffee I'd just bought and then I couldn't breathe." Anna stared off into space as she tried to remember what happened. "I fell to the floor. I felt like I was drowning but I couldn't clear the water from my throat, so I waited to pass out, but it never came. The drowning felt like an eternity. I

286

didn't fully pass out until I felt someone shoving something into my mouth."

"Herbs," Grandma chimed in softly.

"Yes, herbs. When I was able to take a full breath in, I passed out and woke back up in the car on our way here." She looked at everyone in the room. "I didn't see anything out of the ordinary. I didn't see anyone out of place. No one knew where we were going, and I didn't message or call anyone to inform them before we left. We didn't even tell Dan. The barista screamed as I fell and stayed the entire time I was on the floor, so I highly doubt she had anything to do with it, at least not knowingly."

"I'm going to go look around to the mall and see if I can obtain the footage and report back to Queen Leaure." James exited abruptly.

I hadn't expected him to stay long. He looked empty and out of place without the Queen here. Dad followed him out quietly, probably to make sure he could check the scene out and have copies of the footage.

My grandma strolled up to Alaric and, without a word, studied him carefully. It was as if she was appraising a used car. The atmosphere turned awkward as she circled him slowly, but reached out her hand.

"Good afternoon Alaric, my name is Judy," she spoke confidently as if she wasn't speaking to a king at all.

"I know who you are, Judy. I am Alaric, King to the Unseelie people, and it is a pleasure to meet you. Thank you for your

287

continued premonition reports even though you're not staying in the Unseelie Kingdom." Alaric took her hand and clasped it gently in between his two hands. "I hope there is something we can do to help you come home soon," he said sweetly. He spoke to her with admiration and respect, as if she was royalty. Knowing how pushy Alaric was, it sounded almost out of place, as if her coming home would be a huge favor to him somehow.

My grandma smiled slightly and tilted her head. "Perhaps I will," was all she remarked in response. He returned the smile, and they released their hands to look back at the small circle of people. Anna, Grandma, Alaric, Abel, and I all stood together quietly, and it didn't feel like a silence where we were waiting for someone to speak. Instead, the silence helped to reflect on the last two hours of everyone's lives.

My dad walked back into the room with a sullen look on his face. "No one got footage of what happened. James is headed to the mall to see if there is anything out of the ordinary at the coffee stand and then traveling back to the Seelie courts to report yet another assassination attempt on one of the chosen protectors."

"At least it wasn't successful this time," Anna tried to say lightly.

"My men didn't see anything out of the ordinary," Alaric reported, as he was in full 'king' mode now. "They saw Adella run, calling after someone. They followed her and went back to Anna right after Adella found her."

288

I looked at Alaric, bewildered. "You have people following me?"

30

"Of course, I do." Alaric snapped at me. He composed himself carefully before carrying on. "I have two or three personnel on you at all times. Anna is a new protector, and in training often, and it is required you have protection, and I have the means to provide it," he said simply as if I should have known. To some degree, I did see, I knew when I was in the courts at least that there was an extra protection detail on me — I just didn't realize I took them home with me.

I didn't know what bothered me more, the fact that there were four sets of eyes at the mall with us that should have seen what happened or the fact that I was completely unaware of the extra people following me.

"Dells, who was it that you saw?" Dad asked.

"Uncle David. I mean, I think it was him. I looked up, he was there, I looked away for not even a second, and he was gone. I tried to chase after him, but I didn't see him at all."

"Hmmm," Dad hummed, deep in thought. "I doubt it was your Uncle David, he would have told me if he was here for a visit, but I will call him later to make sure."

"Your party is in two hours, Dells," Anna said. "We have to start decorating."

"We don't have to have a party," I replied. The thought of a party after everything that had happened today was absurd, not to mention Anna looked like she'd been hit by a truck.

"Yes, we do," she retorted. "Everyone is already invited, and we're already here, so we might as well finish setting it up and get you dressed."

"The party is here?"

No one responded verbally, but Anna nodded.

"Alright, fine. But you need to rest Anna. Dad and I can handle setting up."

Without putting up a fight, Anna agreed and walked across the room to the couch, where she crashed onto it.

"Don't mind if I do." She looked exhausted

"I will help," Alaric volunteered before calling his men inside with his radio.

The group of hunters were all large and had to file in one by one. My dad took charge and instructed the first two to go back out to the car to grab the boxes of decor in his trunk. As the men walked back in with box after box, I realized I'd signed us up for an over-the-top job. Box after box was filled with fairy lights — fresh deep blue and purple flowers, and table linens. Anna instructed the men on where to hang the lights, and Alaric and I started setting tables.

"This is a bit over the top," I groaned. We were almost an hour and a half in, with everybody helping, and it still didn't feel like we were doing much.

"I don't think so," Alaric argued. I glanced up at him. He paused his work to look at me. "You only turn 18 once, so I think what Anna has planned is perfect."

He looked at Anna, who beamed up at him from what looked like a little throne she had made herself of the pillows that were on the couches, one arm rested delicately on each little stack.

"Dells, you need to go get dressed, people are going to start arriving soon," Anna instructed, handing me a bag that was next to her seat. I took it and headed to the bathroom to change. The bathroom had two stalls, one small and one large, with hooks on the inside of the stall doors, so I could hang my clothes up. The dress we chose was a beautiful deep blue dress, with a tight lace top and a tulle skirt that went just to my knees. Anna picked out matching jewelry. A gold-plated stack of different length necklaces that had little stars hanging off of it (on all but the last chain), and a simple set of lunar phase-inspired bangles. Each one had a different stage of the moon on it. They were amazing.

292

When I was fully dressed, I let my hair down and looked into the mirror. I was wearing no makeup, had dark circles under my weary eyes that seemed brighter after crying today and hair that didn't want to cooperate — but hey, at least my outfit was cute. I did a little spin, watching my skirt fly up. I decided I was ready. I left the bathroom and ambled to where everyone was waiting.

Walking into the main café area, I noticed the difference immediately. The room was dark, lit only by the hundreds of fairy lights strung to the ceiling, mimicking stars — hardly noticeable in the light, but once the lights were off, it transformed the whole room. The candles were the centerpieces on tables. They gave the room a warm glow and a cozy atmosphere. Their aroma reminded me of the fields after leaving the changing tree to enter the Unseelie gates — evergreens, lilacs, and lavender.

"Anna," I gasped, still enveloped in the sweet scent. "It's perfect." I tried to take everything in all at once.

"I knew you were missing the Unseelie Kingdom," Anna whispered.

I nodded, speechless. I couldn't help but look over at Alaric, who was pretending to rustle some papers. He was grinning from ear to ear, knowing I missed his kingdom. People entered the small café one at a time and looked around just like I had. Some had never been to the Unseelie Kingdom, so they took in its replicated glory for the first time. Rachael, from school, walked in and smiled at me kindly. She left a small gift on the table and approached the counter for a drink. MaryAnn followed suit, looking a little stiff and out of place, but she made herself comfortable by straightening and organizing the gifts on the table.

She didn't have to stay busy for long because about ten minutes later, RayRay strutted in. He approached me, grabbing my hands. He gave me a spin and verbally approved my outfit before giving me an air hug. After that, he went off to greet MaryAnn. There seemed to be someone here for everyone, which was perfect because I was able to greet everyone and move on without feeling like I was leaving anyone alone. Anna took charge of the party to make sure everything moved along appropriately. She took two hunters into the kitchen and reappeared holding a large cake lit with 18 candles.

"Happy birthday to you," the crowd sang harmoniously. The front door opened as people sang, and I peeked over the cake to see who it was. The second "Happy birthday to you," was the last line I heard. Luxor stood in the doorway, ogling me. On his arm was Madeline, followed by Jackie, who looked skittish and cautious. Madeline jerked Luxor's arm over to the far side of the room. He hesitated slightly, but since their arms were linked, he had no choice but to follow. I assumed they were late because they heard of the recent assassination attempt and had to take proper precautions.

"Dells. Dells," Anna scream-whispered at me. I looked at her, not quite sure what's going on in the world outside my head right now. "Make a wish and blow out your candles."

I closed my eyes and thought hard, but I couldn't think of a wish, so I blew out the candles quickly and opened my eyes to the eager faces of my family and friends, giving them a wide grin as if I had made the best wish. I refocused on the party, probably with too much enthusiasm, but I did my best to stay far from Luxor, disregarding his attempts to approach me.

Someone grabbed my hand, disrupting my inner monologue, and I flinched. I turned to see Alaric's wounded face staring at me quietly.

"Sorry." I reached for his hands, and he took mine firmly into his.

"I have missed you." He dropped his shoulders in defeat as if he knew he was losing at his attempts to ignore me, as I had ignored him for months. He looked over my hands a couple of times before squeezing them and letting go. I saw the hope in his eyes leave as he released my hands, watching them fall to my sides. "I had hoped — never mind. It's your day." He smiled, but I saw the pain in his eyes.

"To see this?" I asked him, and pulled out the longest length necklace from under my dress, and presented the engagement ring he had given me months ago.

"Precisely — only I was hoping it was placed elsewhere." His face lit up with a huge grin. Seeing his facial expression transform gave me butterflies. He took the ring and twirled it around in his fingers a few times. "You should try it on to see if it fits," he suggested.

"It does," I whispered back, not quite ready for a room full of people to see me put on an engagement ring. I watched his fingers as he dropped the ring to hang freely from my neck.

"Am I interrupting?" A familiar voice asked timidly.

I turned to look at the intruder. "Yes," I said, but Alaric stepped away slightly.

"No, you're not," Alaric said to him, in a voice that was kinder than Luxor deserved after killing his people. "I shouldn't monopolize the birthday girl. If you'll excuse me." I raised a skeptical eyebrow at Alaric, hoping for some kind of explanation.

Alaric walked away quietly, and Luxor took a step forward, hesitantly, as if he didn't want to be here with me.

"Hey, Dells," he said shyly.

"Hey." Long responses lengthened what I needed to say. I knew this conversation needed to end abruptly before I lost my cool in a room full of people whose days I didn't want to ruin. *You can do this, just say goodbye, forever.*

"There's something I've needed to tell you," he began. I took a deep breath and met his eyes, only to be startled at what I found.

He was calm. It was radiating around his whole body. A peaceful white cloud surrounded him. It nearly put me in a trance. The patterns that swirled looked like small clouds. His eyelids were half closed, his hands relaxed at his sides and his mouth parted just enough to show the full curve of his lips. It hurt to miss him, standing there in his tranquility fog, it was hard to remember why I was mad in the first place. He had my full, undivided attention now. Whatever I was about to say to end this short conversation escaped me.

"When I was 18, I was chosen to be part of the Seelie Kingdom. I was chosen by summer, and I wasn't sure why. I assumed that when I received my letter telling me I was assigned to be a protector, that was the reason. Now I can't help but wonder if there was more to it." Luxor no longer looked at me. Instead, he looked through me, as if he was living his memories. "The queen was the one who kidnapped Anna and the rest of the group during your first trip to the court. Alaric told me his plan in confidence, thinking I would be on board to do whatever it took to bring the kingdoms together. I didn't know it was wrong at the time, but I told the Queen. She's the one who encouraged me to persuade you to go on the mission to the Unseelie courts, hoping it would scare you into going along with her plan against the Unseelie kingdom and take your role as Seelie queen-in-training seriously. She thought the Dark Creature groups would be scary and startling. She gave me direct orders to "solve the problem," as she said when it was done. Only, when we approached the shack, nothing was like she explained. When I saw your face and the peace you found amongst the people, I knew I had failed the Queen's orders. So, I did the only thing I could think to do at that point. I finished the job she had sent me to do. I was filled with self-hate, rage, and anger at what I did. I knew I needed to act quickly before I failed to complete the mission. When it was over, those feelings only intensified. I'd known I did wrong, I'd realized the Queen was wrong, and I killed innocent people. I dragged you to the outskirts. I was so exhausted and mentally broken down at that point I passed out with you. When I woke up, I thought I was going to be allowed to see you, so I could explain. I wanted to tell you that I had made a mistake. Those people," Luxor dropped his head in shame, unable to finish that sentence. "They didn't deserve to die, they didn't deserve what I had done, and that is something that I will never get to take back."

Luxor's perfect white cloud darkened slightly. "The Queen had hoped that when you found out Anna and the others were discovered in the gates of the Unseelie Kingdom, that you would blame Alaric. When that didn't work, and you persuaded Jaqueline and Lilah that the Dark Creature group was good — well, Dells, she came up with a plan, that was worse." Luxor's arms shook. His cloud was being taken over by gray completely, until Madeline walked up behind him and grabbed his arm, putting a small object into his hand.

The gray wavered slightly, but remained gray. Luxor leaned slightly into Madeline and took a few steadying breaths. *Seriously get a room.*

"I think that's enough bad news for one birthday. We can talk about this another day," Madeline cooed to Luxor, his white cloud immediately returned, maybe somehow even brighter than last time.

Luxor nodded and gradually looked up at me again. "You don't have to forgive me, and you don't owe me anything. But Madeline

298

told me that you were the one who wanted to free me, even after what I'd done. Please know that I'm here, Dells, feeling more like myself than I have in a long time, ready to fight to be back in your life. Thank you for saving me even when I didn't think I deserved saving."

With that, Luxor walked away, leaving Madeline and me to stare at each other awkwardly.

"We're not together, you know," she explained. "We've been working on meditative approaches to handle his anger and grief because of his actions, that's all."

"You don't owe me an explanation," I told her, even though deep down, for some reason, it did take some weight off my chest.

"I should go find him. He had trouble building up the courage to come tonight, but he will be glad he did, eventually."

"I think we're both grateful he decided to come tonight," I agreed.

I walked away this time, heading for the door, ready for this party to be over. The emotions in the room were becoming too much. I loved the ambiance, I truly felt like I was back in the Unseelie kingdom. Although, I hated being surrounded by so many overwhelming emotions.

"Dells!" My dad called out as he jogged to catch up to me. The room was smaller, so it didn't take too long for him to meet me next to the front doors. "I wanted to be here when you left." He opened the front door for me, and we stepped outside.

299

He handed me car keys, and I passed the unfamiliar set back and forth from hand to hand for a moment before giving him a curious look. I pressed the panic alarm on the keys curious to where they led, and a car midway through the lot went off.

It was a small Kia Rio, dark blue. As I walked up to it, I noticed it shimmered slightly in the light.

"Is it really mine?" I asked him.

"Yes, I supposed it was time I got you something of your own to drive."

I hugged him hard. Happiness and sadness radiated from him. I held on for a second longer because I knew we both needed it. He gave me one hard squeeze before lightening his grip, but I clung on.

"Thanks, Dad," I said to him.

He let go and looked at me for a moment. "It's your party, and you can leave if you want to." He couldn't help but laugh a little as he said it, which makes me laugh too.

"Thanks, Dad, I think I will." I hopped into the car, I looked over and saw a red bob running towards me.

"Waaaaiiiittttt Dells," Anna yelled as she sprinted to the car. She pulled on the passenger door handle, then rolled her eyes as she waited for me to find the button to unlock it.

"Seriously? Did you try to leave without me? Not cool." She climbed into the car and buckled up, taking a quick peek around the vehicle and giving an approving nod.

"Are we both seriously leaving the party? The birthday girl and the host?" I looked over at her.

"Absolutely." She put the visor down and winked. "Let's go home."

31

The second I hit the gas and drove away, the stress from the party diminished. I melted into the seat of the new car and it seemed to mold to the shape of me, and was quite comfortable.

"Let's go to the pizza parlor. I'm starving," Anna suggested.

Now that I thought about it, I had worked up quite the appetite too. My dad wouldn't be home till late and I doubted he would mind. He seemed to be enjoying a conversation with MaryAnn before we left.

"Kay," was all I said.

The pizza parlor wasn't that far out, and air hockey sounded fun. I turned down the familiar road — the same road with the only coffee shop in town. I gripped my steering wheel as we drove by it. Butterflies flitted through my stomach as I reminisced.

The cheesy aroma of pizza greeted us as we approached the small parlor. Italian zest filled my nose and led me confidently through the doors. I walked up to the counter and picked up their small laminated menu, scanning through it quickly.

"I'll have 2 slices of pepperoni and a root beer please." I smiled at the young man in the funny hat behind the counter, who froze momentarily before typing the numbers into the register.

"Wi-wi-will that be all ma'am?"

"Yes, thank you."

I grabbed my purse and unzipped it, but a hand reached in front of me, slapping a $20 bill onto the counter.

"Make that two more slices and a coke please, and keep the change," the familiar voice cooed to the already anxious teenager.

Jackie winked at him, causing his already tomato-red complexion to deepen. Then she turned her gaze on me.

"Seriously," she scorned. "How dare you leave without even saying hi to me!"

A grin crept across her face as she tried to pretend she was mad, but her voice cracked just enough that I could tell there was no real damage done. Letting out a sigh of relief, I threw my arms around her.

"Eh-hem." Anna held her fist to her mouth dramatically.

"Ope! Sorry, Anna!" I let go of Jackie, and we stepped out of the way, so she could put her order in.

"Sorry Jackie, it was all a bit-"

"-overwhelming?" She finished.

"Exactly."

"And I will pay for hers." Madeline's curt voice cut through our conversation. She smiled at Anna who, to my surprise, blushed and widened her eyes.

Madeline gave her a wink, Anna turned quickly, pretending not to see it and grabbed my arm.

"Let's find a table," Anna insisted.

"Can't we sit with you?" Jackie's voice indicated she was curious, but she was also pouting.

"Of course you can."

Anna gave me a look, but I couldn't quite tell what it meant. As far as I knew, she liked Jackie. Jackie sat across from me and Anna, while Madeline took a seat by Jackie. Madeline and Anna seemed to be using an uncanny way of conversing without the use of words, which made the table abnormally silent.

"What have you been up to Jackie?" I watched Anna and Madeline through my peripherals. They both seemed totally engrossed in their silent conversation.

"Oh you know, school, training — more school. Waiting not so patiently for the next assignment."

Jackie sent a funny look in Madeline's and Anna's direction, and held it long enough for me to notice. I followed her gaze and shrugged my shoulders.

"Yes, sadly, I do know. Have you heard anything about it yet?"

"Well no, not yet. I'm hoping we will get word soon. Now that there are only two competitors, I wonder if the trials will finish early. What happens if the trials finish early?"

It was a good question, one I wished I had an answer too. She looked up at me, her hopeful face turning to defeat when she realized I didn't have an answer. The young pizza boy brought us our food, and we ate in silence for a bit. Anna and Madeline still completely ignored us.

"Listen Adella, I have to admit, I have ulterior motives for coming to see you today."

Madeline stiffened, I watched her for a moment, she took in a breath and sat back, looking almost defeated — as if she was losing whatever silent battle she and Anna were having. She rolled her eyes, the movement seemed unnatural, almost forced, and looked to me, waiting with Jackie for my response.

"I don't think this is the best place to talk about this, Jackie."

"You know what happened. Tell me what happened to Lilah," she was starting to get hysterical.

The entire parlor went silent, there was no telling who was listening in to this conversation. I looked into Madeline's and Jackie's waiting eyes, Madeline's were hard, and Jackie's were brimmed with tears. She was waiting for an explanation that would make her feel better — one that will make her feel complete.

"Is anyone expecting you home soon?" I asked her.

"No, my parents knew I was going out, I told them I was staying at Madeline's tonight."

It was a relief that the other contestants were close friends with their protectors. I turned to Anna to see if she was thinking what I was thinking, but she was glaring at me.

Well, okay then...

"Let's have a slumber party at my house?" I suggested. "It is my birthday, after all. I doubt my dad will mind."

Jackie did not respond, she pressed her lips tightly together and nodded. She either understood it wasn't the right place to talk about it or didn't trust herself not to burst into tears if she allowed herself to answer.

I stood up, leaving a tip on the table, and I walked briskly to my car. Anna followed behind closely. As I pulled the car out of my spot in the parking lot, I watched Madeline pull out behind me, and checked my rearview now and then on the way home to make sure they didn't get lost.

My dad wasn't home yet. I parked on the road, so he could have the second spot in the driveway and directed Madeline and Jackie up the steps to my apartment. I went to the kitchen first and put water on to boil. Anna showed Madeline and Jackie where the bathroom was, then took them to the living room.

"Tea?" I called out.

"Please," Madeline, Jackie, and Anna called out simultaneously.

I took the mugs out, set the tea bags in them, and poured the almost boiling water into them. I looked at the four cups of tea, sizing them up.

306

Challenge accepted.

I picked up all four cups, two in each hand, and carefully balanced them as I walked into the living room. Anna took two of the mugs and handed one to Madeline. I gave Jackie's to her, she gave me a polite smile. It was hardly noticeable — a twitch in the corners of her lips really, before returning to her sullen look.

"Okay." It was hard to know where to begin. "On our way back to our room, I felt something, something *weird.* Anna and I veered off course to investigate briefly."

I hesitated. How much of this would Jackie believe? She did help me with Luxor, but was that to gain my trust? *Or maybe she actually wants to be my friend.* My leg began to shake. Madeline took one of Jackie's hands in hers, and I reached for the other. She squeezed it tightly, urging me to continue.

"As we got closer, we heard screaming." She already looked on the verge of tears, no need to scare her further. "We looked into the room, and the Queen was draining her, and she didn't stop." Jackie pulled her hand away and used it to cover her nose, stifling a sniffle I presumed. "We were powerless. We had to get away from that room before we were caught. I couldn't *feel* her presence anymore, Jackie."

That was when she lost it. "Stop, stop. I get it." She managed to force out through sobs.

I didn't know how close she and Lilah really were, but the intensity of her despair told me they were pretty close. Tears ran profusely down her cheeks. Anna handed her the tissues from the island to help her sniffles.

"I'll go grab pillows and blankets," Anna offered.

"I'll help," Madeline said.

Anna gave her a hard look, then nodded her head once, leading her down the hall and to the linens cupboard. I could tell they wanted to provide us with some privacy, I just couldn't think of what to say.

"I knew," Jackie said softly, looking into my eyes. "I knew something was wrong the night they brought out Luxor. I didn't see Lilah, so I went looking for her, but that was when I ran into you, Anna, and Madeline." She clenched her fist into a ball and looked down into her lap, fastening her eyes shut tightly. "I *knew* something was wrong, and I couldn't find her. I didn't save her."

"I'm so sorry, Jackie." My words did not bring her comfort though.

Rage swept through her, pure, seething anger clouded her emotions and swarmed me all at once. I was angry too. Anna and Madeline came to the end of the hall and waited there patiently, checking to see if now was a good time to come back into the conversation.

"We're going to stop her, Adella. We're going to stop the Queen," she decided. "Then, then, she's going to pay."

32

For the next week, I spent every waking moment searching the house for any clue or hint that would help me find the next trial. By the end of the week, I gave up, having found nothing. Instead, I resolved to finally open my birthday gifts. It wasn't a task that I wanted to do. The very thought of it drained me, but it had to be done.

Rachel got me the same perfume she wore all the time. Maryann got me a planner, RayRay gave me a ticket for "Three free and fabulous outfits," during my next trip to the Seelie courts. Madeline got me a knife set, and a holster to go around my thigh. Anna got me tickets to see a band next summer that I'd never heard of, and Luxor gifted me a small jewel that looked like a crystal — the kind used in meditation.

Alaric's gift sat, unopened, on my bed. Not that I didn't want to open it, I just knew that it was probably perfect. I wasn't prepared for the emotions that came with seeing what he'd bought me. For now, it would have to wait. I wasn't ready to open up whatever emotional damage awaited me in that box.

I heard the front door open, which only meant my dad was home. Anna was out training for the entire evening, or at least that was what she told Dad. She and Henry had been sneaking away for little dates now and then. I was happy for her. She had so much going on lately that she deserved a break or two — especially after last week. If he provided her with an escape from reality, I wasn't going to stand in the way for a couple of hours.

"Hey, Dad!" I called out. But there was no response. I listened but couldn't hear anyone walking around the house.

"Dad?" I called out again. Silence.

I climbed out from beneath the mountain of gifts and climbed out of my bed. Walking down the hall, I heard nothing. I knocked on Dad's office door and waited patiently for a response, nothing. I opened it slightly, but no one was there.

"Dad?" I made my way to the living room, but it was empty too. No one was home.

I checked the front door; it was unlocked. It wasn't left that way. I always locked it after Anna left. She had a key to get in. I opened the door and looked out. Again, there was no one. I closed the door slowly and locked the deadbolt again.

Returning to the kitchen, I grabbed a knife from the block. I searched the entire house, armed and ready, like James Bond. I flattened myself against a well, snuck around corners, and almost stabbed myself doing a wonky somersault through the living room. No one. Sauntering back to my room, I threw the door open like I was going to catch someone in an act. But to no avail, it was also empty. Setting the knife on my dresser, I sat on my bed.

I almost jumped out of my skin when my phone buzzed. It was a text from Jackie.

Hey Adella! I just found my second trial…I'm having trouble understanding it, have you found yours yet?

She had found her trial already. I stood up, grabbed the knife, and took a deep breath before I headed into the hall and checked the door again. It was still locked.

Maybe whoever broke in has finally hidden my trial.

When I entered the living room again, I lost it. I tore the house apart. I threw the cushions off the couches, I moved the TV and looked behind it. Nothing. I ran to the bookshelf and knocked the books off. I picked them up one by one and flipped through their pages at break-neck speed. I did the same to the kitchen and the bathroom.

Finally, I hesitated outside of Dad's office door. Summoning the courage. I went in and turned the light on. There were a few things out of place, and I hadn't touched them. One of the books on his shelf was slightly askew and not in the correct spot. I took books off the shelf and stacked them on the desk. He must have had a hundred books, but the shelf was soon empty, with no clue in sight. It would've probably helped if I knew what I was looking for. I walked over to my dad's desk and took everything out of the drawers, I walked around to the front side and got on all fours to look under and around the desk.

The door swung open. I flailed, trying to grab the knife I'd left on the bookshelf. I turned to meet the intruder, swinging the knife around carelessly as if to say, *I'm not afraid to use it.*

"What are you doi-" was all the assailant could say before the knife was at his throat. His silence was satisfying as if he agreed I was the one in charge here.

I looked up sternly and came eye to eye with my dad. I immediately lowered the knife from his neck.

There was an awkward pause. Dad looked at me as if I belonged in a mental asylum. I stared back in utter horror.

"Dad, you see," I began to explain, making large hand movements as if they would distract him from the fact I just tried to kill him. "I thought I heard you come in, but you didn't. There was an intruder. Only there wasn't. Jackie texted. I was a spy. Trying to find clues to my trial." It was all coming out so wrong. He raised his eyebrows at me. Realizing I just waved the knife around like a crazy person with my over dramatic hand movements, I set the knife down, sat on the desk, and looked back at my dad.

Maintaining eye contact, he gestured that I should breathe in and out slowly. I took deep, slow breaths, and let my mind calm down before trying again.

"The door opened and I thought it was you, so I called out but heard nothing back. I went to check and found the door was unlocked but I couldn't find anyone, so I locked it again. Then Jackie texted me and said she found out what her trial was. So, I thought, maybe someone hid it in the house? I began to search again. I've almost looked through the whole house, Dad, I haven't found a thing." I dropped my shoulders and hunched slightly, feeling defeated. If someone had broken into the house, I would have met them down the hall with nothing but a kitchen knife. I realized that was dangerous and stupid. Maybe I did need to go to hunter boot camp.

Dad raised his hands to his temples and closed his eyes for a moment while he took a deep breath. When he eventually let it out, he cracked up and laughed.

"Dells, it was me. I unlocked the door, came in and realized I'd forgotten some papers that I wanted to bring you. So, I left to grab it from the office."

I stared at him, feeling a little silly for running around the house with a knife. Twice. Not that I was going to tell him that.

"I believe I have the details for your next trial," he says. He snickered as he held his hands up, then reached for his briefcase. I recognized the papers he pulled out of the briefcase; they were the same copied book pages that had been in the box containing my present from the Queen.

He laid out the pages on his desk, looking defeated. He ran a hand through his hair and sighed. He shuffled the pages around and put them in some sort of order.

"We didn't think much of it at first," he began, as he shuffled them around. He started writing on a blank piece of paper. "I recognized them immediately as pages from the Tenebris Librir, but in the actual Tenebris Librir, there are no highlighted letters, and when you put the pages in the order, it spells out a message." He finished writing and handed it to me.

Dig to your roots, and you will find,
Something you have left behind,
Find it not and you will see,
A Seelie queen, you will not be.

"What does it mean?" I asked aloud, but it was more of a question for myself and not my dad.

"I'm not sure Dells, I'm pretty sure that's the trial part." I took a photo of it on my to send to Jackie. "Now, clean my office." The front door opened and closed again. "And look, just in time." Anna had followed our voices and entered the office. "Help." He smiled at Anna and left us to it, leaving her to stare at me in confusion.

She scanned the messy room. "What was that all about? Why does the house look like it's been ransacked?"

Instead of responding, I handed her the riddle. Her eyes read over it, and I saw the wheels turning in her head, but she didn't say a word.

She took a seat in Dad's office chair as I started putting books back.

"I think it's obvious," Anna finally spoke. "'Dig to your roots.' It means where you're from, where the life of Adella Shenning began."

"But something I have left behind? I was only a child when I left, Anna."

"There must be something. We need to go there and see if we can figure it out."

"So, a road trip?"

She looked at me with a twinkle in her eye.

"Road triiiipppp!" She sang back.

"Clean house first," Dad sang loudly from the kitchen.

Anna jumped up out of the chair to help me, and I, with more vigor than five minutes ago, began speeding up cleaning. A road trip was precisely what we needed. We could use it as a celebration of my new-found freedom thanks to my new car.

I looked at my phone to find a new text from Jackie.

It would seem the Queen knows something we don't know.

The Queen would have had to go to great lengths to dig into our pasts. Either that or she'd been planning this for a very long time.

Cleaning took the rest of the day. By the time the sun was setting, we were picking up the last of the items I had haphazardly

315

spread across the living room. We went to my room to pack our things. Anna stared at the unopened package on my bed.

"You're not going to open that?" She pointed to the present.

I shrugged my shoulders. I probably should've, so I could've thanked him, especially since we were leaving in the morning for God knew how long. I walked over and sat on the bed, picking the gift up awkwardly in my hands. I gave it a once over before setting it back on the bed.

Anna sat across from me, fidgeting impatiently, her eyes bulging out of her head. Anna's emotions and feelings radiated out of her; she was excited and giddy. I tried to feed off her energy, so I could feel similarly.

Physically I saw her relax more, no longer was she picking impatiently at her fingernails. Finally, I felt a little more ready. I took off the ribbon and slid my fingers under the corner of the paper, flipping the tape off both ends. Instead of tearing the paper off, I unfolded it.

"Oh my gosh." Anna gasped as if the gift was the most exciting thing she could fathom. This was the reaction I felt I should be having. "Wait." She paused, studying the box. "What is it?" She was less excited, more inquisitive now.

"I… don't know," I responded. I held the box in my hand but it appeared to be just that. A pretty, antique box.

Putting it down on the bed, I opened it. Inside sat a light gray, leather-bound journal. It had flowers burned into the leather and it was tied with a thin ribbon. Next to the journal was a beautiful, feathered quill and a small jar of ink. I had never used a quill before. They were outdated, but this one was gorgeous. I didn't recognize the bird's feather; it had streaks of gold and silver.

I took the journal out of the box and untied the leather, so I could flip through the pages a couple of times. Inside, the pages were blank.

My dad tapped on my open bedroom door to make us aware of his presence. I looked up and smiled. He entered and joined us in sitting on the bed.

He motioned to the present in my hands.

"It's a ravens journal," he announced. "Alaric must have known you'd be leaving home for a while. When you write with the quill in the journal, Alaric can read it from a replica journal he has."

"That is actually—"

"—really cool," Anna interrupted. "Like texting back and forth before phones." Anna reached out toward me, so I handed her the journal. She studied it, flipped through the blank pages, then gave it back.

"So, you're going back to Oregon, then?" My dad asked.

"We have to start somewhere," I said. "Rainier, Oregon is where I was born. So, the riddle must want me to go there, to see what I've left behind."

"Dells, be careful. I know you're an adult now, and you can make your own decisions, but some things are better left unknown."

I eyed him suspiciously. *Does he know something that I don't?*

33

I nodded, more confused than anything. My dad leaned over, kissed my forehead, and left the room. Anna and I grabbed a couple of bags from the closet and packed some clothes, not knowing what we would need on our trip. I packed four outfits, two sweaters, and the necessities. Anna, on the other hand, savagely dug through her clothes, my clothes and even made a trip to my dad's closet (why exactly, I did not know), and filled three to four bags full of clothing.

Anna stretched and I heard her yawn as she crawled into the bed, I wasn't quite done packing yet though. I made sure to bring my new journal and the meditation crystal from Luxor. It was odd that I felt like I needed to take the presents from the two men in my life. Thank goodness I had a double bed, because Anna was already snoring, so I knew if I scooted to the far edge of the bed and put my earplugs in I could drown out her snore just enough to fall asleep.

I slept hard. I didn't remember falling asleep or waking up at all. It wasn't total blackness where I felt like I was falling into oblivion, but it was indeed peaceful. Before I knew it, my alarm pierced through my slumber at 5 am. We needed to be on the road before the morning traffic hit, so we could reach Oregon tomorrow evening. We planned on stopping halfway and staying at a motel on route.

If the world wasn't so crazy right now, we would go through the passage to the Seelie Kingdom and exit through the passage leading to California's outskirts. It would cut our trip time in half, but with everything going on, we decided it would have been far riskier, since we had no idea what the Queen was planning.

I threw on a pair of jeans, adding the harness and knife that Madeline gave me for my birthday. I expected it to feel awkward. Instead, it was comfortable, and I soon forgot it was there. It was easy to conceal. I put on an oversized comfy sweater that just covered the edge of the knife. Going somewhere without my dad for the first time made me feel unexpectedly nervous, so knowing I had the small knife helped because I had protection within arm's length.

Packing the car felt surreal. It was just Anna and me against whatever was waiting for me in Oregon. I hugged my dad and climbed into the driver's seat. My feelings were torn between

320

being ready to take on anything that came our way and to head back to the safety of the house and my dad.

It felt like a huge milestone, pulling out of the driveway. The baby bird was finally flying from the nest.

Anna plugged her phone into the dash and cranked the music up, and so the first hour and a half were fun. We sang at the top of our lungs and enjoyed the music. Anna's playlist made a loop, the second time around the music played, it was still enjoyable. We threw our arms up, knowing the words to the songs better this time and trying our hardest to keep up and sing in tune. By the third time, we silently nodded our heads up and down to the music. The novelty soon wore off as the songs repeated themselves. Every song dragged on and felt like an eternity. It dawned on us that we still had 20 more hours to go.

We stopped to get some food and gas. Anna pumped the gas while I went inside. I grabbed the greasiest, worst convenience-store-food I could find. I wanted to make the most of this trip. When I came out, I found her talking to a guy who was at another pump. From what I could hear, it was a conversation that seemed a bit too friendly — in fact, a closer look at the guy revealed precisely why she was cozying up to a so-called stranger.

"Henry?" I asked as I approached the guy.

He jumped slightly and lifted his hands as if he'd been caught red-handed. He turned to face her. "Hey Adella," he said slowly, measuring my reaction. "Fancy meeting you here."

"Oh, I'm sure it is," I retorted. "Seriously, he has you guys following us?"

"Can you blame him, Dells?" Anna piped up. "Someone did just try to kill me a little over a week ago."

"Fine, but stay back, this is a girls-only trip," I announced.

"I'm just your typical bystander getting gas," he said innocently, making exaggerated movements when putting the gas hose back.

We got into the car and I handed Anna her food. She smiled at me.

"How long have you known?"

"I saw them pull onto the exit with us," she shrugged. "It's only a big deal if you make it a big deal. Alaric is just worried."

"Fine."

I shoved a jalapeño popper into my mouth. Fighting was pointless anyways. They were coming whether I liked it or not.

I drove back onto the road. Anna turned the music down. She was probably tired of hearing the same songs. The atmosphere had officially faded, and the reality of what we were doing set in — driving for over 20 hours, to a place I hadn't been to since I was a toddler, to look for something I had 'forgotten.'

I bought way too much food. We ate corn dogs, cheap chili nachos, the rest of the poppers, yet there were still three bags of food left over. Anna carefully bagged the food and put it on the backseat.

"Pretty sure it'll still be good later."

Out of the corner of my eye, I saw Anna stiffen and glance from the side-view mirror to the rearview. I felt the stress and anxiety spilling out of her. I peered into the rearview mirror.

I spotted the guard's car close to us, alongside two other cars that seemed to just be other people. However, a fourth car was accelerating in the left lane, trying to get past the guards. I shifted my gaze to the road, but kept glancing into the rearview mirror. The unknown white car relentlessly accelerated. I shot a look at Anna, who kept flitting between the mirrors.

"Dells, drive. We need to get away from that car." Panic filled Anna's voice.

"I am. Let me know what they're doing, Anna, okay?"

Fear washed over me. My heart thumped in time with the engine as I accelerated hard. I was above the speed limit now. I no longer felt completely in control of the steering wheel as the speedometer ticked upward.

This car wasn't made to speed, and it protested as I accelerated further. I flicked the 'sport mode' but it didn't shift. Anna leaned over and switched the joystick from D to M.

"This is manumatic," she announced proudly. "I'm going to shift down so you can speed up quickly, and then when we get to the right speed, I'll put it back."

The car whined again as she shifted down but began to pick up speed with a little more enthusiasm. We were inching toward the end of the speedometer.

Is this the Queen's doing? Why would she do this if she wanted me in Oregon?

Anna interrupted my thoughts to give me a commentary.

"Okay, Dells, eyes on the road but…the white car and the guards are neck and neck."

Bile rose in my throat, and I couldn't help to disobey her and see for myself.

They were indeed side by side, but the guard's car kept veering into the white car, clipping it. I looked back to the road, so we didn't crash, but then I heard the worst screeching noise. My gaze snapped back to the rearview mirror and the scene unfolding held me there.

The guards veered once more into the unknown car; both lost control and spun off the freeway.

Eyes snapped back to the road, I slowed down, so we didn't crash too. Both cars were nowhere to be seen.

Anna was hyperventilating in the seat and I returned to the rearview mirror. The hairs on the back of my neck rose as we saw a black car right behind us. I heard a gasp, and looked at Anna. There was another black car on our right. I checked the left. We were surrounded.

"Step on it, Dells! I've never seen them before," Anna yelled.

Fear poured out of her, matching my own. I accelerated once again, trying to make sure I remembered to breathe.

"Go to the right! Take the exit!" She screeched and pointed.

I followed her instructions to a tee, waiting until the very last moment before I swerved, shifting lanes. I pressed my horn and cut through a few cars in the lanes. One of the slick, black cars caught up to us on our right, getting closer and closer. I semi-panicked and almost froze. I accelerated further, passed the car and Anna yanked the wheel farther to the right to overtake it and get into the next lane after. It was clear we had won this dangerous game of chicken. We made the exit, scraping passed the car and almost crashing. I remembered to breathe, but it wasn't over yet. Two out of the three cars had made the exit.

Anna had spotted them too. "Now, let off the gas a bit and keep driving straight, even when the road ends, keep going."

I did as she said, but couldn't help but look back. The cars were getting closer. The knots in my stomach tightened as I turned around to spot a sign in the middle of the road, blocking our way forward. It indicated that I could turn left or right, but not straight ahead.

"Anna are you sure?"

"Yes, Dells, do it!"

I stepped on the gas again and drove straight over the sign, denting my new car and taking the sign out. Relentless, the cars didn't hesitate before following me off-road and into the desert.

"Now really step on it, Dells," she yelled, shifting the car back into M.

I didn't know if the car would survive its first trip at this point. In the distance ahead, I saw a row of grey buildings. As we approached them, I saw they were covered in colorful graffiti. I started to turn but Anna grabbed the wheel again.

"No, speed up, it's a passage to the Unseelie Kingdom." She sounded confident, but one look in her eyes told me she was anything but.

I sped up, placing my trust in Anna's snap judgment. Hopefully, she was right. Before we hit the buildings, the graffiti caught my attention. The word, "Unseelie" was clearly scrawled across the building. Before my head processed any of this, we reached the walls.

We reached the other side of the wall, and so did one of the cars, following closely behind. I put a little distance between us and that was when I heard it. The roar of a different engine. We watched with bated breath as a black SUV T-boned into the side of the car. I slammed on my brakes, jerking us both forward slightly. Not the smoothest of breaking. I slowed and veered to the right to park.

Anna opened the door frantically and fell out onto the ground, throwing up. After all the greasy food, the adrenaline, and fear from being chased, mixed with the smell of her vomit, my stomach was close to puking too.

"You are so lucky you got to drive during that," Anna said in between heaves.

"Next time, be my guest and take the wheel," I told her. The adrenaline coursing through me made my hands shake on the wheel.

I opened the driver's door and took a few gulps of fresh air. Alaric stepped into view, blocking the opening my car door had created.

"Take the exit on the north side of the Kingdom; it will put you out by Salem, Oregon, I can't guarantee no one will know the route you take or follow you there, but I will have the guards follow close behind and keep an eye out for any other unwelcome guests. We have caught one of the people that was in the car following you, the other one died in the crash. We will question him as soon as he's awake."

I looked back at the mess that was the car that'd followed us. Smoke drifted up from the bonnet. The SUV had destroyed it.

Alaric grabbed my car door and slammed it shut abruptly. Clearly, stretching my legs wasn't an option. I rolled the window down, and Alaric bent down to tell me something. Only he said nothing. Instead, he did something that shocked me. He brought his lips to mine for an abrupt and very public goodbye kiss, only making it harder to want to leave. My cheeks flushed as all of his guards stopped in the background to watch the display.

He pulled back just enough to whisper, "Have fun," sweetly against my lips.

He took a small step back. I looked past him and spotted Luxor amongst the small crowd that had gathered. Luxor was silent, but I felt his eyes bore into me.

I took a deep breath and pushed the button to turn the car on again. It groaned to life. I didn't say a word as I stepped back on

327

the gas and left, not enjoying the audience surrounding the car. Saying goodbye to Alaric felt too permanent, so I didn't. Anna slammed her car door shut.

"And we're off," she forced out. Everyone standing around the vehicle stepped out of the way to let me pass. I drove off, making my way to the north edge of town as fast as I could.

34

Salem was beautiful. The air's humidity tripled within moments of exiting the gate. The sudden change made it hard to breathe at first. The air was saturated with the scent of evergreen — a familiar, pleasant aroma that I hadn't been around in a long time. I rolled the window down slightly so I could take in the scent. Trees, moss, and green surround us as we wound down the hillside roads, making our way to Rainier. The clear view of the snow-tipped mountains was undeniably stunning. I couldn't remember the last time I saw snow.

The journey to the house Dad had rented for us lasted a little over an hour and a half. It was roughly 15 minutes' drive from the house I grew up in. I switched places with Anna, letting her drive the rest of the way. This way, I was able to get some rest and take in the luscious green scenery around me. I tilted my head against the window and watched the deep browns and alternating shades of green pass us by.

Anna's driving was much faster than my own. I didn't know if she'd even kept to the speed limit. Driving through Clatskanie, she managed to slyly talk herself out of two tickets, then receive three more tickets, which was impressive considering I was pretty sure there were only five people in the small town's police force. After she received her third ticket, I saw the frustration coloring her face. She always had a way with words, and for some reason, people here saw right through her. She slowed down to only going 10mph over the limit. She sat at a comfortable pace until we reached the little brick house where we spent the next seven days. The outside of the house was simple and charming, the brick was painted white, and it had a pine-green door and yellow shutters.

I was anxious to leave the car. My legs were stiff, and my tailbone officially numb. I stepped out into the thick fresh air that reminded me of my childhood. When we stopped, I attempted to get out of the car but Anna stopped me, holding her hand up, gesturing for me to wait. She locked the car doors and proceeded to march up to the front door of the house. She typed in the code and searched the building.

It felt like an eternity before she came back, and I was stuck there like a sitting duck. I fidgeted and flicked the lock on my door up and down repeatedly. I knew she'd be upset if I left without her giving me the all-clear, so I stayed put. Five minutes later she appeared in the doorway and gave me a thumbs-up, before jogging back to the car. We fetched our belongings from the trunk and headed inside.

As I looked around, I realized that this house was way too big for just two of us staying here. But it was just us in the house.

The decor was homey, almost cabin-like. Everything was made out of small pieces of logs; the decoration on the inside consisted of different shades of tans and browns — very shabby chic. I could tell it was someone's home, from little touches like homemade quilts and personalized pictures on the walls. It was immaculate and welcoming. In the living room, I thought there was a fireplace inside, considering there was a small chimney on the roof. Instead there was a small pellet stove with instructions on how to fill it taped to the nearest wall.

I tossed my bag into one of the three bedrooms. There was a queen bed, and although I probably wouldn't use it, an empty dresser. My dad rented this house for a month. He hoped we would come home sooner, but made sure we could use it for longer if we needed to. This was one of the only available homes in Rainier on the site he used. There were a lot of motels a town or two over, in Longview, Kelso, and even more so if we drove 30 more minutes to stay in Portland. I really wanted to stay back in Rainier, where I was born and lived the early years of my life.

Rainier had a strange, yet familiar feel. I remembered the scent of the evergreen trees and the thick green moss that coated the ground as I ran barefoot when I was little. I didn't have any solid memories in Rainier, though, I was only four when we left. I

331

looked out the back windows of the house into the dense forest behind it. There were a couple of deer and bunnies in the forest, which I certainly didn't see in Arizona. I thought I'd feel more at home looking into the dense green fairytale-like land, but sadly it appeared strange and foreign to me.

Anna, in an attempt to not startle me, carefully walked up behind me. I could scarcely hear her footsteps.

"What now?" She questioned.

I took a deep breath. "Now, we have to go back to the home I was born in and pray whoever is currently living there is willing to humor us."

"We could come up with a story," Anna suggested. "Like we're weary travelers and need a place to sleep for the night."

I couldn't tell if Anna was joking or not. Her idea sounded like the beginning of a terrible horror movie.

"Probably not, Anna." Something caught my eyes and I turned to look out the window that Anna was already staring out of. One of the bunnies was gone, but it was so quick I missed how it had happened. "What was that?"

Anna's eyes widened as she leaned closer to the window to get a better view of something. "I'm fairly certain I saw a gremlin."

"Fairly certain?"

Shrugging her shoulders, she said, "I've only ever actually seen a few."

"Are they supposed to be in the forests here?" I asked, curiously.

"Technically, they can live anywhere, but it's not very common to see them around the human world. At least it's not supposed to be very common."

I stretched my arms out and fell onto the bed. Anna joined me, pushing the bags onto the floor. It was only then I realized she had also brought her things into this room too. It looked like we'd be bunking together again, which did not come as a huge surprise, as the other rooms were down the hall, and it wasn't safe to have too much distance between us.

"I think I'm going to end things with Henry," Anna said out of the blue.

"If you can say it like that, without a hint of remorse, I probably would too."

"I shouldn't feel remorse though. Things just aren't working."

Things looked pretty friendly back at the gas station, but who was I to judge? It wasn't my business to decide who she did and didn't date.

"Also, I want to get my hair done while we're here. I need a change," she laughed but it sounded forced.

"Let's do it now!" I suggested, although I really didn't want to get back into the car. Anna needed a pick-me-up, and I needed lunch.

We grabbed our wallets and headed back out the door. Driving into downtown Rainier, I remembered there were a few food options, but it was smaller than I remembered. We settled for what looked like a little convenience store, but had a restaurant seating area in the back and boasted of having "the best burgers in town." The decor was simple, black and white tiles, and shabby signs, it seemed shabby was a common theme here.

I couldn't attest to whether they were the "best burgers," but they were indeed astonishing. The menu boasted of the homemade, thick juicy burgers, topped with sliced cheese, local produce, and their own special sauce. They didn't disappoint. I couldn't quite place the ingredients in the sauce. It was tangy and sweet at the same time. Unlike the last food we ate from a convenience store, this surprisingly felt and tasted like a meal from home. We were the only ones in the restaurant area. Not many passersby were in the storefront, which was nice because we didn't have to be on edge while we ate.

We stayed a few more minutes at the booth to let the food settle down. There were two nice ladies behind the counter who checked on us a few times. I was enjoying the friendly-small-town atmosphere just as much as I enjoyed the food. Though Tombstone was a small town, it didn't always feel like it, especially with everything going on. We left a decent tip on the counter and headed back to the car. There weren't many hair salons in town, so we drove across the bridge into Longview.

In town, there were four or five salons. Anna wanted a dramatic new change, so we opted for the most expensive one — a little boutique on the corner of Commerce. It had a pink awning out front and decals on their windows in the shapes of scissors. Walking in the room, the scent of high-end beauty products was heavy. Upon closer look at the products, it turned out to be their personal line. The bottles were pink with tiny ribbons around the top and fancy black script writing on the bottles.

We were greeted by a friendly receptionist. "Do you have an appointment?" She asked. Anna shook her head. The receptionist pursed her ruby-red lips. "I'm sure I can squeeze you in if you go take a seat over there."

She pointed to a cozy waiting area with small white leather couches. We sat down in silence as the hairdressers worked around us. We heard snipping of hair being cut and several hairdryers. Anna anxiously waited for her turn and bounced her leg up and down, running her hands through her long red mane of hair.

"Anna?" A stylist called out. Anna rose from the chair and gestured for me to follow, so I did.

As she sat in the small black chair, the stylist examined her mane. He lifted it, zhuzhed it, and threw it up and carefully observed where it fell. His eyes lit up as they made eye contact via the mirror.

"You have stunning hair. What am I doing with it today?" He asked.

"Well, whatever you want."

My eyes widened — she didn't even have a plan. She was putting the fate of her hair into the hands of a total stranger.

He clapped his hands and jumped up in excitement. He gave her hair a thorough second examination, tsk-ing a couple of times, then turned her away from the mirror.

"I know just what to do," he said as he began tying a small white piece of paper around her neck and gave her a black apron.

Anna was radiating calmness, completely at ease, where I seemed to be more nervous than she was. The stylist took out sheers, a razor, a water bottle, and a pick, and went to work. He didn't waste any time. He parted her hair so only a small section on the right was on the left. Picking up his razor out, he shaved the whole section off. She raised her eyebrows as I detected a hint of panic in her aura.

"Trust me, you will look fabulous." He promised.

He then used the same sheers with a different tool to carefully draw a design into the smooth part of her head. I couldn't make out what it was. He didn't wet her hair as he cut it in layers, sifting through the curls while making each cut. I could tell he was experienced with cutting curly hair. While cutting, the ringlets fell precisely in the place he wanted them. Her hair started to look more natural and tamed.

My eyes followed hers to where she eyed up the mass of hair on the floor. She had so much hair, it only made sense for there to be loads on the floor. After every snip, it was almost like he hadn't done anything at all because of how much there was.

He finally dampened her hair, brushing it entirely out. He used his fingers to rake through what looked like their signature leave-in conditioner. The stylist stepped back for a moment, studying her face, before holding up his hand for her to wait a moment. He disappeared from view before he reappeared with a tray of tools. He clipped in a few feathers in different spots on her hair.

"When you shower, as the conditioner sits in your hair, brush it well, and only after you brush it, do you rinse the conditioner out. When you get out, do not brush it again, it will help your curls dry together. Put a little of this in it, run your fingers through and let it air dry." He handed her an unopened jar of the conditioner he had just used on her hair. He gave her a reassuring smile before spinning her chair around in a dramatic fashion, so she could see her reflection.

She gasped quietly when she saw the new Anna. She still had a wild mane, but it was carefully placed on one side, showing off the side shave that was feminine, but somehow made her look edgier, more threatening. In the side shave, he had carefully sculpted a little flower, giving it a delicate touch. The feathers stood out slightly, but held a slight curl as well, which made them also blend in. The rest of her hair sat in perfect, frizz-less, ringlets on the side of her head. It was a little past her shoulder and it was still long enough to tie up for her training. He had taken some of the volume out, so while it did have body to it, it no longer took over her whole head anymore.

"It's perfect," she whispered. The stylist grinned at her, clearly pleased with his handiwork. "Thank you so much."

"You are very welcome." He began sweeping around her, cleaning up the endless amount of hair from the floor.

Anna stood up, playing with her hair for a moment before throwing her arms around the stunned hairstylist. Leaving him shocked, she bounced off to pay with the receptionist.

As we left, she ran her fingers through her ringlets a few more times. Using the mirror above her, she began admiring herself for a bit.

"We should go out tonight!" She exclaimed.

35

To prepare for our night out, we had to return to the house —
my current attire of leggings and a baggy t-shirt weren't fit for our
night out. Meanwhile, Anna was wearing a black pair of skinny
jeans and a simple black blouse, which she could wear literally
anywhere and fit in. We Googled places we could go. Since we
weren't familiar with the town, we settled for a small club called
"Fae" in Portland — quite an ironic name that amused us greatly.

I lamely dug through my luggage, realizing that I hadn't
brought a nice outfit to wear out. I tried two of the three outfits I
had before sighing and admitting defeat. Anna held up one of her
bags with a confident I-told-you-so grin. She opened the top and
pulled out two neatly packed going-out ensembles.

"You can never be too prepared," she pointed out.

"Speaking of prepared Anna, who the heck do you think was chasing us earlier?" Even thinking about the car chase gave me anxiety, the hairs on my arms raised.

Anna picked a loose sequin blouse and a tight mid-thigh length leather skirt. Her outfit was gorgeous. After, she began laying an arsenal of weapons out on the bed. Her face turned serious, I could practically see the thoughts swimming around her head.

"Honestly, I can't help but wonder if it was the people killing protectors, although I have also considered that maybe it was the queen."

I considered this information for a moment "Why the queen though? I mean yes, we saw what she did with Lilah, but she couldn't drain me if I was already dead." *Could she?*

"You assume she wants you dead, I assumed she was trying to scare you into failing your trial, if those cars really wanted to catch us, they could have. But, I think there was some hesitation." She laid the last knife onto the bed.

"How are you going to bring all of those?" I asked curiously.

"Carefully," she said, as she began attaching holsters to herself — one on her right thigh, and one around her waist under her loose blouse. She had a built-in holster on her bra and used the back of her skirt to carefully conceal a small handgun. By the time she was done, she had managed to conceal three knives, two guns, and I think about five throwing stars — not to mention the pepper spray in her purse, and a small, pink pocket knife.

"What's the small knife in your purse for?"

"A distraction from the real weapons. Now it's your turn. Get dressed."

I had no clue what she meant by the distraction, but I looked at the little black item she had taken out for me on the bed next to her.

"But if we see them again, I'll pay more attention," Anna promised me, or maybe it was a promise to herself. "I was so overwhelmed by what was going on, I completely missed the details that mattered, faces, plate numbers and even how many there were eluded me. I saw the few that were directly behind us, but I was so distracted I didn't bother to check if there were others." Anna looked down and away from me, shame clouded her thoughts.

Anna carefully threw me the mini black dress and I held it up to myself. I slipped my shirt off, then put the dress over my head and down, before sliding my pants off. It was just long enough to conceal my thigh holster that had my new knife. Anna handed me a pair of black, sparkly flats to wear, put my hair into two French braids down the sides, painted my face for me, and threw in some hoop earrings. Looking into the mirror, I almost didn't recognize myself. The black eyeliner and fake lashes she'd put on my eyes really brought out the gold hiding in amongst the dark, murky brown. I was wearing no lipstick either because she handed me a clear lip gloss — probably because the makeup around my eyes was so dark.

The drive to Portland wasn't too long. We arrived just as it was getting dark. I stopped to grab a couple of my favorite energy drinks on the way. It had been a long day, and Anna had an endless amount of energy that I wanted to match. Turning onto the road to the club, we spotted the line stretching out the door. I parked a block away. It took me an embarrassing amount of time to figure out how to pay for parking, but we managed it. The anticipation from the club outing seemed to be putting Anna in a better mood.

Walking to the club's entrance, I tried to remember what other clubs looked like as we passed them, just in case this one doesn't pan out. Lights and music filled the tiny street, as people milled about waiting to go into clubs.

The line was long and it was chilly out. Apparently, Anna had no interest in waiting, so she headed straight past the people waiting patiently in line and marched up to the bouncer whom, I might add, was a lot less intimidating than I thought a bouncer would be. There was no way he was over five feet.He was abnormally scrawny and had bright blue hair. He stood somewhat confidently, puffing out what chest he had out as if he was holding his breath.

He didn't object to Anna as she approached and asked him, which made the girl in the front of the line roll her eyes.

"Purse, please." The guy requested, in a deep voice that didn't match his outward appearance.

Anna handed her purse over to him, he gave her a stern look as he pulled the pink knife out. She looked at him with a face of pure innocence.

"Would you like to go put this back in your car?" It was phrased like a question, though it sounded more like an order. Anna didn't like to be ordered around like that.

"No, you can just throw it away." She gave him a genuinely sweet grin and a flirty wink as he gestured for us both to enter. Unbeknownst to him, he had just let a whole weapons store walk right past him.

For my first club experience, I was surprisingly unimpressed. The stench of feet and sweat hit us as we entered. People's bodies were mangled together in the low light. It looked smaller on the inside. The outside gave off a huge presence. I attempted to make my way to the bar, but Anna grabbed my wrist, shook her head, and pointed to a set of stairs where a couple was walking up. We followed suit, up the flight of stairs. We went through a door to the right, where there was another door guarded by a bouncer. He was only letting in certain people.

This bouncer was much larger, with broader shoulders and a face that said, "try me, I dare you."

Anna smiled at him, and his eyes widened as he gave us a once over. A single nod of the head and we were both in. He watched us go all the way into the room before shutting the door securely behind us.

This room was significantly bigger, however people were still dancing in a mass form in the middle of the floor, all touching in one way or another. However, the outskirts had enough room to maneuver around to get drinks, and the music was faded enough so I could hear what people were saying.

I had a funny feeling that I was being watched. I turned around and found multiple sets of eyes staring directly at me, proving that I wasn't wrong. Anna came back from the bar and handed me a gorgeous neon purple drink. I took a sip.

"Ehhh," was pretty much the sound that escaped my lips. I felt my face scrunching up. I tried to play it cool, but I could still feel the odd burning sensation of the weird drink. It had tasted like a mix of lilac, rubbing alcohol and habaneros. "What is that?" I asked Anna who is sipping on her drink nonchalantly.

"It's the signature "Fae" drink. The guy at the bar said it was his specialty."

I glanced over to the bartender who was watching me with hopeful eyes. I quickly wiped the sour look off my face and gave him a big thumbs up. He gave me a thumbs-up back and returned to his work. This was alcohol. That explained the weird taste. I looked at the bar behind the bartender. It was covered in rows and rows of liquor.

Anna was fanning herself with something dramatically, she paused and handed me the small item she was fanning herself with. The picture was her, but the name was unfamiliar.

"Denise Townhowser, 34? Seriously, Anna, you could barely pass for 12!" I examined the card in my hands, and noticed it was a fake and there were bubbles in the laminating job.

"He seemed to believe it." She gave the bartender a wink and a small wave, and he nodded her way.

"I think he drinks one too many of his own cocktails," I responded. "No more of those for me please, I'll drive home."

Anna shrugged and grabbed my drink, too.

"Your loss." She grinned and downed both drinks. She glanced at her watch, "Oooooh. Come on! We need to dance!" She pulled me into the middle of the crowd on the dance floor.

The music was so loud I felt the vibrations from the speakers through the floor. In the one spot I was trying to stay in, I felt five different bodies moving to the beat around me. I was not much of a dancer, but it was easy keeping up with this group. Most weren't dancing — well all except one, who made me feel inadequate compared to her smooth dance moves.

It was Anna, twirling and shimmying in front of me. Her sequins dazzled under the lights. She was dancing gracefully without a care in the world around and through the crowd, managing to not touch a single person. I could tell she was starting to feel the effects of the alcohol, as her emotions heightened and clouded slightly. She wasn't drunk so I wasn't worried, but it was enough for me to notice.

She glanced at her watch again. She'd been looking every few minutes as if she was waiting for something or someone. She

345

looked at me and started yelling a countdown, and without even knowing why, everyone around her joined in.

"...7, 6, 5, 4, 3, 2, 1. Happy birthday, Dells!" Anna shouted to me above the music. I'd forgotten it was my birthday.

All around me, everything shifted and changed. What I thought was a crowd of overly sweaty young men and women, transformed into people of many colors and sizes, varying from dark blue to neon yellow — some of which I was hoping was some type of neon paint. I watched in wonder as the world transformed around me. The dancers still danced together, but now they seemed much more diverse, as the entire crowd upstairs, belonged to the Fay world. I looked over at the bartender, who now I saw was a bright blue elf. He held up his glass, smiled, and shot it. I threw my head back and joined in, feeling freer than I had in weeks — months even. The atmosphere was euphoric and I fed off the crowd's energy. It was almost like a high. I mean, it could have been the effects of the alcohol that I had, but either way, I didn't care. The world around me was bright, colorful and happy, and it was intoxicating,

I started feeling dizzy. I looked around, and it was as if everyone moved in slow motion. I felt a heavy tap on my shoulder and turned to see a familiar face in the crowd. Luxor. I grinned, grabbed his shoulders, and planted a big sloppy kiss on his lips. He grabbed my arms and held me. Not for the kiss — he was holding me upright.

346

"Hey, Luxor!" I pulled back slightly and shouted to him gleefully.

He tried to coax me into sitting down and not dance. It didn't work entirely as I managed to still dance to the loud hypnotic beat.

Luxor gave me one of his swooning smiles, and I nearly melted. "What has she had to drink?" He called over to Anna.

"Not nearly enough," she yelled back, laughing. She stopped dancing to watch me for a minute. I didn't know why, but she was looking at me weird. I was having a great time. Anna came close to me, so on impulse, I grabbed her shoulders and gave her a big kiss too. She seemed like she needed cheering up. She stepped back, aghast, causing me to let go of her shoulders. I fell into Luxor's arms, the world spinning faster and faster around me.

The euphoric feeling was now overwhelming as it clouded all my rational thoughts and feelings. The music around me pounded in my ears, and I held onto Luxor to stay upright. I could feel the permanent cheesy smile plastered to my face as I swayed to the beat. I attempted to dance once more, still hanging onto Luxor for dear life, but I was the only one moving. Anna and Luxor didn't look like they were having much fun anymore.

"I think she's feeding on the intoxicated emotions in the room," Luxor yelled to Anna.

Half understanding what they were saying, I looked back and forth between them as if I was watching a tennis match. Concern filled her face, as she walked back over to me, put her hand on me lightly and closed her eyes. I sensed her calm aura and pulled my arm away. It was killing my buzz.

"Let's get her out of here," Anna said. But I stood my ground.

"I don't want to go," I whined. I was happy where I was. I tried breaking away from Luxor so they couldn't make me leave, but he held my arms firmly but gently. I had no choice but to let them lead me out of the club, just when I was finally able to see the real world around me — the world I belonged in.

"Noo."

I felt the buzz fade quickly as they loaded me into the backseat of the car. Out here, in the fresh air, around only the concerned emotions of my friends, the dizziness disappeared and my mind began to clear. Thinking back to just moments ago, I realized how out of character my pleas to stay at the club sound.

I took a moment to analyze what was happening around me. Anna climbed into the front passenger seat and Luxor into the driver seat. They were whispering about something I couldn't quite understand. But things were becoming clearer by the minute.

"What are you doing here, Luxor?" I asked slightly annoyed that I felt as if I had a babysitter in town.

"I was invited to come here."

"By who?" Certainly not from me; this was our girl's trip.

"That's the weird part. It didn't specify. There was just a date and address on the invitation. I thought it was too close to you to be a coincidence and decided to come down immediately. Thank God I did." He gave me an exacerbated look as if he was scolding me. "No way Anna would have been able to get you out of that club alone — who knows what kind of trouble you would have gotten into."

"And the date and address happened to lead you to the club we were at?" I looked accusingly at Luxor.

"No. The date and address are for tomorrow. I hacked into the Ring security system at your rental, so I could pick my room and saw the footage of you two leaving, all dolled up. So then I followed the location settings on your phone, I linked them to mine when I was assigned to be your protector, and ended up here," he paused awkwardly for a second. "For your protection of course."

Luxor was so matter-of-fact about all of this. It was almost as if he didn't see what was wrong with his story, how odd all of this sounded. *How creepy it sounded.*

I thought over this for a moment. "What happened to me in there?" I asked.

"I have two theories. One: someone slipped something into your drin—"

"—not a chance in hell, I was super careful." Anna interrupted.

"Precisely, which leads me to believe that the intoxication was like an emotion, and Dells was able to feed off of it. It makes sense if you think about it." He paused, before continuing. "Alcohol

350

alters a person, I could see how it could be fed off like it was an emotion of its own."

"Wow," I whispered. *I now have my head back to myself.* My eyes felt heavy, drained from the night. I had to concentrate hard to try to stay awake. The car halted, and I jerked awake but soon felt my eyelids grow heavy again.

"Don't worry, Dells, I've got you." Strong arms picked me up from the backseat of the car, cradling me close to his chest and carrying me with ease to the house.

The arms set me on the bed lightly, and Anna came crashing in behind them.

"Night Luxor!" Anna called as she shut the door, crashing into the bed next to me

"Night, guys!" He called back.

Despite my sleepiness, slumber didn't come easy. I was so tired that it was hard to sleep. Tossing and turning all night, I must have kicked Anna a couple of times because I felt her turn and put her arms around me, I relaxed slightly when I sensed her calmness and drifted into a deeper sleep.

Waking up was hard, I felt safe and warm. Anna pulled me in for a tighter hug and it felt nice, cozy even. I drifted back off for a while, but half an hour later I opened my eyes fully, alert. Something was amiss, but I didn't know what. Anna hadn't stirred yet, but I knew I should've pried myself away before I slept the day away. My hands were on her arms, only my fingertips brushed past hair on her arms — a lot of hair. I looked down and my

351

stomach dropped as I realized I wasn't in Anna's arms at all. I looked around me to see Luxor's head close to my neck. Panic flooded me. Luxor stirred.

"Morning, sunshine," Luxor said to me, sleepily.

"Oh my God."

I broke free from his grasp and jumped out of bed. He, too, jumped up out of bed and assumed a fighting stance, as if we were in danger.

"What were you doing?" I asked him accusingly.

"What do you mean? You came into my room."

I looked around the room. It was hard to tell whose room it was because the only difference was the bed sets and bags that were kicked under the bed.

"How did I even get in here?"

"Uhm, you walked in here around 2 am."

Just then, Anna busted through the door in her pajamas and hair in a super messy bun. "Where's the fire?" She yelled. She paused as she took in the scene before her. I was on one side of the bed in nothing but a pajama shirt and black underwear. Luxor was on the other side of the bed. To make matters worse, he was only wearing a pair of grey pajama pants. "Well, then." Anna's eyes were wide as she turned around to leave quickly.

"It's not what it looks like!" I yelled after her as she rushed out of the room.

"Wasn't it?" Luxor raised his eyebrows suggestively.

"No!" I picked up a pillow and threw it hard at his head. He caught it with ease and set it back on the bed. "Seriously, what happened?"

"Nothing." He chuckled. "You came in here half-dead around 2 am, mumbling about how Anna kicked you off the bed. You jumped into my bed — without invitation might I add — and started kicking me. I held onto you to stop your crazy leg spasms, and you went back to bed."

"I'm dating Alaric." *At least I think I am.*

"I didn't say you weren't, but here you are, in bed with me."

Groaning loudly I exited the room, slamming the door on the way out. *Why does dating have to be so complicated? Why does Luxor have to be so complicated?*

I stomped back to my room and slammed that door behind me also, just to make a point. Anna was lying on the bed, looking at me accusingly but saying nothing.

"Nothing happened. Apparently, you kicked me out of bed last night," I explained to Anna.

"I did, but I assumed you would go to the empty room, not the one that was ocupado." Her eyebrows raised in suspicion.

"It was probably because his room is the closest one to ours, and I was exhausted. I don't even remember walking into there. We just slept."

"He's half-dressed, though, and you're half-dressed..." She prodded.

"Because that's how we went to bed in the first place."

She put her headphones back in and turned around slowly. I grabbed a towel and a pair of clothes before running into the bathroom across the hall for a shower. I needed an emotional break from these two.

I turned the water on as hot as it could get as if it could wash away last night, not only waking up in bed next to Luxor but my hazy memory of a swift and extremely messy kiss. There were two baskets on the shelf next to the shower. One said bath bombs, and the other said vapor bombs. I took one of the vapor bombs and threw it into the shower's corner. As it disintegrated, the sweet scent of lavender and roses filled my nostrils and the room.

The soaps that were stocked were homemade — maybe not made here, or by these people, but certainly bought from a farmers market as the label was simple and sweet. I jumped into the scalding water and let it run over my head and neck, washing away the worries and stress I'd been carrying on our trip so far. I was aiming to relax so I could fully enjoy our day of exploring.

I turned the water off and dried myself off with the large, fuzzy towel. I picked my clothes up off the floor and realized I'd forgotten my bra. It was a good thing the towel was big enough to wrap around me. I threw it on, ran a brush through my wet hair, grabbed my clothes on the floor, and headed out of the bathroom.

I went to shut the door, but it wouldn't close. I pulled on it tight a few times, and it finally closed. I turned to walk away, and my towel pulled right off, dropping to the floor — leaving me completely nude. I dropped my clothes and yanked frantically on the towel, realizing it was stuck in the door I had slammed shut.

I heard a door close behind me. I stood up straight and turned around praying it was Anna that was behind me. It wasn't. Luxor and I stood face to face. I used my hands to do my best to cover my privates and act natural, he raised his eyebrows at me and walked a little closer. We were almost nose to nose.

I heard another door close behind Luxor.

"Seriously, guys, get a room!" Anna went back into the room.

Luxor leaned down, reached behind me, and forcefully pushed the bathroom door open, releasing my towel from its grasp. Then he stepped back so I could move without touching him.

He watched me amused, as I tried to bend down casually to grab the towel. Had he no decency? My cheeks were on fire. I snatched up the towel and wrapped it back around me.

"I knew you always found doorknobs tricky. Learned that on day one." He chuckled as he walked away.

Hot tears of frustration flooded my eyes. It had been one hell of a day already and it was only the morning. I wiped them away, picked the rest of my clothes off the floor, and stormed into mine and Anna's room.

"If you guys want me out, you can just tell me," Anna mused.

"Seriously, Anna, not today," I warned.

She shrugged her shoulders and got up. I assumed she was going to get breakfast, which was probably where she was heading when she bumped into Luxor and me again.

I yanked my bra off the closet door knob, where I had hung it yesterday since the black dress didn't require a bra, and got dressed for the day. I had a lot to get done today, but comfort was the only thing I wanted. Heavy drops of water ricocheted off the windows and thumped onto the roof. A baggy sweater, leggings, and the only pair of soft boots I had would have to do. I pinned my hair up into a carefully placed messy bun and put on a bit of gloss. There was no need to pinch my cheeks as they were already red from today's events.

I marched into the kitchen, I dreaded facing Luxor but I needed food. I fetched a bagel out from next to the bread cabinet and made a coffee with a couple of packets of sugar, then turned around to face my friends. Luxor barely glanced up from behind his coffee cup, reading today's newspaper, and Anna was texting wildly on her phone, probably giving my dad a complete recap of our first day in town, no doubt. I sighed as I joined them at the table.

I sat in silence for a while and listened carefully to the birds chirping outside. They were much more sweet and lively than the ones back home. Whistling little tunes and joining into other songs to create perfect little melodies. I grabbed the journal out that I brought so I could send a message to Alaric. Putting my small jar of ink and quill on the table in front of me, I opened to the first page and concentrated.

"You know you need the quill to write, right?" Luxor asked.

"Why don't you just text him Dells?" Anna chimed in.

"Because I wanted to do something personal, something special. I really miss Alaric." I made sure to put extra emphasis on the "really" part, so everybody got the picture.

"Weird," Luxor said as he frowned. "It sure didn't seem like it last night." He sounded annoyed, but I didn't look at his face. I didn't want to give him the satisfaction. I just looked down at my journal. Anna resumed her furious typing.

"Well, good luck with that," Luxor said dismissively. "If you want company that's always around and actually here for you, I'll be back in a couple of hours. I have a meeting."

"Hmm, probably wouldn't even notice if you came back," I remarked snarkily.

"Then maybe I won't." He stood abruptly up, knocking his chair into the wall behind him and headed out the front door, slamming it loudly.

Anna looked up at me, speechless. I wasn't in the mood to talk. We both jumped up, grabbed the keys, and sprinted to the window to watch Luxor leave. The second he pulled out, we ran out to the car and pulled out after him. I wanted to know where he was going but didn't like asking.

Following him down the road, there were only two cars in front of us. I prayed we were far enough back that he didn't notice us following him. It wouldn't take him long to ditch us. Turning onto Atkins Road and driving what felt like up into the mountains, we both lost phone signal. I hoped Luxor hadn't spotted us and was now taking us to a dead-end road to leave us there. He finally pulled into a long wraparound driveway, and we followed through casually, watching him park in front of the little yellow house with a vast barn outback. Looking at the house, I felt it was familiar.

"Pull back around to it," I told Anna.

She looped around and drove by slower this time. I pulled out a slip of paper from my glove box and compared the two addresses. They were precisely the same.

"This is my old house, Anna."

37

"What do you think it means?" Anna drove a block away then parked on the other side of the road. We could just about watch Luxor's car in the driveway of the house.

"I don't know, it could be just a coincidence, I wish we had a glance at who owns it."

"I could drive back around?" Anna suggested, reaching for the button to start the car.

"No," I said, stopping her. "Even if we did, the shutters on the windows were closed. I doubt we could see anything or anyone in the house."

We sat there waiting for Luxor to leave, hoping that maybe we would get a glance of the house's owner.

He stayed longer than I had expected. We waited for around four hours before impatience set in. We started playing Doodle on our phones (apparently the only app that didn't require service or internet) and telling boy stories to pass the time. Every time we saw any kind of movement, we both looked up quickly, only to be disappointed when it was nothing but a bird or small animal. They appeared to be much more common here than they were in Arizona. Eventually, we got hungry and decided to drive down to the convenience store diner down the road for some lunch. I could certainly go for another burger.

On our way back, something felt amiss. As we drove up the hill this time, it felt like several pairs of eyes were watching us. The hair on the back of my neck stood up and goosebumps traveled up my arms.

Anna turned down the music as if that would make a difference in whether we could hear someone out there. I looked over at her. Anna was white-knuckled, gripping the steering wheel. It was affecting her, too. The ascent up the hill was longer. I kept wondering if we had missed a turn off somewhere. I followed every road sign, trying to remember anything about the drive up here for the first time, but nothing seemed right. Everything was a bit darker with tall trees looming over us. I couldn't shake the feeling that we shouldn't be here. Anna pulled the car off onto the side of the road.

"I don't think we're going the right way." She looked at me with large fear-filled eyes.

"I'll pull up the map on my phone." Pulling my phone out and opening up the app, it gave me a no service signal. "Or not."

"Let's just go home and wait for Luxor. We can ask him when he gets home who owns the house and to write down the directions."

"Agreed." We turned the car around and drove down the hill.

The second we reached the main road at the bottom of the hill, the feeling of being watched lifted. It was like a weight that was on our shoulders was released, and a hand pressing down firmly on our chests was removed. I hadn't realized my leg was shaking, but it stopped moving now.

"Wait a second," Anna said, turning the car back around. She looked at me curiously and put her foot to the floor, heading back up the hill. She wound quickly up the roads, running stop signs and blasting through potholes like I owned a 4x4 truck.

The second we get back onto the hill, the feeling that we were in the wrong place, at the wrong time returned. But this time, Anna and her lead foot blast right through it. Near the top, I saw a few familiar houses this time.

"There's a jinx." Anna focused hard on the road as she spoke. "Anyone driving up this hill will be warded off. They released the jinx when Luxor was driving up, and we followed close enough behind that we missed it too." Anna swerved off the road about a block before we reached the house. "This only makes me want to know who owns that house, that much more. They don't want uninvited visitors."

I looked back at the little house, but Luxor had already left. I wouldn't have been surprised if we'd passed him at some point on the way up or down the hill but were too distracted to notice.

"Well, there's only one way to find out." I opened the door, hopefully walking up to the house would be less daunting than finishing the drive up to it.

Anna got out behind me, and we walked for what felt like forever, up the hill to the tiny house. A rustling sound came out of the nearby bushes. Anna snapped her head round to the left. She crept closer to the forest and squinted as if trying to see in the dark.

I walked up behind her. "What are we looking for?"

"Nothing. I thought I saw-" She moved a couple of bush branches to the side carefully and found nothing. "Oh well, let's just keep going."

Abandoning the search for the origin of the noise, she turned and approached the driveway to the house. We continued up the path. The wrap-around driveway was much bigger than it looked as we were driving toward it. We walked for at least five more minutes before walking right back out the other side — where there was no house in sight.

"Seriously?" Anna exclaimed, clearly agitated. "It's another jinx. We have to hop their fence, anytime we enter into the driveway on either end, it will lead us right back out the other side."

I looked at the eight to ten-foot fence surrounding the house; it appeared to be completely flat and there weren't many edges we

362

could grip and use to climb up on. It was intimidating since I wasn't much of an athlete.

"Of course, we do," I barely whispered, walking up to the fence.

Anna clasped her hands together, and I stepped into them. She boosted me up, but even with that extra help, I could barely reach the top. I dangled there for a moment and started to swing my legs back and forth. It took me a few tries, but I finally hooked one of my ankles around the top of the fence and hoisted myself up onto it. Sweat dripped from my forehead. I looked down at the other side which was also a straight drop.

Anna stepped back about ten feet, to get a running start. She sprinted toward the wall, kicking off a tree that was about four feet away from the actual fence she'd launched into the air. It didn't look natural, how far her tiny body ended up in the air. She grabbed the top of the fence with ease, hoisted herself up then threw herself over the side. I made a note of how she landed, on all fours almost in a frog-like position, before straightening herself out. I flung myself after her, landing much less gracefully. If I was an animal, I would be a cat — a blind cat with three legs. I fell hard. The ground slipped from under my right hand, which caused me to face-plant and bury half my face in a pile of mud.

"Oh no," Anna moaned.

I stood up, dusting myself off to see what she's so upset about. I look around, no immediate danger noted. I took a step or two back from the fence, and that was when I saw it.

The street was behind me, which meant we didn't hop over the gate as we'd thought. I stuck my foot out and tapped the road to make sure it wasn't an illusion tap; it was real. I looked over to Anna, who had her hands on her head.

"Whoever set these jinx's in place were extremely crafty." Anna scratched her head, confused.

"Let's go home. I'll write a letter to Alaric to see if he knows a way for us to counter the effects of the jinx or anything about who owns the house," I told her.

Anna nodded. We went back to the car, defeated. Waves of frustration and heat emitted from Anna's frigid body. I could tell she was fuming. She used the word crafty, but I was sure she had a few other choice words she would have preferred to call them.

We drove in silence. I took the wheel this time to give Anna a chance to calm down. When we pulled into the driveway, Luxor was outside, loading his bags into his car.

I parked, got out of the car, and walked up to him.

"You don't have to leave." I tried to be as gentle as possible, knowing we didn't leave this morning on the best of terms.

He tossed his bag into the trunk and slammed it shut as if he was angry, only I sensed that he wasn't.

"Yes I do," he says abruptly. "Clearly, things aren't working with us, and you're too hard for me to be around."

I laid my hand on his shoulder, not to try to persuade him to feel a certain way but to try to get a sense of what he was feeling. He jerked away quickly, but it was too late. Hatred and disgust

364

enveloped him and when I faced him, his eyes said it all. The green that circled them somehow seemed so much darker. His eyebrows scrunched together and heat rolled off of him in waves of rage.

I stumbled back a few steps and tensed. He didn't want me near him and that shocked me. Tears streaked down my face uncontrollably and I began hyperventilating.

He looked down at my face .As he met my eyes, his expression softened, but it was too late. I felt myself spiraling, so I sprinted away before I lost control. I heard him call my name, but I didn't stop. He could leave, that was fine with me. Leaving, and pretending I didn't exist was something he and Alaric had in common. I ran into the forest, not wanting to go inside and face Anna, immediately needing to find peace in nature. I ran until I was out of sight of everyone and I couldn't feel or hear Luxor. I tried to stay on a straight so I didn't get lost. I sat on an overgrown root on the ground, hugged my legs, and put my head between my knees. I let the tears fall, no longer fighting them.

Even after the tears ran out, and I stopped sobbing profusely, I sat there with my head down, not wanting to move yet. I enjoyed the silence, the rustle of the trees in the wind rushing over a river nearby. A tap on my shoulder sent a jolt through me, but I didn't lift my head.

"I'm not ready to come back yet, Anna."

There was no response, but another tap on my shoulder. I turned to look at her, only no one was there. I stood up and looked around, trying to see who it was. I heard rustling all around me, less like it was coming naturally and more like there was something in the forest. I ventured back the way I came, as I suddenly realized I might not have been alone.

Something popped out of the bush near me and grabbed my hand. I flinched away slightly, but whatever it was kept a firm grasp. I wiggled my fingers a bit, to try to free them as I kneeled to take a closer look.

It was a small gremlin child, barely over a foot tall and abnormally scrawny looking. Its little ears pointed straight up, and its skin had a luminescence similar to my own. It looked at me as if confused about what I was, too. The peculiar little guy had an innocence to him as if he was still learning about the world. Despite this, he wasn't shy at all as he grabbed my hand and tried to pull me farther into the forest. I planted my feet firmly in place and hesitated, not knowing where it was planning to lead me. It pulled my finger a little harder, the insistent child. I looked back toward the direction of the house, sighed, and followed the sweet little imp into the darkness of the woods.

38

We were officially far enough into the woods that I couldn't find my way back on my own. Hopefully, the little one could help me back when we were done.

The sun had nearly set. The moon was our only source of illumination on the path, but it wasn't enough to save my shins, which I kept banging on rocks and scraping through unknown bushes. I felt and heard my leggings snag on the branches, again and again, tearing them up. I felt damp and I couldn't feel my legs, so the wetness could have been from the leaves or blood from the scratches made by branches.

We walked around three to five more miles before the little creature sat on the ground and gestured for me to join him. I was so tired that I sat without hesitation, hoping whatever surprises were next, would include some water.

The gremlin and I sat quietly in the dark for a while. I wasn't sure what we were waiting for. He patted a rhythm onto the ground over and over again. After a while, I was so bored that I joined in. He gave me a pointy-toothed grin of encouragement as we made little musical sounds on the ground in front of us.

I heard a bell sound coming from the trees behind us. I stopped patting to look at what made the chiming sounds, but the noises stopped too. An older gremlin froze as he spotted me, and glared. I shifted around a bit and continued the little gremlin's rhythm. Almost like clockwork, the older gremlin ran her nails delicately against the chimes again.

The child stood up and clapped in tune with the little song he started, dancing around me excitedly, clearly happy with the song. He threw his head back and closed his eyes while he danced. Suddenly the forest came to life. First, the sprites came bouncing in from the trees, lighting up the spot we were in and hummed along with the song. Then what I thought to be an imp came along, although I'd never seen one in person. He came up to me slowly and stopped right in front, following my hands and repeating it in a much lighter tune of the pattern that I was doing. I focused on the little hands drumming for a while. I could hear more little hands, or maybe feet, joining us.

I hadn't looked up yet, as I didn't want to startle the new comers. Soon the forest around us filled with the hypnotic little tune. In my peripherals, I saw the leaves bouncing up and down to the vibrations, and I heard the echoes of our little song drifting out into the open night. I slowly raised my head, keeping the rhythm going, and saw a swarm of creatures of all colors and sizes surrounding me.

Gremlins were drumming, elves were dancing, and imps were swinging from the tall branches on the trees. The sprite's tune became more prominent as they doubled in numbers, dancing colorfully around the dark forest ground. I stopped patting, allowing the magical little tune to surround me. The tree branches now swayed with the rhythm, almost so much, I couldn't help but wonder if they were alive.

An elf approached me. She was only about three feet tall. She took one of my dirt-covered hands in her own and looked at me. I didn't know if she was waiting for me to say something, or if she was capable of speaking and understanding English, but having her hand in mine felt significant.

I rose to my feet slowly, allowing the little elf to lead me around the illuminated forest floor. The sprites jumped up and danced around me as we walked. The tune faded out slowly as the creatures returned to the forest. One by one, they left, turning the once lit ground, back to the darkened forest floor.

The elf let go of my hand and waved before walking back into the forest as well, leaving the small gremlin child and me alone again in the woods. I sauntered back up to him and sat back down. He looked up at me with his large round eyes, before he too, nodded and walked into the dark trees.

I was utterly alone, lost in the forest, in the dark. Somehow though I wasn't afraid. I knew there was an abundance of magical creatures on the outskirts of the trees. The night was warm, the ground surprisingly soft, and my eyelids were extraordinarily heavy. I lay back onto a pile of moss and closed my eyes, letting the quiet calm night and the harmonious tune that still played in my head draw me into the darkness.

"Where are you?" I heard Alaric speaking calmly to me, but I couldn't find the words to respond.

"Adella." His angelic voice screamed my name, "Where are you?."

My subconscious didn't want to respond, though, sleeping peacefully, not wanting anything to disturb this tranquil rest.

My eyelids fluttered open as I roused slowly. It was bright. I opened one eye and realized that the sun was high in the sky — I'd slept through the night and right into the afternoon. I let the heat warm my skin up, hoping that it would give me the energy to walk back. I propped myself up using my elbows and gave my muscles a quick flex for good measure. Sleeping on the ground had done less damage to my muscles than I thought it would. I was surprised to feel so relaxed.

I paused to take in my surroundings. The faint scent of smoke wafted through the air. As I looked around, I realized I was no longer in the small clearing where I'd fallen asleep. I didn't know how, but I had been moved. I followed the smell of smoke, a few trees, and jumping over a small river, I found myself in the backyard of my old childhood home. The chimney was roaring and grey smoke poured out of it.

The back porch was empty. The porch swing made a light screeching noise as the gentle wind rocked it back and forth. I saw shadows in the window, figures that appeared to be fighting. I walked up the back porch and took a deep breath, preparing myself to meet the owners of my childhood home.

The door swung open before I could even lift my hand to knock.

"Adella." The woman in front of me held her arms out as if expecting me to embrace her.

I stood there for a moment in disbelief. The stranger who stared back at me, said nothing. She dropped her arms slowly, and we just stood there staring at me. She was exactly my height, only a bit darker than myself, but her black hair was pulled into tight braids and woven with different fabrics. Her familiar eyes came into contact with my own, and how I reacted next, no one could have anticipated.

I pretended she didn't exist, just as she hadn't only moments ago. I walked right around her to the emotional pull coming from

371

the living room. Happiness, excitement. It was like a magnet pulling me into its gravitation.

I looked at the small TV in the corner of the room and the image on the screen stopped me dead in my tracks.

"Two people have been found dead in a fatal car crash this afternoon." The lady reported on the screen.

They showed an image of the crashed vehicle. This was a car that I'd seen — hell, I'd even sat in there before.

I covered my ears and squatted as the blackness consumed me, but the picture of the car was there, playing as if on repeat now, with images of Luxor's face next to it. I felt myself pushing my despair onto everyone in the room as I lost control. I scrunched my eyes shut in the hope that if I didn't open them again, it wouldn't be true.

"I wouldn't do that if I were you, Jennette," I heard an unfamiliar male voice warn.

A hand on my shoulder pulled me back into reality. I could just about hear the high pitch scream and wondered if it belonged to me. I grabbed my mom's wrist roughly and pulled her into the black oblivion with me.

39

A car door slammed loudly outside. I peeked out and saw Luxor's car racing away. I sat up a little higher but couldn't see Dells.

"Gggaaaaahhhh," was the sound I made as I rolled myself off the couch. I slid faster than anticipated, bringing my hand down to catch myself, but I slipped and face-planted anyways.

Clumsiest protector ever. I felt a searing pain in my nose and quickly brought my hand to it to catch any blood that might come out. I left my hand there for a moment while I ran to the door. Satisfied that my nose wasn't going to bleed, I opened the door.

There wasn't much going on outside, a small cloud of dust.

"Dells," I yelled. No response. "Dells?"

She wouldn't have left with Luxor and not told me. I checked my phone just to be sure. Nothing.

I turned the GPS tracker I'd installed on. It took a moment to kick in. The service here wasn't very reliable, so I didn't know if the direction was going to be accurate.

The little red dot beeped a couple of times, then went off for a minute, but then started beeping again. This couldn't possibly be right.

It showed Dells heading straight into the woods, the opposite direction to where Luxor drove off. I let the red dot come back and beep a few more times, which only seemed to be getting farther and farther away from me the longer I waited.

I sighed and started for the woods, having to stop every few feet to let the red dot pop back up again. I lost signal about a quarter a mile in and started calling around. "Dells...Dells?" I called her name a good few times, though I wasn't entirely sure she was out here in the first place. I looked for footsteps or any sign that she was in the woods. I found nothing.

I headed back to the house, hoping to get enough service inside to message Luxor. The little red dot didn't come back on my phone, even as I neared the house. Dells must have turned her phone off. I took my phone out and dialed Luxor's number, waiting through the trilling rings. Voicemail.

I hung up and sent a text instead.

Where are you and Dells?

Once inside the house, I ran a hot shower. It had been a bizarre day and I needed to relax. *Those two can do whatever together, it just would have been nice to know.* I turned to see the steamy water

374

going down the drain, and decided I wanted a bath. Watching the hot water collect in the tub relaxed my muscles almost instantly. I run out to the living room and turn the news station on full volume. I liked to listen to other people's misfortunes while I soaked.

I removed my clothes slowly, relishing in the feeling of being unrestricted. I dipped my toes into the water, sinking my foot slowly to the bottom. The burning sensation of the scalding water traveled up my body as I climbed in fully. I didn't bother putting anything scented in the water. *I'm a fierce protector, I don't want to smell like peach trees.*

I closed my eyes and tipped my head back, the tantalizing water eased the soreness from my muscles and warmed me to the core.

From here I could still listen to the TV. It was time for the news, though I could only hear bits and pieces from the reporter's announcements.

There has been a huge house fire…few sustained minor injuries…there were no deaths…

Well, that's good, at least. I kept listening.

In other news…a car crashed near Salem, Oregon.

My eyes flew open. I stood up in the water, got out as quickly as I could, and ran over to the TV. I grabbed the remote and turned the volume down just a bit.

I patiently waited for the clip to play on the TV. The news reporter, all dressed up, smiled for the camera, standing directly in front of what I needed to see. She was talking, I was sure, but I was ignoring her. If the wreck had just happened, she wouldn't have any more information than I couldn't see by looking at the scene. Finally, she stepped out of the way. The camera slowly panned out over the scene of the accident, once, twice, and a third time.

They panned to the men carrying the black body bags to the ambulances. I sank into the couch and turned the volume up so I could hear the report. An uneasy feeling rose in my chest.

There have been two deaths as a result of a car collision. One male and one female... That was all I heard before I lost it.

I screamed, and I screamed loud. I wanted to cry, fall apart, and lose myself completely, but the tears didn't come.

I ran into the room and jumped on the bed, face down, and let out another scream, wanting so desperately for the tears to come so I could get them out of the way, but they refused. I sat up and grabbed one of my large shirts from the end of the bed, and threw it on with a pair of undies I had nearby. I sat crisscrossed and gave my mind a moment to catch up with my heart, clearly, there was some confusion here. I knew I wasn't this desensitized to death.

I fetched my phone from the bathroom, unsure of who to call. I checked my messages and the zero sign ensured I went over the edge, I hurled my phone at the wall; I watched it hit and hearing the glass shatter in a satisfying break. I screamed louder, throwing myself onto the bed, this time, the tears followed suit. I was like this for a while before I stood up and wiped my face. I sniffled a bit to make sure my nose was under control and I headed out of the house.

This couldn't be happening. There was more to this story, they couldn't be gone. Especially — no. I wouldn't let my mind go there. I didn't know where to begin, but I needed to find her. I was going to find her.

CPSIA information can be obtained
at www.ICGtesting.com
Printed in the USA
BVHW080748220221
600765BV00002B/65

9 781087 944043